The Playground

The Playground

A Novel

Jane Shemilt

An Imprint of HarperCollinsPublishers

THE PLAYGROUND. Copyright © 2019 by Jane Shemilt. All rights reserved. Printed in the United States of America. No part of this book may be used or reproduced in any manner whatsoever without written permission except in the case of brief quotations embodied in critical articles and reviews. For information, address HarperCollins Publishers, 195 Broadway, New York, NY 10007.

HarperCollins books may be purchased for educational, business, or sales promotional use. For information, please e-mail the Special Markets Department at SPsales@harpercollins.com.

FIRST HARPERLUXE EDITION

ISBN: 978-0-06-294473-3

HarperLuxe™ is a trademark of HarperCollins Publishers.

Library of Congress Cataloging-in-Publication Data is available upon request.

19 20 21 22 23   LSC   10 9 8 7 6 5 4 3 2 1

To my husband, Steven Gill, and our beloved children:
Martha, Mary, Henry, Tommy, and Johny

The Playground

PART ONE
The Truth

I t was surprising how quickly things took off in the end, like a bonfire, one of those big ones the children loved so much. Some nights I hear that sound of crackling again, like a bomb ticking down. I wait for the roar and see the flames; the scent of scorching fills the air. I can feel that searing heat.

The children danced around fires all summer, lit up and yelling like wild things. We left them to it, watching from a distance, watching each other more. We were kindling ourselves those long hot months, parched and waiting, though we didn't know that till far too late.

I used to think truth was a simple thing. That there could only be one truth, single and essential—like light, say, or water. Now I know it comes in layers, some more transparent than others. If you look carefully—

and we didn't—you can see through the top layer to the darkness beneath. I'm thinking of ice on the surface of deep water.

Eve told the truth: she told the police she loved her children and that her marriage to Eric was happy. That was true, the top layer of her truth. She didn't tell them that she hadn't watched her children carefully; she didn't tell them about the affair. She didn't say how upset Sorrel had been or that she hadn't listened to her properly, but I don't think she was hiding that on purpose; she hadn't seen the truth either though it was staring her in the face.

And Melissa—designer, wife, mother, hiding under that perfect exterior, we didn't look deeper, not until later, and by then the damage was done.

The children, well, it never occurred to them to tell us the truth. But then it probably never occurred to them they were lying. They were simply surviving. We were all skating on ice, thin ice. No one was looking at the depths beneath, which was pretty stupid, considering what happened.

The day it started began the same for all of us, with blood and sunshine, with hope, with no idea at all.

1. May

Eve

Eve is in her kitchen making bread; her hands knead and press and throw. The sound will travel up through the ceiling to the beds where the children drowse. They'll remember this, the sound and the scent, the light through the curtains, feeling safe, being safe. Beyond the open windows, the garden rolls to the wood, the long grass fringed with sun. There's warmth in the air already. Eve divides the dough into rolls and fills a loaf pan with the rest; she takes the croissants out and stacks them on a rack.

Everything is ready: books, piles of paper, the pencils for each child, and the name tags in bright blue ink: Poppy, Isabelle, Blake. She glances at the certificates hanging by the sink: EVE PEMBERTON, BA (HONS) IN PRI-MARY EDUCATION; the smaller certificate means more, the diploma in teaching learners with dyslexia, the course she did online this year, for Poppy.

Eric comes into the kitchen; he reaches for a crois-sant, which disappears in a couple of bites. "Nervous?"

She pushes the lines of pencils on the table together until they meet with a little click. "A bit."

"I hope it's worth it." He kisses her, the stubble scraping her cheek, and smooths a strand of hair be-hind her ear. "You don't have to put yourself through this; school will sort Poppy, given time."

She shakes her head and moves away, sliding the kettle onto the stove. "Time isn't on Poppy's side. If you feel stupid, every day, every minute matters. I have to try for her sake. It might seem a little crazy but—"

"You must do what your heart tells you to." It's a fa-vorite expression of his and it usually helps. He smiles at her; he's hardly changed since they met twelve years ago, back when the garden was still her father's and he was shaping beds and planting trees. His eyes are the same sky blue as they were that hot morning in June, the week before her finals. She'd been lying on a blanket in her bikini making notes. Her parents' cocktail party was in full swing on the sun-drenched veranda above;

the babble of chatter and chink of glasses reached her hiding place behind a bed of roses. She could hear her mother calling her, thinly disguised impatience in that well-bred voice. Eric had almost stepped on her.

"Now there's a coincidence," he'd said, as he lowered the wheelbarrow. "I hate parties too."

When her parents died and it came to choosing, her brother chose the shares, the cars and the yacht, the racehorses. She'd wanted space. The villa among the olive trees in Greece, and the house where she'd grown up, this very house with its two acres of planted land between the road and the railway. The chance to be barefoot in a kitchen with children in the garden, running in and running out. Her mother had been too busy for her, too occupied with friends and parties. Eve's kids would have a normal childhood, though as Eric pointed out, it wasn't normal at all. Most mothers had a job nowadays; if you wanted normal you had to model it. Well, now she was.

Privately she wonders if Poppy inherited her dyslexia from Eric; he had talked late, and says little still. Her father had liked his silences, finding them restful. The old man had walked with him in the garden each evening, sipping wine, gesturing with his pipe to the wood, the planted slopes, the wildlife pond in the paddock where his donkeys lived. He'd put his arm around the young landscaper's shoulders, growing expansive with drink. All the same, when Eric asked for Eve's hand after three short months, her father was cautious. He advised her to wait, but Eric had been what she wanted, she had been quite sure. She'd wanted peace back then, not words; a kind man, a garden, children.

Eric pushes the window open and stares across the meadow to the wood. "Those trees need thinning."

"Those trees are just fine." She tucks her arm into his, resting her head against his shoulder. She loves the soft mass of leaves; the way the branches mesh together, blocking out the railway at the back. They cast shadows, making secret places for the children to play. All children should have the chance to escape from their parents, though he doesn't agree.

"I'll take Sorrel to school and drop Ash at playgroup on my way," he offers.

"It's half term; there's no school today and no playgroup." She lifts her head from his shoulder. "Don't tell me you forgot."

He doesn't reply; he's not listening. His gaze shifts between the wood and the meadow, working things out. He wants a Japanese garden. A landscape should have shape, according to him, symmetry preferably, a proper sense of order.

She takes her arm from his. "You promised you'd look after Sorrel and Ash, remember?"

"I promised I would if I was here." He shakes his head, his mouth turns down, there's a trace of guilt in his eyes. "We've just been handed the contract for felling in Crystal Palace provided we do it quickly. I'd happily take both of them, but it would be far too dangerous."

She closes her eyes, praying for patience. He could have told her before, but she won't lose her temper, not today. Today has to be perfect for the children, as perfect as the cloudless sky over the garden and the warm sunshine that's beginning to creep through the kitchen windows. There is no point in getting annoyed.

"They'll have to stay then; they can join in once I've finished teaching." She puts paper on the smaller table. "I warned Melissa and Grace that Sorrel and Ash might have to be around sometimes. It's not all bad; little ones are supposed to be calming for dyslexic kids, it gives them a sense of control."

"So I'm forgiven?"

"I'll just have to hope they don't mind." She straightens, staring across the lawn to the wood, imagining the group of children playing together after the lesson, their laughter drifting back to her through the open window.

"I'd keep them inside," he says, following her gaze. "I don't want to tell Paul we lost track of his daughter. He's not the forgiving type."

"This is Dulwich, my darling, not the Amazonian jungle." She touches his cheek. "If it makes you feel happier, I'll ask Igor to mow a path through the meadow; they'll be easier to spot."

"I'll do it. Anything for my princess." A mock bow; he doesn't like her calling on his coworker to do jobs.

The two men had met during a landscaping project in Dulwich Park. Igor was living in a hostel at the time, scraping a wage to send back to his family in Poland. Eric offered him a job and a place to stay in the old staff bungalow on the grounds; it had been empty for years. Eric and Igor make a good team: Eric designing and planning; Igor following his lead, a giant of a man with the jowly face of a bulldog, the same steadfast loyalty in his eyes.

A heavy footstep sounds on the stone veranda outside the kitchen.

"Talk of the devil." Eric vanishes to confer with Igor. Eve hands a croissant and a mug of coffee through the window; Igor nods as he takes them, his face half hidden behind a large beard, cap pulled low. He seldom speaks to her; whether he's shy or sullen she can't quite decide.

"Who's a princess?" Poppy appears, dressed for the day in a red sequined jacket unearthed from the dress-up box. She'd been listening outside the door. Her beloved eldest with thick auburn braids, a splash of freckles over her nose, and toenails painted blue; eleven going on sixteen.

"You are of course, my precious one." Eve swoops for a hug, but Poppy grabs a croissant and makes for the door. Eve watches her go, registering a small tug of sadness; she used to be allowed to hold her eldest daughter. She'd hold all three children so close it was hard to tell in the tangle of limbs where her body ended and theirs began. Poppy disappears as Sorrel tumbles over her sister's feet and into the room. She scrambles up, used to this. Six years old, a smaller edition of her sister but rounder, more disheveled, sunnier in nature.

"May I have one, and one for Ash?" She lisps, her tongue catching the wide gaps between her teeth.

"Of course you may, my little darling." Eric has returned for his boots. He lifts her to the table and she frowns, breathing deeply as she chooses two croissants, one for each hand; put down on the floor she tiptoes out, silent as Noah, Sorrel's little Labrador puppy asleep in front of the stove.

Eric shakes his head. "We should have breakfast round the table, Eve."

Eve holds on to an image of her daughters upstairs, whispering under the tented sheets, littering fragments of pastry, the filtered sun rosy on their skin. They will have brought Ash into bed with them.

"We should just let them be," she replies.

"Kids need a structured life." He laces his boots; this is an old argument, one they've tossed back and forth for years.

"They need freedom," she calls out as he shuts the door. She hears him clomp down the path in his boots. It doesn't matter; she lets them stay outside for hours when he's away, playing until dark or the cold brings them in. She gives them the run of the garden as a secret gift, the childhood she wishes she'd had.

A croissant falls from the rack into a shaft of dusty sun. Eve checks the fridge: carrot sticks, small sandwiches, homemade pizzas. She pulls butter from the middle shelf, strawberry jam from inside the door, and lathers both on a warm croissant with a knife, nicking her finger. She leans her elbows on the windowsill, sucking the blood off her skin, eyes half closed like a cat in the sunshine. The garden spreads out in front of her, the blue hydrangeas nodding their great heads near the house, roses and lavender against the side wall by the drive. The donkeys in the field, and beyond them the grass in the meadow and then the trees, which are larger than they were when she was a child, much taller. They cast shadows that are darker and stretch farther than they did back then. As she watches, the little wood seems to shiver in the breeze, as if readying itself for the children.

Melissa

Melissa spends an hour in her basement gym, the cross trainer first and then the rowing machine, working out until her hands are too slippery to hold the handles. In the bath afterward her body is visible from all angles in the steamy mirrors. There is a new softness at her hips and her shoulders look stringy. Shaving at the bikini line she misjudges the angle and cuts the skin; blood ribbons into the water, staining the foam. She watches as though it belongs to someone else. Thirty-five is still young. There are always things to try: a personal trainer, a new diet. She steps from the bath, wraps herself in her dressing gown, and pads barefoot to the kitchen. She waits for the kettle to boil, placing her palm against the kitchen windowpane equidistant from the metal edges. She spreads the fingers; hand as art. The spaces between the thin digits are shaped like knives, there are hollows beside the tendons, some blue veins are scarred. The tips of the fingers tremble. The kettle flicks off; she turns her face from the light. The sun is already heating the curved lines of brick and gravel outside. The landscaper talked about flow and focal points, but Paul took over and the results were disappointing. She makes chamomile tea and takes it to her office, where she sifts through her emails; an architect wants bespoke blinds for his garden room in Dulwich, then there's a mural to commission for the flat in Chelsea; the clients expect her to be on hand whenever they call. Her desk is awash with computer-aided designs for their kitchen, but it's unlikely they'll agree on anything. The plans have been sent back twice already. She's painted sheets of paper to try against the walls of their flat in soft yellow and burned orange, the colors of happiness, though in reality she suspects those clients are miserable; like us, she thinks as she glances at the glowing hues; like me.

A tapping noise picks at the silence, a tiny woodpecker of sound. She ties her dressing-gown cord more tightly and walks upstairs to the sitting room. Her daughter, up early, is focused on her laptop, legs tucked under her on the leather sofa. She's in pajama bottoms and a skimpy vest through which breast buds are visible. Melissa leans against the door, pride and fear curdling. Thirteen. She reaches back for her own thirteen, but the years are blurred with misery. Her father's taunts about puppy fat had sparked a frantic determination to lose weight. The starvation became extreme, the exercising desperate. She was taken to the hospital twice. Recovery was slow and incomplete; Izzy must be allowed to be the person she's been becoming since she was little, at all costs. Happy or at least content or at least not cowed. It's worked so far—shame seems to be the last thing on her daughter's mind.

"Hi, sweetie."

Izzy jolts and snaps the lid shut. She glares up, her pretty face contracting.

"Can't you knock?" Her fury is palpable. Melissa feels automatic guilt, a low-down flooding like waters breaking. Ridiculous, she's done nothing wrong.

"This is the sitting room, Izzy. Everyone's space."

"Where's Daddy?"

"His flight arrives at three. He'll be here when you get back later."

The blue eyes blaze. "Back from what? What have you arranged now?"

"Your day with the teacher, Daddy's landscaper's wife. You met her when they came to lunch. You liked her."

Izzy jumps up, her laptop clatters to the ground. "What's the matter with you? It's half term. Why are you doing this?"

"Calm down, darling. It's about finding you the right kind of help—"

"Why pretend it's for me when it's actually for you? You want to get rid of me so you can work, it's pathetic."

Isabelle chucks a cushion across the room; it hits a vase, which topples to the floor and smashes on the marble. She reaches for another.

"There'll be a couple of other children too," Melissa says quickly.

The cushion lowers.

"How old?"

"Eve's daughter's eleven and there's a boy coming of about the same age." She glances at Izzy, hurries on. "Her other children may be around sometimes, a girl of six and a little boy of two."

"You have to be joking." Izzy's eyes narrow.

"Everyone will look up to you; you'll be leader of the gang."

Izzy's face becomes thoughtful. No one waits with her by the entrance to the school lane where Melissa finds her at the end of the day, slumped against the railings by herself. Friends never last. The only person she goes to the movies or shopping with is her father; she must yearn for friends of her own.

"How much will you give me if I go?"

"How much?" Melissa is confused.

"As in a hundred pounds," Izzy replies impatiently.

It's impossible for her daughter to look anything other than beautiful, the thick fair hair, the fierce blue stare, the way she stands on long legs as graceful as a colt; strong bodied. Dyslexia is better than anorexia. Funny how flowery they both sound, like girls' names, pretty girls.

"Fifty."

Everything comes with a cost. Izzy's cooperation is cheap at the price; she's so angry these days. It's just frustration, the teachers say, common with dyslexia, and then there's her age of course. They organized a tutor and extra lessons in school, but nothing has worked so far. At the same time that these thoughts run through her mind, others are speeding beneath them, like traffic on motorways that twist one under another. Izzy's right; Melissa can finish her work if her daughter is occupied, she can even fit in a run.

Izzy smiles as though she can read her mother's mind; she probably can. "Done," she says, letting the cushion drop to the floor.

"They live in College Road; it'll take us ten minutes to walk there," Melissa tells her. They could chat. Izzy might open up on the way. She can see them now, like those advertisements for mini-vacations: a mother and daughter making their way through a park with flowers in the background, linking arms and laughing, special bonding time.

"Walk?" Izzy sounds horrified.

"Okay, I'll pop you over in the car." Melissa steps forward and holds her daughter tightly for a few moments, inhaling the clean scent of her hair. Izzy's agreed to go, that's the main thing—she won't push for anything else.

"Drop me off before we get to their house, though," Izzy warns, stepping back. "It's not like I'm some little kid who needs to be handed over at the door."

Melissa nods obediently and retreats to the kitchen; she'll catch up with Eve when she collects Izzy after the lesson.

The kitchen is in the basement of the house, next to the gym and newly equipped. The gray concrete work surfaces are pristine, slatted pantry doors hide a small room of shelves. The dark slab of marble topping the island was specially quarried, an immense fridge-freezer hums quietly in the corner. Paul stores the old stuff in a shed; he prefers new things. He's always updating something in the kitchen, the units or one of the machines. It's important for an architect to be at the cutting edge of design, he says. He shows clients around their house from time to time. Double doors at the back lead to the courtyard and beyond that to the curving walls of the landscaped garden.

A dark-skinned young woman in ankle-length black is washing the floor and humming a tune under her breath; her symmetrical features are framed by a hijab. The kitten, Venus, jumps out of the way, toying with the mop and shaking her white paws. Lina comes from Syria; she worked for colleagues of Paul before, other architects who moved to America. Her references were excellent. When Melly's interior design business took off, they needed someone to look after the house and cook. Lina sleeps in their converted loft; it's hard to remember how they managed without her. She's probably in her early twenties, though it's impossible to tell exactly with the clothes and the makeup she always wears. Paul pays her in cash, calling her up to his office every Saturday. She seems content. Lina looks up and gives a solemn wave; Melissa smiles, warmed. She feels close to her silent little maid, closer than to her daughter sometimes. They share more time together; she tells Lina her thoughts. Last week she found her working late, cleaning cupboards. Paul was away. She had sat at the table with a glass of wine, allowing herself to chatter. Lina listened and for a brief moment rested her hand on Melissa's shoulder. She's not quite sure how much Lina understands; she hardly talks but she listens closely, like an ally. Her presence feels gentle, healing even, though Paul would laugh at the notion.

"It looks perfect." She glances around the shining kitchen. "Thank you, sweetie; did you remember the flowers?"

Lina nods. She squeezes out the mop and puts the bucket in the pantry; she remembers everything. The white lilies, the special scentless kind Paul prefers, will be delivered later.

"Dinner?"

Lina nods again. The daube of beef, his favorite, will be ready in the fridge, beautifully cooked.

"You're an angel. I literally cannot remember how we coped before you came." She wants to hug Lina but doesn't quite dare.

A red stain creeps into Lina's cheeks. She sets out cereal and bowls on the island, adds cutlery and a little vase of flowers.

"Take the day off," Melissa says impulsively. "Izzy will be out and I intend to work. Everything's ready for Paul. You deserve a break."

Lina has a boyfriend, a thickset, bearded man who looks older than her, a little surly. He waits outside the house in the evenings; perhaps they could spend the day together. Lina bows her head in acknowledgment.

Melissa returns to the sitting room; Izzy is still glued to her laptop. "Here's Venus come to see you. I'm going to catch up on work till it's time to go." She tumbles the kitten on to her daughter's lap; Izzy's hand closes around the soft little ears.

Grace

"Shit. Shit. Shit."

Grace pushes against the glass; the jammed window gives way on the third attempt, her hand scraping on the frame. She jumps off the bathroom stool and holds the bleeding palm under cold water, which seeps up her arm, soaking the new white shirt, the neat black suit.

"Fuck."

Receptionists should be immaculate, but there's no time to change and nothing to change into. She trips over Martin's shoes left in the doorway of the main room.

"Bloody hell."

She pulls the curtains back; the sun floods into the room. The sky looks flawless, that deceptive English blue. You can see a long way from the thirteenth floor. Thirteen was unlucky, Martin had worried; beggars can't be choosers, she'd shot back. Charley likes it. She watches foxes in the community gardens from here, sleek shapes slipping by the rows of beans in the dusk. Blake wants a garden but he'd need help and there wouldn't be time; there's ten minutes left some nights, half an hour if she's lucky—just enough time to slip the red notebook from its hiding place on the top shelf under the pile of cookbooks she bought from Zimbabwe. She writes at night in secret, battling tiredness.

A muffled groan comes from the sofa. Martin is lying flat out with a cushion over his head. An ashtray brims beside him, three empty beer bottles on the table, papers on the floor. When she narrows her eyes, his outline becomes a sleeping animal, a beast from the plains, lifeless on the back of her grandfather's truck, chugging into the village at sunup, blood dripping on the dust. Cocks crowing. Smoke from early fires. Miles and years away. Before success, before failure. Somewhere inside her husband is a young student with burning eyes, the English boy she'd followed over the sea. In the flat above a door slams as the tenants leave for work; that's exactly how it began for them all those years ago, with the sound of a door slamming.

It had been late; most of the drinkers had already lurched out into the potholed streets of Harare. Beneath a layer of smoke, the tables were littered with empty glasses. The door to the bar banged open against the wall then slammed shut, followed by footsteps and the noise of something heavy being dumped on the counter.

"We're closed." Her back had been to the bar, as she counted the register.

"Oh gosh. Just my luck. Any chance at all of a glass of water?"

The voice of the radio: white, old Rhodesian, upper class, everything her grandparents hated. She turned to bawl him out, but the mud-splashed face above the orange backpack was grinning at her, his eyes more alive than any she'd seen in here or anywhere else for that matter. She retrieved a cold beer from the fridge and handed it over. "On the house," she said. "Be quick." She came back in five minutes. "Finished?"

"What's the rush?" He handed her the empty bottle.

"Like I said, we're closed." Then, because he was still smiling, because his backpack was spilling books, she added, "I've got to study."

"For?"

"English A level, next week."

"Ah." He pulled out a book from the backpack and put it down. *Great Expectations*. "Have you read it?" A pickup line, something to keep her there, he told her later. She'd loved that book so she nodded. He slapped down *Middlemarch,* she nodded again. They'd sat outside in the parking lot afterward; he was studying English at Oxford, he told her, in his final year. They talked till dawn about the books they'd read, about their secret dreams of writing. The sun had come up hot and clear like today, the future had glittered like the cars parked beside them.

She touches the graying hair and turns away, giving him five more minutes of sleep. The kids are sprawled, eyes shut, mouths open, arms spread. After yesterday's shift she'd come home to them sitting with glazed expressions in front of the television, sated with pizza and french fries. Martin's arms had been around each child, pretending it was a treat, not laziness.

Charley wakes at her touch and slips from the bed, a neat rush of smooth limbs. Blake falls out like a puppy, growling as he hits the ground. They know better than to argue. They fill the bathroom, elbowing each other; it's hard to imagine that these jostling kids will grow into their names: Charley for Charlotte Brontë, her choice; Blake for William, Martin's. She pushes them into the kitchen, watches again as they down milk, juice, cereal.

"Do I have to go?" That whine, the hunched shoulders; she buries a fist into his Afro and pulls gently, forcing his face up.

"Yes."

"Why?"

She doesn't want to say it all over again: that a child of eleven should be writing better than his sister of nine, that he should be reading fluently by now. It's not his fault that he's way behind, but he has to try. She's paid for the course that she found on Facebook, a nominal sum but hard-earned all the same.

"Because." She loosens her grip and jerks her thumb at the door. "Dress."

"Can I go?" Charley shoves Blake with her shoulder, he kicks back. Grace holds them apart.

"Please." A drawn-out whine from Charley, pulling on her hand.

"You can collect him later, with Dad."

"They've a puppy, you said. And donkeys."

"I've paid her to teach Blake, not babysit you."

"What about her other kids? You said there's a toddler and a little girl. I could help look after them. I'm good with kids, Miss Howard told you."

Charley helps out with the younger children in the after-school program. She's right, the teacher has mentioned she's efficient for nine, very kind, especially to the youngest ones. Grace studies the hope in her daughter's wide brown eyes. "I'll put it to Eve, but she's probably made other arrangements by now. Stay in the car when I ask, okay? I don't want you twisting her arm."

Charley makes a victory fist.

"Get dressed now," Grace tells them both.

Martin has pulled himself upright on the sofa; he yawns, his eyes still closed.

"We're off in a minute. Charley's coming with us, but don't leave yet; I may have to drop her back with you."

"Wow." His eyes snap open, his face looks wider when he smiles. "The chance of a day to myself. I can go to the library. Chapter seven's a bitch." He fumbles for his watch.

Writing. Code for cigarettes, coffee, reading the paper. Films in the afternoon, lunches in the pub. Her writing means chewing paper to stay awake, grinding out words, exhaustion the next day. She picks up Blake's shirt from the floor, his scattered socks, and bundles them into the washing machine.

"I am grateful." He's watching her. "You do know that, don't you?"

Gratitude is easy; it doesn't cost much. He fell in love with her energy, but he's using it up. She opens the giant candy tin that sits on the draining board behind the kettle and takes ten pounds for parking from the deep pool of saved coins and puts them in her purse, struggling with the broken zipper on her bag.

"You jolly well should be grateful," she tells him. "My turn next."

He smiles, the special melting smile, and kisses her; she softens, kissing him back.

"Yuck." Charley looks away.

While Martin hugs the kids goodbye, Grace reaches for her red notebook from the shelf and slips it into her bag. The hotel allows thirty minutes for lunch most days, ten more if it's quiet; useful writing time.

They wait for the lift on the narrow landing outside, Blake sighing and kicking his feet against the wall. The lift smells of vomit and piss, denser than in the stairwell. The landlady should hire a cleaner. Grace glimpses her sometimes, putting rubbish in the bins; a large woman with red hair and bottle glasses who rarely emerges from her ground-floor flat. She greets her politely on those occasions, receiving a grunt in reply; their landlady's the kind who seems to resent her tenants.

The children follow Grace outside. The patch of grass by the parking lot glistens with discarded bottles; her shirt feels sticky already. The usual four adolescents are bunched in a group by the dumpsters, thin boys waiting for drugs. A new one has joined them today, older, taller. The green soles of his sneakers flash as he twists, walks, turns, and starts again; head down and hooded, seventeen at a guess, scrawny, already scarred. He flicks a cigarette butt her way and she feels a faint crackle of fear. It's the way he looks at her, half grinning as though biding his time. Grace's father had been a veteran of the Second Chimurenga in Zimbabwe. He had fought with ZANLA against the ruling whites and witnessed the atrocities his people suffered; she grew up on his stories. It took her a while to convince her family that Martin was different, that she would be safe with him. She didn't tell them about the UKIP graffiti on the walls of the flats when they moved in; she had been pregnant with Blake at the time and they needed a home, it was all they could afford. She watches her kids getting into the car and gets in herself, heart thumping. She pulls out and turns on the radio for the children. Her story starts up again, running below the music like a bright river.

*P*oppy lies on her bed, watching the dust jumping in the light. The minutes drag already. There is literally nothing to do. She closes her eyes. Ash is crying; Sorrel is complaining in a whiny voice because Poppy won't let her onto her bed. The smell of hot bread hanging in the house makes her feel like vomiting. She wants to tell her mother to stop with the fucking baking. She wants to walk out of the room and down the stairs and out to another house, a normal family where the kids are allowed screen time and junk food and normal bread and they don't have to look after their brother or sister or play games in the garden, like kids in a fucking fairy tale. Everyone at school thinks she's an idiot. Izzy— the girl coming this morning—will think she's stupid when they start their lessons together. She'll arrive any minute and it'll be embarrassing. Her mother's laugh is embarrassing, like she's escaped from some mental hospital. She's not even wearing a bra today, Izzy will think it's gross. Poppy rolls over onto her stomach, squashing the croissant. She covers her ears to block out Ash and her whiny little sister. She wishes she had some of those earphones that cancel out noise. She'd cancel out her whole family if she could.

Blake stares out the car window. When they pass the park, some of his friends are playing soccer already. He doesn't want to go to special lessons for stupid people; if he can't do the work he'll look even more stupid. He puts his legs up on the back seat to the halfway mark. Charley has her legs up too, but she's over the mark so he kicks her and she laughs. He kicks harder and she goes on laughing; that's exactly what the whole day will be like.

Izzy chooses the jeans with rips; she wants to look cool but not like she cares. Through her bedroom window she can see her mother running in and out to the car, putting stuff in, yelling for her. She's wearing the scarf again; the bloody scarf. Izzy feels anger rising up hard and hot. She shoves her feet into her oldest sneakers and saunters down, purposely slow.

2. May

Eve

"Oh hi, you must be Martin. Grace said you'd be picking up. Charley and Blake are outside with the others. They needed a break, they've worked so hard. My son's napping so this is a good moment. Gosh, it's hot, I hadn't realized. They say it's going to be a barbecue summer."

For God's sake, shut up, calm down. He's just a man, an ordinary bloke. Invite him in.

"Sorry, do come in."

He seems shy for someone so well known, hovering at the doorway, his head ducked like a boy's. He towers over her, but whereas Igor's height seems brutish, this man's size appeals. He's rumpled like her father was, glasses on his head, the same kind of soft cotton shirt rolled to the elbows. That familiar tobacco smell. He puts the pile of books he's carrying on the table, slips off his jacket, and smiles around at the room as if he were at home. She's imagined *his* home often: Martin Cowan, Booker winner. A manuscript spread out on a table in a high-ceilinged loft, balls of paper scrunched on the floor. His wife hovering in the background, bringing tea, hushing the children, shepherding them away. She adds cigarette butts overflowing in a saucer, no, a heavy ashtray, made of African malachite. He spent time in Zimbabwe, she's read, for the book, the famous one. He gave away half his prize money to the school that inspired it.

"Tea? The children made cakes."

"Now how could I resist a homemade cake?"

He wanders around looking at the books on the shelves. She pours tea and he sits down with a little sigh; she needn't have worried. He seems content, relaxed even. She sneaks a glance; he has graying hair straggling over his collar; a good nose, beaked; brown eyes that gleam from little folds of skin. He's watching her as if waiting; should she tell him how much she loves his book? She sits opposite, suddenly tongue-tied.

"So how did they get on?"

He wants to know how his son performed, of course. "Oh, really well."

"Really well?" His eyebrows peak comically. "Blake?"

"He was reluctant at first, but we went back to basics with alphabet blocks and phonic cards. Once he'd gained a bit of confidence I set him a writing task with templates, and he didn't make one mistake."

"I'm impressed." The brown eyes shine.

She pushes a plate with a couple of little cakes toward him, the icing splotched and scattered with lavender. "He helped bake these too."

"Wow." He takes a bite. "We never make anything like this at home."

She glances at the coins of hardening cake mixture on the stovetop, the sticky bowls in the sink. Grace had been wearing a suit at drop-off, makeup and nail polish, one hand neatly bandaged. Eve had felt dowdy by comparison, but Martin is smiling at her as if she wasn't sweaty, with her apron around her waist and hair in her eyes, possibly a dab of flour on one cheek.

"We finished with a chapter from a novel and Blake predicted precisely what happens in the end."

"Which one?" A storyteller, he leans to hear.

"*Lord of the Flies*."

"Isn't that a bit—"

"Dark? It was only the first chapter. Izzy brought it in; I don't think she had any idea."

"You obviously brought out the best in him." He nods, taking the second cake and inspecting the empty plate. "Unusual." He traces the ellipse on the glass, the black circle in the middle. "A hand-painted plate; are you an artist as well as everything else?"

"It's from a village in Greece." She laughs. "The eye is supposed to keep people safe from the glance of a blue-eyed intruder. I bought lots."

"Do they work?"

"We're okay so far."

"Gosh, a dimple. I haven't seen one of those for years."

The blood rises in her cheeks. It's been so long since anyone mentioned her looks, she's forgotten how to manage a compliment.

"Sorry, the writer in me. I notice faces." He puts the plate back on the table. "Where's the village?"

"In the Peloponnese. We have a house out there." Does that sound like boasting to him? She never knows; she begins to bite her nails as she did when she was a child. "It's very run-down," she adds quickly. "The garden's wild."

"Sounds exactly like my kind of place." His eyes meet hers; his smile deepens.

"Let's find your children." She gets to her feet, flustered. "It's time I woke my son."

"Grace didn't tell me you had a baby."

"He's almost three, but he seems younger; he hasn't started speaking yet. I'm worried it could be dyslexia, like his sister Poppy." She begins to bite her nails again. "I think my husband might have had it as a child; it can run in families; I expect you know that." She's talking too much, drinking in his interest the way you swallow water when you hadn't realized how thirsty you were.

"I didn't say a word till I was five." Martin grins. "I've made up for it since. I wouldn't worry; he'll be fine."

He's kind, the sort of man who understands. "I'll introduce you." She leads him outside, but when they reach the little makeshift bed under the willow tree, the heaped nest of blankets is empty. Ash has disappeared; his red tractor is lying on its side in the grass.

"He'll be down in the garden," she says breathlessly. "He must have gone to find the others. They'll be together somewhere."

Martin follows, gazing around as she walks rapidly toward the meadow, passing Igor at work under the hood of a large green truck. His dusty-looking head is close to the engine, blue overalls smeared with oil.

"Did you happen to see which way the children

went, Igor? I've lost track of Ash." Her cheeks burn. Eric was right. She should keep a closer eye on the children; perhaps she should have kept them inside as he'd said.

Igor lifts his head and stares at her then Martin. He frowns and shrugs heavily. She hurries along the path Eric mowed earlier, Martin keeping pace.

"It's as though we're in a fairy tale." Martin stares at the donkeys in their field as they pass, and at the pond glittering in the sun. "I've never seen donkeys in a London garden before; it's impossible to believe we're in the middle of a city."

"My father bought this place for the garden; he was mad about trees. He taught us to ride on those donkeys."

"It must have been fantastic to grow up with so much freedom."

"We didn't; the nanny kept us on a leash." It sounds like a joke, though it wasn't funny. She doesn't talk about it much, but Martin feels like a friend somehow and she hasn't many. She lost touch with her old crowd years ago; Eric didn't like them, he found them phony. Family is enough for him, family is everything, but she misses her old friends at times.

"Actually, Eric thinks our kids have too much freedom."

"Is it possible to have too much?"

He calls it neglect, but she doesn't tell Martin that; she pushes the gate open and they are immediately in the little wood. The quiet is dense, like entering a soundproof room with thick green walls.

"Poppy! Sorrel!" The words don't carry very far; perhaps Eric's right, they should cut down some trees. "They'll be here somewhere." It's dark under the crowded branches, too much undergrowth, so many thorns. She begins to hurry, her feet catching on roots, her breath hot in her throat. For a place where the children spend most of their time, she doesn't come here often enough.

"Girls?"

A soft giggle comes from the right, the red of Poppy's jacket flares beneath a young horse chestnut tree. She steps closer, Martin holding aside the brambles. The children are grouped in a patch of green-gold shade; Ash is sleeping on Izzy's lap. The young girl is leaning forward, her body sheltering his, her long hair brushing his face. She is talking quietly, telling a story from the look on their faces. Poppy is lying in front of her playing with Ash's foot, Blake is flat on the ground with mud on his face. Charley has her back against a tree, her eyes on the puppy in her lap, Sorrel near her.

"See?" Martin whispers. "Babes in the wood."

"I hope not," she whispers back, light-headed with relief. "We don't want them to starve to death under the leaves."

His snort of laughter is so loud the children look up, except for Ash, who is sleeping, and Izzy, who smiles.

"Thanks, Izzy. Hello, my little one." She bends to take Ash. He feels warm in his green onesie; he whimpers then settles again, his cheek against hers, his mouth on her neck. There are little scratches on his hands, new ones, easy to tell, she knows his skin by heart. She kisses Sorrel's head and reaches for Poppy, who moves out of range, flushing angrily. The children get to their feet, they seem dazed. Blake looks cross. Martin rumples his hair but he shakes him off, moving closer to Izzy. Poppy maneuvers herself to her other side. Sorrel takes Charley's hand; allegiances shaping up.

"I should have been watching more closely." Eve leads the way out of the woods, back into the warm sunshine of the meadow. She holds Ash tightly; the warm weight against her chest settles her heart.

"I lost Blake in the supermarket when he was just four. I found him in the confectionery aisle tipping Maltesers into his mouth from two packets at once. I'm not sure Grace has ever forgiven me."

She glances at his rueful expression and smiles. He's nice; a nice man as she'd thought. Near the house Igor has closed the hood and is leaning against the green truck, arms folded, watching their progress.

"We found Ash. He wasn't lost after all," she tells him.

Igor stares back. "Aha. So that's why I couldn't find him under the hood." His lips twist into a grin, a joke of sorts. Sorrel giggles and waves to him. Eve steers her toward the house, feeling sick; the image of her son's warm body crammed into the greasy workings of a truck is vivid.

Farther down the drive a woman steps from a red sports car, a slim blond with a scarf around her neck and her hair pulled tightly off her face. As she walks toward them, Eve recognizes Melissa, but she looks different today; thinner than Eve remembers, more tense.

"Am I late?"

"Not at all. They were all down in the garden. Your daughter's been working hard and having a lovely time." Eve puts an arm around Izzy, who is staring at her mother from under her bangs; her smile has vanished.

"Has she?" A tremor runs over Melissa's lovely

face; Eve wonders for a moment if she is going to cry. "Thank you, that's good to hear."

"Come in." Eve gestures to the house. "I can show you what she's done."

"I'd love to see it . . ." Melissa glances at the house, then at her daughter as if uncertain.

"I'll make us some tea." Eve smiles. "There's homemade cake."

"Actually, I better go." Melissa's face seems to tighten. "Would it be okay to scan and send her work instead?"

"Of course," Eve says smoothly, masking her disappointment; there will be other chances to get to know Melissa, lots of them. "See you on Sunday, maybe?"

"I'll have more time then," Melissa replies. "Say thank you, Izzy."

Izzy follows her mother to the car without a word, wrenches open the door, and climbs in. The children watch the car drive away.

"She didn't even say goodbye." Sorrel sounds disappointed. Eve puts an arm around her and cuddles her into her side. She looks for Poppy, but she has gone back into the house.

Blake is scuffling the gravel of the drive into little piles with his feet; Charley leans against her father looking tired.

"Your wife must be wondering where you are," Eve says, feeling guilty for keeping him so long.

"Oh, Grace won't be back yet, she works full-time. It'll be me bringing the children from now on," he replies.

Eve's heart lifts at the thought. It had been so easy to talk to him; their conversation had slid seamlessly into a place in her mind that must have been ready and waiting.

The wrinkles around Martin's eyes deepen as he nods goodbye. "Thanks for the magic," he says.

Grace

"Fairyland? What the hell, Martin?"

She shouldn't raise her voice or stand with her hands on her hips, a parody of a shrewish wife, but he looks so complacent. Stories. Homemade cake. A day trip then, not a workshop, money gone to waste. She is tired, so tired she can hardly stand. The website had crashed at work, a drunk guest had been insulting, then a woman told her to collect her suitcase as though she were a porter, not a receptionist. She said nothing in case she lost her temper, but then the woman complained about her silence anyway.

"It's imperative we engage with the clients." The

hotel manager, a plump little man, had inspected her face and, more slowly, her body. She had walked away, swallowing rage.

"They had fun," Martin replies mildly. "That's the main thing."

"The main thing is his work; he'll have exams to pass one day."

"You don't have to follow every rule in the book—"

"Yes, we do." She turns away and walks into the kitchen; he should know why Blake and Charley have to follow rules, that she does too. Ten minutes ago the tall bloke had stepped out from a doorway in front of her as she reached the entrance of the building.

"What do you think you're doing here, bitch?" he'd muttered, standing close enough for her to catch that nail-polish smell of cocaine.

She walked around him, didn't reply, didn't look back, and didn't run, though her heart had been thudding in her mouth. It wasn't dark, she was wearing work clothes, her hair was tied back, the keys had been ready in her hand. She'd been following every bloody rule in the book; her grandfather had made her learn them by heart. The youth laughed as he watched her go, the type who didn't give a fuck about rules.

Martin follows her to the kitchen and pours two glasses of wine, offers her one.

"We can't afford wine."

"We ought to celebrate, it's been a good day."

"Let's celebrate when something good actually happens." She dumps the dirty supper plates and forks in the sink and begins to wash them.

"The kids had a great time and I wrote five hundred words this morning." He raises his glass, smiling. "Isn't that good enough?"

"Good as in when your next book sells," she continues, scrubbing the forks. Or my first one does, she adds silently.

He doesn't reply; there's nothing to say. He knows the prize money is almost gone and her earnings are barely enough. She puts the cutlery on the draining board, takes the wet clothes from the washing machine and hangs them on the rack. She doesn't want to discuss her writing, not yet, it feels safer that way. She pulls the broom from the cupboard and starts sweeping up the crumbs.

"Stop for a second, Gracie. Eve's kitchen was a mess, but it was kind of relaxing."

"They have the space for mess; you have to be rich to be that untidy." She can't remember the last time he picked up a broom, though that was the deal. He'd write for now and keep house, she'd go to work, then they'd swap. She's too tired to go into it all again now.

She sweeps the dust into a pan, tips it in the bin, replaces the broom, and walks past him into Charley's room. Her daughter is asleep and snoring. Grace kisses her cheek, strokes her hair, and eases *The Sheep-Pig* from her grip, puts it on the table, and turns off the light.

Blake is sprawled on his back; he's fallen asleep with a streak of mud on his face. She sits on his bed and watches him, feeling her face soften. If she'd gotten back earlier he might have told her something about his day, she could have said good night. She's missing things, important things; she's not around to see anything the kids do, or even hear about it afterward. There must be a way to arrange life better but she hasn't found it yet. Blake's toes are still hooked into his sneakers; as she inches them off, a penknife falls out, a small metal one, cold in her hands. She flicks it open, feeling sick; the blade is surprisingly long. She closes it and turns off the light. In the sitting room, Martin is watching television.

"Look what I found in Blake's shoe." She puts the knife on the table. "God knows what he's doing with a knife." She sits close to him for the warmth, shivering a little as if with shock.

He picks it up, looking bemused. "Where did it come from?"

"I have no idea."

"Maybe a friend lent it to him—I used to love playing with penknives at his age."

"It's completely different now; the police came into school the other day to give them a talk about knife crime. He'll be in real trouble if he's found with this, perhaps he's in trouble already."

"Blake's a good boy, there'll be an explanation. I'll talk to him and get the story." He puts his arm around her. "Leave this to me, Gracie. He'll be fine, you'll see. You look exhausted; come to bed."

She puts the knife in her bag where Blake won't think to look. It slips down out of sight, beneath the coin purse and the keys, her wallet, makeup, the spare tampon. Maybe Martin's right; questions might be better coming from him, man to man.

In bed Martin turns toward her with his smile. "Hello, stranger," he murmurs as his arms wrap around her. There's always this, she tells herself as their faces meet, this at the end of the day, when they are together and warm and everything else melts away.

But it isn't quite the end of the day; once he's asleep, she gets out of bed again and sits down to write at the kitchen table. Now and again she stares out at the trains passing beyond the community gardens, beads of light traveling in the dark. Thousands of miles away the sun is rising in the mountains in the north of Zimbabwe where her grandfather lived on his farm. He used to tell her to walk slowly, look carefully in case you miss a sick calf or the moment when the maize is ripe for harvest. She wishes now she'd asked him how the hell you do that while you fit in everything else; no one walks slowly in London, not when you have a job and kids or hostile youths near your home. She misses him, she misses her whole family, the neighbors she used to have, all the friends. Life had seemed so much easier back home.

"What do you think you're doing here, bitch?" she whispers to her reflection in the window.

Melissa

"You actually look scared." Paul gets out of his chair and comes around the table with the wine; he seems amused. His suit is tighter, his high cheekbones obscured by new padding. "Were you frightened she'd force you to eat it?"

She should never have mentioned the cake. Perhaps she should have accepted Eve's invitation; she could have brought some home with her. He might secretly love cake. He might consume it on his plane journeys or maybe his secretary smuggles it into the office for him, hidden in damp paper napkins. The last secretary used to ask for him in breathy whispers on the phone. Melissa didn't really mind; she didn't last long, they never do.

"Izzy's going to show me her story after supper." He pours himself another glass then sits down. He's drinking more than he used to, but she can't possibly point it out.

"Oh, Eve was going to send it to me." How childish that sounds.

"She must have sent it to Izzy instead." He smiles, head to one side with a mischievous look, the one she fell in love with years ago. "Does it matter, Melly?"

The light is harsh in here, the new decanters glitter on the sideboard, the lilies cast stark shadows over the tablecloth. He likes to examine what he's eating in the same way he'll examine her later. He wants to see what he's doing.

"No, it doesn't matter." She'd wanted to see Izzy's work for once, but she shakes her head. "It doesn't matter at all."

Paul begins to eat rapidly. "I can't remember when I last saw her like this, she's really excited."

Izzy had been silent in the car on the way home but her eyes had looked different, hopeful somehow, brighter, as though a light had been switched on inside.

Melissa picks up her knife and fork and starts to cut her beef into very small pieces, pushing them under the lettuce. "Tell me about your project."

"It's not mine yet. It's a shareholder decision." He shrugs. "It could take a while. Everyone was there, plus the other architects, of course, the competition."

"Everyone?"

"Senior partners, their wives. The odd girlfriend." He holds the wine in his mouth before swallowing, then he smiles. "They loved my design, especially the windows. When it's built, the atrium will dominate the Seine . . ."

She stops listening. He'd have been conspicuous in Paris, tall, fair-haired, a little fleshy. Handsome. The kind of looks that hold women in thrall, that can catch at her heart even now. He might have caught someone's eye. Someone young, he prefers younger women. She pushes another piece of beef under the lettuce. She's being stupid. He was there to be judged; he would have been on his best behavior, there wouldn't have been time.

". . . take Izzy to France with me on the next visit," he finishes with a fond little smile.

Melissa puts her fork down. She'd looked forward to showing Paris to Izzy herself for the very first time. She'd planned it out: they'd go to the Eiffel Tower first then the Louvre; the next day there would be time to explore Montmartre and, after that, maybe clothes shopping from little boutiques.

"What a good idea," she makes herself reply. "Izzy will love that."

He comes out of his daughter's bedroom an hour later, smiling to himself. He halts when he sees her hovering outside on the landing. "She's shown me what she did today. She's tired now. Best leave her be, my love."

She hesitates, disappointed. She had wanted to see the work, put her cheek against her daughter's, kiss her good night. She daren't insist.

"I'll take the day off tomorrow." He takes her arm very gently; his breath in her ear makes her shiver. "We might go to the sea."

She spends half an hour in the gym before bed, aware of Paul's voice murmuring in the kitchen next door, Lina's quieter answering one; hopefully he's thanking her for supper and not ordering her about. He's asleep by the time she's finished on the treadmill. She slides in beside him and lies still, keeping her breathing very quiet, but he wakes and reaches for her anyway. He turns on the light and runs his hands over her body, her stomach and thighs, as if assessing her flesh. Her muscles tense. He likes women slender, very slender.

She closes her eyes. After a while he asks her to turn on her face. She keeps very quiet; they mustn't disturb Izzy, she's probably asleep. It's over quite quickly. He falls asleep but she lies awake in the dark, tears sliding from her eyes. Tomorrow there'll be waves and a beach, she doesn't care which one. She'll watch Paul and Izzy playing together, Paul holding his daughter close, lifting her over the waves in his arms like a baby while she waits on the shore. He'd do anything for Izzy, nothing else matters. The father-daughter bond she never had, that's the important thing. Izzy's lucky, Paul adores her. Nothing must get in the way, least of all her.

The house is quiet when she wakes the next morning, though it's past nine o'clock. The sky is cloudless, already bright. She overslept. Paul must be loading the car, Izzy showering. She dresses quickly, winding a soft blue scarf around her neck, blue for the sea and the sky. The scarf is new and patterned with little flowers. Paul prefers block colors, but she'd been unable to resist. Patterns on a scarf don't matter, they won't count, surely.

In the kitchen Lina is spooning cat food into a bowl while the kitten winds around her long skirt, purring loudly. Lina looks tired, there are shadows beneath her dark eyes; she might like a break from her routine.

"We're going to the sea today, Lina," Melissa says cheerfully. "Why don't you come with us?"

Lina shakes her head, her cheeks redden.

"Please, sweetie. You might enjoy it and I'd love your company." She means it; it would be comforting to have Lina's calm presence on the blanket next to her while Paul and Izzy swim in the sea. She'd love to see Lina enjoy herself for once. They could stroll along the beach together eating ice cream; well, she'd pretend to eat hers. They'd breathe in the salty air and look at the boats. She opens the fridge. "I'll make the picnic. What would you like? I'm certain we had some Manchego—"

"Mr. Chorley-Smith said they'll buy something on the way." Lina studies Venus, who is eating her food with small, savage bites.

"On the way?"

"They left an hour ago." Lina doesn't look up.

The kitten steps away from the bowl. The sun is pouring through the windows, illuminating the dirty metal; fragments of leftover cat food are squashed at the edges of the bowl. The sea will be very blue in this light, very clear. The kitten twists her head to lick her sides, it looks as though she's turning herself inside out. Melissa closes the fridge and walks from the room, unwinding the scarf as she goes and letting it fall to the ground. She phones the clients in Chelsea to let them know she is free today after all, she can bring the curtain fabric to their flat to try against their windows at any time that suits them. The walls in Melissa's upstairs studio are painted black; the darkness works well as a background, colors glow, things stand out. You have to be careful with your choices, though; dark materials tend to recede. As she assembles the bolts of fabric, she catches sight of her reflection in the mirror; in her black shirt and jeans she seems to be disappearing into the walls.

*B*lake's actually looking forward to going back to
Eve's house. That first time was way better than
he thought it would be. The garden especially, you can
get lost in that garden and no one knows where you
are. There were ants and stuff under the leaves, balls of
rabbit poo. The mud was sticky like some kind of cake.
He was good at making cake, his was the best, Eve had
whispered. He can't remember being the best at anything before. That first time he'd pushed his fingers
into the mud and smeared it on his face, like a soldier
tracking people in a forest. Next time he could make a
shelter with the branches. He could kill rabbits for food
and skin them, like that guy on TV. He could make a
fire then spear the rabbit and cook it. He'll share it with

Izzy. She'd gotten a knife especially for him, though he's gone and lost it. For you, she'd said, smiling. She made him feel good, like he's important or something. He's looking forward to going to Eve's again, mostly so he can see Izzy.

Poppy crosses *off the days in her homework diary: five, four, three. She starts to feel excited. She used to hate Sundays, but it's different now; everything's different. She doesn't care about coming last in spelling anymore, or having to work on her own because no one wants her to be their partner in science. She goes back to the woods after school to see the place where Izzy had been lying under the conker tree, her arms and legs spread wide. She had lain down next to her; the leaves had looked amazing, patterns and shapes she hadn't seen before. After a while they'd heard her mother calling. It was funny because she'd sounded panicky and she never panics—she hasn't got the slightest clue where she and Sorrel are most of the time. She was probably only worried because of what the other parents would say if everyone was lost. Poppy had looked at Izzy. Izzy had been looking at her and she was smiling; Poppy had smiled back. She felt brilliant. She had actually felt like bursting out laugh-*

ing. Today the wood is very quiet. It's getting a bit dark. Poppy lies down in the same place and closes her eyes. She stretches out her arms and legs as widely as she can. Three more days. She feels happier than she's ever felt.

3. June

Eve

The weeks have settled into a shape, the days tilting toward the Sunday lessons. At least once a week Eve walks the half mile to the bookshop in Dulwich Village. She collects a basketful of children's books, glancing at a copy of Martin's in the adult fiction shelves. The new jacket carries a photo of him from fifteen years ago, looking like a young Harrison Ford. She sees the assistant watching and shuts the book with a snap, replacing it on the shelf.

Then it's Sunday again, the fourth session. After a game of letter snap, she scatters photos on the table in front of the children. Jamie Oliver, Tom Cruise, Steven Spielberg, Richard Branson, Joss Stone, Keira Knightley, Holly Willoughby. "They all have dyslexia," she explains. "But they've all got to exactly where they wanted to go."

Blake is quiet, his eyes flicking between the faces. Poppy inspects the women closely, but Izzy glances at them briefly then laughs. Poppy laughs quickly, joining in. Eve takes the photos away and hands around the set of words she has cut up for them to use in their writing. Blake chews his pencil and begins to work; Poppy frowns, writing slowly. Izzy scrawls a few sentences then gets down from the table and starts to play with Sorrel, whispering behind her hand. Ash reaches to touch her shiny fall of hair; he looks dazzled, as if staring at a bright light.

Eve calls Izzy back to the table for the math session. Izzy and Poppy sit side by side, so close they are almost touching; her daughter's face looks soft with happiness. Eve wants to tell her to be careful, hold back a little, she's been hurt so often. Blake stares across the table at Izzy, looks down when he senses Eve's gaze, then looks up again; Izzy exchanges little glances with Poppy. After half an hour, Blake stops writing and puts down his pen. Poppy looks out the window toward the trees.

"Break time!" Eve says quickly.

They run into the garden like puppies off a leash,

Ash stumbling to catch up. Eve watches from the door, she mustn't interfere. This is what she'd hoped for, all the children playing together; after half an hour she calls them back for painting, then at the end of the morning they rush outside again. As Eve is clearing up paint pots and washing brushes, fingernails tap against the window like the rattle of little stones; Melissa arriving early. Eve looks up, smiles and waves. Few people call in at the house; it's set far back from the road, the grandeur is daunting. Her father had liked the peace; the idea that his children might feel lonely had never occurred to him. She takes a tray outside and they sit on the grass, sipping coffee. Melly's red MG is parked in the drive, the top down.

"I know what you're thinking," Melly says, catching her glance. "It's lazy of us not to walk, but Paul gives Izzy lifts all the time, she's got used to it. He spoils that child."

The air is lime-sharp with the scent of grass. The noise of Igor mowing the meadow merges with the children's voices from the wood. Melissa shades her eyes, staring across the garden. "Listen to them," she says wistfully. "A whole family of children having fun."

"A bigger one than I'd planned for, counting Charley and my little ones—they're here more than I thought they would be. I don't teach them, but they join in the games afterwards." Eve touches her arm. "I should charge you less; that's only fair."

"You don't owe me a penny. Izzy's happy, she adores everyone. I think it helps, having the younger ones around. Paul says her homework's improved. He checks it every night." She tightens the scarf around her neck. "I'm not allowed."

"He does the homework?" Eve raises her eyebrows. "Gosh, the perfect husband."

Melly shakes her head, smiling faintly; her eyes glisten.

The children appear soon after that, shrieking as they scatter across the lawn, chased by Izzy. Ash tumbles into his mother's lap, laughing hysterically. Izzy stops in her tracks when she sees her mother, then stalks off to wait in the car.

"We better go." Melissa stands up. "Paul's home; he gets lonely without us."

"You're covered with grass." Eve helps her brush off the clinging fragments; as they walk to the car together she stoops to pick a bunch of red peonies from the border and when they reach the driveway she puts them into Melly's hand.

"Thanks." Melissa clutches the flowers. "For everything."

The children are silent after Izzy's departure. Sorrel leans against Eve as she picks Ash up and wraps her spare arm around Poppy, but her eldest daughter shrugs her off. She walks down the drive, staring at the grooves Melissa's car has scored in the gravel as if she wants to follow them to her friend's house.

"I really want to do something for Melly." They are clearing supper, the children settled in bed. "She seemed down today, a little tearful. I imagine Izzy's a handful at times." She passes Eric the plates, which he loads into the dishwasher. "It's Ash's birthday at the end of term, let's have a party. I'll invite Charley, Blake, and Izzy. Melly and Paul can come, Martin too, of course, and Grace if she's free."

She'll lay out a feast, buy a new dress, wear makeup for once. She hasn't bothered for months, years even. Eric has never liked makeup. He thinks it makes her look like someone else; she is prettier without, he told her. At the time she was charmed, but she can't help thinking it would be fun to look like someone else for a change.

"What about Ash's other friends?" Eric takes a glass from her hands.

"I think he likes these ones the best. He likes their parents as well."

Eric rinses the knives without replying, then slots them carefully into the dishwasher basket.

"All right, I'm fond of them too. It's not like we know masses of people round here." Eve addresses his back; she bends to stroke the dog's ears. "It's strange, but I feel as if we've known them for years."

He nods without replying, so she stops talking, and they continue to stack the dishes side by side in silence.

Grace

"How was it today?" Grace asks.

"How was what?" Martin is comparing the prices of organic and ordinary bananas and doesn't look up.

"I wish you wouldn't do that." Grace puts a giant bag of potatoes in the cart and pushes it on down the aisle. Martin hurries after her.

"Do what?"

"Pretend you don't know what I mean."

He knows she'd want to hear about the session, she always does. She had wanted to see the children's work for herself, and though she won't ever admit this to Martin, she'd wanted that friendship with Eve. She'd met her before Martin did, but she can't say that either, it would sound so childish. Back in the winter, when she was first considering whether to put Blake's name down for the sessions, she went to Eve's house to meet her. Eve had flung open her door and taken

Grace's hand in both of hers, her great ring flashing red in the frosty December sun. She'd seemed larger than life somehow, more colorful, more friendly, than most people Grace had met in England. "Hi, I'm Eve Kershaw," she'd said, smiling a warm smile. "I'm thrilled you got in touch. I'm certain I can help your son." She'd brought Grace into her brightly lit kitchen. She'd been brimming with hope and ideas; the hope was infectious. Grace had handed over the cash for a term's worth of sessions there and then.

"We'll chat after each lesson," Eve had promised. "I'll fill you in as we go."

But then the sessions turned out to be on Sundays to fit with the children's commitments. Sundays were workdays for Grace, extra long because of double time. That first visit was her only one; Martin takes the children instead and collects them too.

Grace pays for the groceries at the register and they wheel the bags to the car.

"Blake's doing fine," he tells her as they fill the trunk with the shopping. "Just fine."

"You always say that; you said that about the knife in his shoe—"

"And it was fine. A friend had lent it to him as I told you; he wasn't going to use it. I believed him, I thought you did."

"I just wish I shared more of his life, Charley's too, rather than a few minutes at the beginning and end of the day." She dumps a box of washing powder in the trunk. "I feel excluded somehow."

He hefts in the potatoes, slams the trunk, and gives her a bear hug. "Why not do a few of the school pick-ups? Melly and Eve share some already; you'd feel more included then."

"I thought of that, but I wouldn't have time to get round to all those schools," she replies, getting into the car.

"They'll be at the same ones soon." Martin sounds surprised that she doesn't know, but that's exactly the point; she's never there to know. "When Blake starts at the Charter next term, he'll be with Poppy and Izzy; Charley's already with Sorrel at Dulwich Hamlet."

"Okay." She stares out at the parking lot as Martin starts the engine. At least that way she'd get to exchange a few words with Eve, be part of it somehow. "I'll try to swap for more early shifts."

At home they make the journeys in the lift up and down until there are just a couple more bags left in the car. Charley and Blake beg Martin for one of his made-up bedtime stories. She watches them sprawl on the sofa, cuddling close to their father as he begins to weave a magical tale involving a heroine and dragons.

She'll manage the last things on her own; they look so happy together. She descends in the lift, hurries outside, then stops abruptly. The tall guy with the green-soled sneakers is standing near the door, a foot against the wall behind him. He turns to look at her, his eyes cold; menace seems to throb in the air between them. There's a smaller boy by the path and another in the parking lot; there could be more in the shadows. She walks to the car, heart thumping, staring straight ahead. She takes the bags from the trunk, locks it, and walks back. The boy by the door has moved; now he's blocking her way, head lowered, like an animal about to charge. She steps around him, catching a guttural laugh, more of a growl than a laugh.

She reaches the doorway and, once inside, runs into the lift, pressing the button to the thirteenth floor. She leans against the side of the lift as it rises; her legs feel separate from her body, as though they might give way. Martin needn't know. He'd tell the landlady, though there's really nothing to tell; things might get worse. They put the shopping away, then Martin goes to bed, but she makes herself reach for her notebook. Her fingers are still trembling, so it's difficult to form the letters at first, but gradually she becomes absorbed in the world on the page. The only sounds she can hear are the familiar ones of her husband snoring, Charley breathing, Blake muttering in his sleep; her family close by, practically within touching distance. The threat outside fades as she writes; gradually it becomes something she might have imagined, almost as if it had happened to somebody else.

Melissa

Melissa paces the landing waiting for Paul to emerge; she is determined to see Izzy this time. The sparkly "I" on Izzy's door glistens in the security lights shining through the landing window. It's getting late. Her footsteps are silent, cushioned by thick carpet. Their home was designed for quiet and she tries to quiet herself. The house won an architecture award the year it was built, but when Melissa returned from Eve's a few hours ago and went down to the kitchen, the gray walls had closed around her like a prison. Eve's kitchen is chaotic, her colors clash, the red of the sofa against the orange walls and the faded pinks of the Persian carpet. Cookbooks are piled on the table along with recipes torn from magazines, children's drawings are stuck to the walls, clothes are left on chairs. The windows are flung wide; the garden was alive with the noise of children today; Ash had been laughing joyously. Strange to think she can't remember Izzy laughing at that age, but then she hadn't spent much time with her, at least in the day. They'd had an au pair so Melissa could work; at night she'd sneak from their bed and lie down next to her sleeping child, breathing her in.

Izzy had hurried to her room on their return to finish her weekend homework and Paul slipped in later, as usual, shutting the door. She needed his help, he'd said; he asked her not to disturb them. She paces to the window. The gravel garden looks pale and lifeless in the outdoor lighting. Eve's lawn had shone in the sun at lunchtime; the smell of grass is still on her palms, the same scent that had been in the air the day she met Paul. He'd been sprawled like some god by the side of the grass court in the tennis club, twenty years ago. "Look at that," her friend Julie had whispered. "Bet he's got loads of girlfriends." Melissa could feel him staring at her as she played; she'd felt exposed in her tennis skirt, babyish in the ridiculous socks, but she'd seemed fresh, he told her later, so innocent, so young. As the summer progressed he took her to the theater and for picnics by the sea in his sports car with the roof rolled down. She was fifteen, bowled over by the attention. When she told him about her anorexia, whispering with shame, he seemed refreshingly unperturbed. Her parents didn't mind the age gap; her father said Paul was a man after his own heart, ruthless like him. Ambition should be rewarded, he'd said. He'd set him up in his own architecture practice. They were married after her interior design course. She spent a couple of years building her business before she was allowed a pregnancy, back to work after. Sometimes she wonders if they'd planned it all out between them from the start.

The door of Izzy's bedroom opens after a further ten minutes and Paul emerges, but as she moves forward he shuts it quickly behind him. "She's tired out again, poor lamb. Come with me," he whispers, and leads her downstairs. His clasp is firm on her arm; cheated again. He pours them some wine. "She's doing okay." He raises the glass to her. "Those lessons were a smart move, Melly. Good thinking."

His praise hooks her back, still. She moves closer and holds her hands out. "Smell, right here. Does it remind you of anything?"

"You know I can't stand perfume." He frowns.

"It's just grass, not perfume. It took me back to that tennis club where we—"

"Can you wash it off before bed?" He picks up his glass. "I ate at work; I've got accounts to go over."

She's not going to cry, it's her fault; she picked the wrong moment. He's tetchy with tiredness, that's all. Lina is laying out their food in the kitchen: pink salmon, green broccoli, and tiny new potatoes.

"Please eat with me, Lina, Paul's busy."

Lina sits down obediently. She must wonder why Melissa is so often on her own and why their house seems empty of friends. Melissa pushes her potatoes to one side. The stark truth is that she doesn't invite friends around, or go out with them, because her husband doesn't want her to.

"I simply want to spend time with my wife at the end of a busy day," he'd said, sipping wine. "Fair enough, surely?" She'd nodded, but the days had become weeks, months, then years. The friends had stopped phoning, stopped coming around. She touches the peonies that Lina has put in a vase on the table, a splash of scarlet against the gray; the petals feel very soft. The days are different now; there are Sundays to look forward to, conversation and laughter. The whole week feels warmer, richer, more colorful. It must be the same for Izzy.

Melissa smiles at Lina. "It seems crazy we don't know more about your family after all this time, Lina. Tell me about them."

Lina shakes her head, perhaps she doesn't understand.

"Your father, for instance. What does he do?"

"He is dead," Lina says after a pause, turning her head to the window. Melissa puts down her fork, walks around the table, and sits next to Lina, slipping an arm around her shoulders.

"I'm sorry, sweetheart." She feels guilty for having stirred the memories, guilty for not having discovered them before.

"The war." Lina makes a horizontal movement with her hand, as if sweeping something away.

After a while, Lina gets up and they clear the table together in silence, but one that feels companionable. When they finish Melissa makes two cups of tea. Lina picks hers up with a little bow and walks softly from the kitchen.

Melissa checks her watch, it's late. Paul will be in bed, waiting. She hurries upstairs in a panic and stands in the shower for a long time, soaping her wrists again and again.

*P*oppy tells Izzy her secrets because Izzy listens; she says she wants to know all about the family. Izzy thinks Mum doesn't look after things properly.

"Look at that ring your mother wears," she says. "She's got bits of food stuck in it like she's been cooking with it on. She doesn't give a toss about anything. It's all a mess in your house."

Poppy nods meekly. They're in the wood; Izzy's smoking. She offers one to Poppy but Poppy doesn't dare.

"Suit yourself." Izzy shrugs. "There's whole boxes of cigarettes in my dad's office if you change your mind; he's got a drawer where he keeps secret things, his bottles of booze and stuff. There were knickers in there once, black ones. I bet he has sex on the desk." She blows out smoke in a ring.

Poppy's skin prickles. "Who with?" She tries to sound bored like Izzy.

"God knows," Izzy says. "Could be any one of his girlfriends."

"What does your mum think?" Poppy asks.

Izzy shrugs, her face closes up. She doesn't answer, but then she never talks about her mum. She stubs out her cigarette on a tree trunk, gets some chewing gum from the pocket of her shorts and gives some to Poppy. They walk out of the wood together, chewing.

"Ninety-nine, a hundred," they shout, smothering giggles. "Ready or not."

Blake watches them from behind the rain barrel. Izzy said they'll play better games soon. She told him they'll need the knife, so he had to admit he lost it, and she said don't worry lots more where that came from, e.g., the shed. She came up really close and smiled and he felt amazing. The last time he felt like this was when they went camping and they played soccer and he got more goals than anyone else, and that was over a year ago.

Sorrel is hiding behind a tree. She can hear Izzy growling; she's being a monster. It's supposed to be fun but it's scary. She's coming closer and closer and it's too late to run, then suddenly Izzy starts laughing and she turns back from being a monster into a friend. Poppy starts laughing, so Sorrel does too. She doesn't tell anyone about being frightened because that would be silly, it was only a game.

PART TWO

Summer Holidays

Later the police would pore over the videos we took that summer, play them over and over, looking to see where it all began. They start—as everything does—with the children. Poppy and Sorrel waiting by the door, wearing dress-up clothes. Charley and Blake being dropped off, Izzy arriving. Ducklings swim on the pond and the trees in the distance become a denser, darker green. Eric waves from a ladder by the trees, Igor trudges past with a spade. The clothes get brighter, lighter, skimpier. It was hot for months. Poppy walks with Izzy, linking arms, they look as though they are whispering. Blake is close behind, his head lowered. Sorrel and Charley play with the dog on a blanket. Ash runs toward them over the grass. For a little boy he ran surprisingly fast, surprisingly far. We didn't realize that until later—would that have made a difference? Then shots of Charley giving Ash donkey rides around the field, Sorrel walking beside her. They are all smiling.

If only we could stop the film, right there. Stop, re- wind, and play again on a loop.

Flicker, flicker. Food on the table. A fruit cake, a chocolate cake, cupcakes. Lemon drizzle then a sponge cake smothered in strawberries and cream. There are lots of Martin arriving and leaving, books under his arm, blowing kisses to the camera. His shirt becomes tighter, all that cake.

Bonfires flare in the background; Eric made so many, there was a bonfire every Sunday to burn dead stuff from the garden; the children loved them, begged him for them, danced around them. There's one long shot of them running into the woods, disappearing among the trees, bleached out by the light like little ghosts. Eve was filming from the veranda by the house; so far away that you can't really see what they are doing, but then, none of us saw what was happening at the time. We weren't looking. It seems incredible now, when you think about it, that we were all too busy to see what was right in front of our eyes.

4. July

Eve

The holidays arrive with a bang. Ash's birthday party. Everyone's coming: all the kids, plus Melly, Paul, and Martin. Grace hopes to join them after work. That's twelve, counting Eve's own family.

The kitchen is messy, messier than usual. The girls hang around Eve as she rolls dough, smooths icing, and pipes cream. Scraps of pastry litter the table, lemon halves lie on the floor and eggshells in the sink. Eve's face is wet with sweat. The kitchen is a furnace. At lunchtime the children are hungry. Poppy asks for food, pushing against her mother impatiently. She gives up after a while, grabs an apple from the fruit bowl, and goes outside. Sorrel follows. Eve leans her elbows on the windowsill to watch, blowing the hair from her eyes, her hands sticky with icing. The girls trail after Eric, who is sawing wood and hammering lengths together to make the roof of a playhouse. They clamber over the planks, used to his silences; his quiet focus settles them down. Sorrel squats near him, patting sawdust into cakes on a length of wood. Poppy sits in the shade eating her apple and watching closely. The little house is taking shape quickly as if by magic; Ash's birthday present, due to be unveiled at the party later. The slide and swing have arrived and Igor is assembling them, grunting with effort.

Eve remembers her cooking and turns to the oven with a gasp. The papery cases of filo pastry are dark brown at the edges; she throws them away and starts again. They scorch again. On the third try they are perfect. She fills them with lemon cream, fresh dill, and tiny shrimp. Martin likes fish. She's made the bouilla-baisse, marinated the salmon, and baked crab patties, all with him in mind. Ash climbs on the table. He runs his fingers through a glistening heap of broad beans in oil, pushes his hands in her mouth, makes a face. She laughs and lifts him down, holding him to her for a moment, the small heart beating against her hands as he wriggles. She breathes in the warm smell of his hair as she sets him on the floor. Released, he tumbles into the cushions on top of the dog. She takes the cream from the fridge, then purees the raspberries. She is folding them together, absorbed by the red bleeding into the white, when Eric comes in from the garden, his face dripping with sweat. Noah runs to him limping slightly, wagging his tail. Eric glances at him as he crosses to the fridge, the bottles jangling as he yanks open the door. He drains half a liter of orange juice from the carton then puts it down.

"Dog's hurt," he says, wiping his mouth with his arm.

"Ash fell on him just now. He'll recover." She draws near, touching his hand; the skin is wet. "Do you remember it was hot like this, the day he was born?" Labor had been long and sweaty; Eric had been by her side throughout, attentive and tender, overwhelmed when his son arrived. She smiles. "It's hard to believe that little baby is already three!"

"He's not a baby anymore." He walks to the door, turns back, grins briefly. "He said 'Dad' by the way." He disappears and she stares after him, stunned. Ash's first word.

Through the window, Ash is now sitting on a pile of bark chips trickling them through his fingers. He must have escaped from the kitchen unnoticed. She hurries out the door after Eric and bends down to Ash in the new playground. "What did the birthday boy say?"

He picks up a handful of bark chips and shows them to her.

"What's Daddy called, poppet?"

Ash rolls on his back, squeezing his eyes shut against the sun.

Sorrel slips off the swing and squats near. "I heard him say 'Dad,'" she whispers.

Eve puts an arm around Sorrel and they watch Ash as he rolls from side to side. "Lucky girl," she whispers back. "Wish I'd heard too."

"The house is s'posed to be a surprise." Poppy's angry voice comes from the top of the slide. "You're s'posed to be keeping him inside."

Eve carries her squirming son back to the kitchen. She puts champagne in the fridge and watches Eric's tall figure through the window, trundling pieces of wood away for the bonfire, too busy to celebrate this special moment together. She bastes the salmon, watching the dark soy and honey slide over the pink flesh. She knew what he was like when they married; has he changed or has she? She didn't mind the silences at the beginning, she was busy with babies. It hadn't mattered then but now it does. She puts the salmon back in the fridge and takes out the steak to marinate in oil and garlic. He's a wonderful father and a loyal husband, but if she never said another word, he might not either. She rubs garlic into the meat, imagining the silences stretching for hours, days, weeks. She has a brief vision of their lives going forward into the future, spent side by side in wordless quiet, like life in a monastery. When she tells Martin that Ash has said his first word he'll laugh and clap his hands. They'll talk; the chat might open into a discussion about language and books, the novel he's reading or the chapter he's writing. It could be something else like the view from his balcony or the people in the streets. Anything. Small talk, Eric would say, but it's talk that expands, the conversations swirl outward. Eric's statements are like the shutters that close over shop fronts in the evening, metal ones that clang. *Dog's hurt; he's not a baby anymore.*

She bends to Noah, running her hand over his leg. He whines when she feels around the left hip joint; perhaps she needs to get him checked out by the vet; family concerns flowing into the cracks in her marriage, filling them up and sealing them over, disguising the damage.

"The table's finished." Poppy appears in the kitchen, jerking her thumb at the window. There are two tables on the veranda, each set for six with candles already lit, colored glasses and beakers of flowers filled with meadowsweet and buttercups.

"Thanks, Pops. It looks lovely." She puts an arm around her daughter's shoulders and cuddles her close although the slim body is rigid with resistance. "Shall we push the tables together? That way we can all talk to each other."

"Izzy said separate ones."

"Okay." She drops a kiss on the bright auburn hair. Don't fuss, she tells herself, it doesn't matter. It's a party, anything goes. "So what are you wearing tonight?"

"Whatever. Jesus." Poppy spins around and heads for the stairs. Eve crushes a basil leaf from the pot by the window, inhaling the peppery scent. She recognizes Izzy in Poppy's words, in the way she'd turned her back. What did she expect? The two girls have become close, whispering in the lessons, disappearing together in the garden. They are friends, and friends leave their mark. Outside the candles glow in the dusk. It's getting late, she should hurry.

"Let her be," she mutters to herself. "Let her grow." Children change and then change back. She'd wanted freedom for her kids, she should be prepared to take risks.

After her shower she dresses and inspects herself in the mirror. Her body isn't thin like Melissa's or shapely like Grace's, but her arms are turning brown; the dusty pink of the new silk dress suits the color of her face. She doesn't look like a thirty-four-year-old mother of three;

she doesn't feel like one either. Anticipation seethes in the pit of her stomach. She puts on eyeliner, eye shadow, mascara, lipstick; picks up her wrap and then steps back, looks at her reflection in the mirror and smiles.

Eric has started the barbecue; she hands him a beer. He drops a kiss on her shoulder, it feels like a truce although they haven't fought. Perhaps that's the trouble. Fairy lights sparkle in the olive trees, lighting the drive along its length to the front of the house, around the side, and all the way to the garage and barns at the back.

The girls appear with Ash. Poppy has glitter on both cheeks. Sorrel has smeared some unevenly on her forehead. Both must have found her lipstick. They look older, a little unfamiliar; even Ash has glitter on the back of a plump fist. They take him to the playhouse with an air of ceremony, exclaiming as they point to the windows, but he runs out and falls into the bark chips, crowing as he throws them about. The girls follow slowly, disheartened. Poppy frowns at her mother, her fault for letting Ash see the house earlier.

The girls brighten when Martin arrives with Charley and Blake. Poppy takes them on a little tour of the equipment, pointing out the smooth joints and bright colors of the house, proud of her father's work. Charley hangs upside down from the bars, her hair touching the ground; Sorrel laughs, clapping her hands. Blake careers down the slide, Ash on his lap.

"Grace can't make it after all." Martin's eyes follow his son as he carries Ash up the steps and down the slide again. "She's waiting for the plumber; the washing machine broke down, tonight of all nights."

Eve can see he believes what he's been told though she recognizes an excuse, a lie. She gives him a flute of champagne and they tip glasses. He laughs aloud with pleasure as she knew he would when he hears about Ash's first word. Eric glances over from the barbecue and then back to the coals, his expression unreadable.

Melissa and Paul arrive with a huge bunch of flowers in crackling cellophane. Izzy is wearing ripped jeans and a T-shirt; Poppy glances at her friend and quickly wipes the glitter from her cheeks. Paul looks elegant in white linen, a leather bag slung over his shoulder; Melissa is stunning in a silk trouser suit with a matching scarf. Paul propels his wife forward, one hand on her elbow, another at her back. A perfect couple, as handsome as film stars, though when Melissa hands Eve the flowers, Eve sees there is a mark under the creamy foundation, a dark swelling like a bruise on her right cheekbone.

"Stupid me; I slipped in the flower shop," Melissa explains with a little laugh. "The floor was wet."

"Oh, poor Melly."

"I bought this for Ash," she says quickly, handing him a little teddy in a sparkly blue waistcoat; he hugs it to his neck, his eyes disappearing in a wide smile.

"Just look at this food!" Melissa's gaze sweeps the table hungrily as she takes in the piles of little pies, gleaming slices of salmon, bowls of salad, thick slabs of homemade bread studded with olives. Both women watch Paul as he produces bottles of ginger beer from his bag, deftly unscrews the tops, and hands one to each child with a low bow.

"You have a very clever daddy," he tells Ash, shaking the small hand. "He did good work for me too." Ash stares at him wide-eyed, Sorrel giggles.

"May I have a grand tour?" he asks her; she takes his hand, pulling him over the bark chips to the little swing. Eve glances at Melissa, smiling. She hadn't realized Paul could be so charming to children, but Melissa is staring at her husband, her face expressionless. The fall must have shaken her up; beneath the glamour she seems tired, a little fragile. Eve turns back to watch Paul swinging back and forth with Sorrel by his side and Ash on his lap.

"Excellent!" Paul puts Ash down, kisses Sorrel swiftly on the head, and climbs the steps to the veranda. He joins Eric at the barbecue, handing him another beer and chatting as he pokes at the food with a fork. Eric adjusts the coals, lays out the steaks, and turns the sausages. Eve watches, interested. This is probably what happened when they worked together in Paul's garden: the older man talking, Eric getting on with the job at hand. It seems to work; they look comfortable together.

Beneath the steps Izzy is inspecting the faces clustered around her, one by one, as if choosing a favorite; she puts an arm around Poppy, who grins widely, and they retreat to the little house. Blake takes Ash by the hand and follows them. Sorrel and Charley walk in after the others, and the door is shut. Eve meets Eric's eyes, she raises her glass to him, he tips his bottle of beer to her, his playground has just been christened. She sits down at the table, Melissa next to her and Martin on the other side, so close she is conscious of his sleeve lightly brushing her arm each time he lifts his glass to his mouth.

"Izzy's told us how well she's doing." Melissa places cool fingers on Eve's other arm. "Especially math. We're thrilled. How on earth do you do it?"

Eve studies her friend's face, masking surprise. She

sends weekly reports home with Izzy. They are clear: Izzy's work is careless. Her problem is different from Poppy's and Blake's. They reverse numbers, struggle with order, and have trouble with columns of tens and units; the kind of difficulties she was expecting. After a good start, Izzy fails to finish her sums; it's as though she's bored. It occurs to her that Izzy could be discarding the reports before they reach her mother.

"Izzy's doing well with writing and reading." She puts her hand over Melissa's. "Her math still needs a little work."

"Paul said it's getting better." Mclissa falters, slipping her hand away.

"I sense a clever mind; once she decides to improve, she'll fly, I know it."

Melissa stares at the playhouse where her daughter has disappeared; she looks mystified.

"Well, we love what you're doing." Martin's whisper in her ear raises goose bumps. He reaches to pour champagne into Melissa's glass and then hers, his hand resting briefly, burningly on her shoulder. By the time Eric has straightened from the barbecue, calling to the children, Martin's hands are back in his lap. Eric circles the table, a steak drops onto Martin's plate, spattering a little blood. Melissa jolts and reaches for the salad. The children settle noisily around their table, Blake elbowing Charley to sit next to Izzy. Poppy is on her other side. Eve pours a tiny amount of rosé into a cup, diluting it to the faintest pink with water; she gives it to Sorrel.

"Is it dreadful of me?" she whispers to Martin. "She adores it, I think it makes her feel grown-up." He shakes his head, laughing.

Eve raises her glass. "Happy birthday to my special boy."

Izzy has taken Ash on her lap. Sorrel kisses his cheek, and Poppy gives him a sausage from the barbecue, which he crams into his mouth. The children sing the "Happy Birthday" song, everyone joining in except for Izzy, who wraps her arms around him as if he were her present, a birthday gift especially for her.

Grace

Blake forgot his inhaler, it's been left on the table.

She tries to ignore it as she pulls the clothes from the washing machine. Martin believed the story about how it was broken though his clothes were spinning around at the time.

She unlocks the glass doors to the little balcony and hangs the clothes on the rack, careful not to tread on

Blake's tomato plants. The air is very warm. Up here you could be on the balcony of a hotel or the prow of some great ship. Today has been perfect, another missed perfect day. The rim of the sun is sinking fast. A plane sweeps by, ripping the peace; the red tail-lights puncture the blue. A point of scarlet flares in the parking lot below like an echo or a warning. A man is smoking down there; she can't see his face but he might have clocked her, outlined against the window. Grace steps back inside, shuts the doors, then lowers the blinds. Two or three hours of peaceful writing time stretch ahead, time she'd never normally have, though she's had to sacrifice the chance to be with everyone and she'd wanted that too. She pulls her notebook from its hiding place, opens it at the marked page, and starts to write, then pauses. Her eyes flick to the paragraph above, she crosses out a line, writes another, changes the last word, looks up for inspiration. Her gaze meets Blake's inhaler again, his fingerprints in chocolate outlined on the blue plastic. He doesn't need it often but he just might be wheezing tonight. Charley said there'd be a bonfire, the smoke could set him off. Martin might not notice until it's too late. She puts her pencil down, slowly closes her notebook, and climbs on the stool to slide it back on the shelf.

She strips out of her jeans and finds the red beach dress scrunched at the back of a drawer, something in nylon, bought online for a weekend at a campsite in Devon last year but never worn. She snaps off the label and slips it on, then she shoves her feet into Charley's jeweled flip-flops and slings her bag over her shoulder. She takes out a few coins from the candy tin; she'll buy a present for the little boy on the way, Martin won't have remembered. At the moment of stepping outside the block of flats, she realizes her door keys, the ones with a little red tab, aren't on the main key ring, which has opened up a little. They must have slipped off in the flat. Martin will have his keys; it doesn't matter— but a moment later she realizes it does. The boy with the green-soled sneakers has appeared from the shadows and is standing in front of her, blocking her way; without keys she can't escape back into safety. He steps nearer, so near she can see the yellow of pustules on his cheek and the pitted scars of older ones, white powder clogging the hairs of a nostril. There is a low-pitched humming noise in her head, like a warning, but it's too late. In her hurry, she forgot the rules. The boy chucks his cigarette down in a violent motion; that was the red light in the parking lot. He must have been waiting for her since Martin left.

"Just fuck off, will you." She turns her head away,

trying for an exasperated tone though her heart is banging so hard her voice trembles.

"Fuck off?" He's not taken in. The ribbed wall of his chest pushes at her. "Fuck off?" he whispers in her ear as he clutches her hair, pushing her violently around until she faces away from him. He shoves something against her face, a small plastic bag full of white powder. "Want some?"

Something slides around her neck, leathery, pulled tight. The fear in her head ratchets up, there's no room for thought. He pulls hard and she chokes, struggling for breath. Their feet shuffle together as if in a dance, as she is pushed, stumbling and gasping, behind the high wooden screen where the garbage is kept. He thrusts her forward till her chest hits the dumpster. Her mind is empty of thought, hot fluid trickles over her feet. Urine, hers. He clamps her neck so her face is forced down onto the lid of a bin as her dress is yanked to her waist. He releases his grip; she hears the grating whisper of a zipper. His thighs are tight against her buttocks; he fumbles at his jeans.

Scalding fury takes over; he thinks he can do this, thinks he can get away with it and he might, man against woman, white against black. Her thoughts switch on. He's forgotten her hands are free; he doesn't see her slide them into her bag, which has swung forward around her neck. While his fingers are scrabbling at her underwear, tearing cloth and skin, hers push aside the coin purse and inhaler and close on Blake's penknife. She flicks open the blade, her hands still deep in the bag as he snarls in her ear. "You've had this coming, stuck-up bitch."

She jabs back fast and hard. The knife is snagged by his jeans. He doesn't pause, doesn't notice, he is beginning to straddle her, putting both thighs alongside hers, pushing into her, missing, swearing. He bends to bite her neck and she jabs backward again, higher this time; the knife glides through the cloth of his T-shirt and into skin, a layer of firmer tissue after that. He screams, a high-pitched shriek, and falls away from her; his shoulders and then his head hit the pavement with a bang. She runs to the car, her breath hurting her throat, her bag swinging about her neck, the dress around her waist. The car key misses the lock twice. Once inside she doesn't look back. She drives fast, swerving out of the parking lot then along the road; she takes the second left, skids half up on the sidewalk, and brakes sharply. She raises her hips, pulls off her underwear, and shoves them in the glove compartment, DNA from his skin if it comes to that. She leans forward and takes slow, trembling breaths, trying to calm herself; her heart is still pounding, her head still full of noise, but none of it makes sense. After a few minutes she wipes her face with her palms and pulls out her phone. She jabs at a number three times.

"A pusher on the Blackberry Estate's been stabbed; he's loaded with coke. He's by the rubbish bins behind the fence." Her voice isn't like her voice. She gives the address and cuts the call; she won't hang around. Her father's stories about white police swell the roaring fear, about what they did to his countrymen; he'd warn her she could be blamed for her own assault. In any case, the police don't need her story; that boy has enough coke on him for months in jail, years maybe. He'll say nothing about her, surely. Attempted rape would mean extra years. She'll say nothing to Martin, either; he comes from a different world; he'd make her go to the police or even tell them himself, not understanding the dangers. She could end up in jail. She'll cope, she always does.

She lifts her head. The gray metal strips of a drain cover gleam dully from the gutter a few meters away. She inches the car forward and brakes just beside it; she looks around, checking the street is empty, then opens the door and, leaning out, drops the knife through the grating. She hears, or imagines she hears, a faint answering splash. She straightens, straps on her seat belt, and begins to drive; lucky it's not far—it's difficult to see through eyes streaming with angry tears. Fury and triumph are hot in her throat. She shucks off the wet flip-flops when she arrives and gets out. Fireworks bang and crackle beyond the house, shooting sparks high above the roof. She can hear Blake's voice with the others, shouting loudly. The inhaler wasn't needed after all; she could laugh if her stomach wasn't twisting with longing for Martin and her kids, for alcohol and warmth.

The gravel of the drive digs into the soles of her feet. The great front door is open, wide open. Don't these people care about what they have? She shuts the door behind her and looks about. The high-ceilinged hall disappears into shadows at the far end beyond the stairs; she could be in the entrance of some grand munici-pal building, surprisingly impersonal. There is a faint smell of damp, the floor is chilly under her feet. She came in through a door into the kitchen when she vis-ited that first time, somewhere at the back of the house; the room had been warm and full of color, like Eve herself. This part of the house feels different, as though the place belongs to strangers; she could be an intruder gaining entrance. A dog barks from somewhere deep within the house. She runs up the thickly carpeted stairs in front of her to a wide landing. The door to her left opens onto a disordered room, an unmade four-poster bed heaped in clothes. She shuts that door and tries another, a bathroom that's almost as big as their flat. She steps inside and locks the door behind her. The room is warm, the steamy air scented with the oversweet smell of ripe strawberries. There is an oval bath and a walk-in shower with shampoo bottles strewn on the tiled floor, pink liquid oozing out. Grace wipes a patch on the misty window, glimpsing a great bonfire down in the garden. Blake is scampering around the flames without a T-shirt and Charley is following him. Eve's kids are there, of course, and a girl with blond hair waving her arms and shouting as if in charge of a game. That must be Izzy. The adults are at a table directly below the window, heads together; three of them are strangers to her. Martin's shoulders are hunched forward, Eve is next to him, her youngest on her lap. They are talking, almost touching. Martin throws back his head in a laugh. The wave of anger takes her by surprise. If Martin spent more time writing and less having fun, they would have more money. They wouldn't be living on a cheap estate; she might not have been assaulted just outside her home. He turns to Eve; she can't see his face but imagines his laughter continuing in a carefree, happy chuckle. Her face burns. A different world, as she'd thought.

A thin woman with blond hair is sitting on the other side of Eve, fiddling with the scarf around her neck and glancing at the food spread all over the table, masses of it. A tall, sunburned guy in shorts is turning slabs of meat on the barbecue; a bloke in white linen lounges next to him, gesticulating with his cigar. He has one of those smooth, actor-type faces with lots of white teeth and seems to be watching the children closely. Well, at least somebody is.

They pass food, lean across each other to chat or nod, laughing easily like any group of good friends. They have no idea she is watching them from above, wounded and invisible. Thick towels lie twisted on the bathroom floor and she steps over them to reach the sink. There's a jar of glitter by the taps and little fingerprints on the mirror. She leans close, inspecting her face: a cut under her hairline, a bruise on her forehead, another on her cheek. A thin stream of blood has trickled from the back of her neck around to the front. There are more bruises on her chest. She lifts her dress, there's one forming on her abdomen where she was forced against the bin, an uneven triangle with irregular edges. Like Africa, and she wants to laugh. Blood is running down her legs from where his nails tore her flesh. There's no pain, not yet, just the sharp stink of his sweat and of garbage. She picks up a pink shower cap from the floor and tucks her hair inside. The shower is powerful. She tips her head back, letting the hot water cascade over her face and her dress as well. She waits till the water washes away all the stains then takes off the dress and sluices her body, gritting her teeth until the stinging stops. She towels herself dry and stuffs the towel in the laundry bin under the others. There are bandages with little teddy bears on them in the glass cabinet; she sticks one over the wound on her neck then draws a fingerful of glitter along her cheeks to disguise the bruise. She slips on the wet dress again and shakes her hair over her forehead. Weirdly she looks good, very good.

She leaves, descending the stairs at a run as the dog barks again. She closes the front door behind her and walks around the drive to the back. Farther down in the garden the children are still running around the bonfire, leaping and whooping. Blake is hollering at the top of his voice though she can't make out the words. No one notices her at first as she walks toward them. Martin and Eve are leaning together. The thin blond looks up first; the two men she saw by the barbecue are now sitting down but both turn and stare as she walks into the candlelight. They get to their feet, a chair is knocked over, the smooth-looking man is still chewing.

Melissa

An unfamiliar woman is striding barefoot toward them, not smiling but blazing, as though for battle, coming from or going toward. She's easily the most beautiful woman Melissa has ever seen. The light from the bonfire licks along her limbs so her dark skin gleams as though wet. She walks the way models do, dipping on each side with every step. Her dress is red, her cheekbones glitter. She looks like a warrior, Melissa thinks, and finds herself wanting to cheer.

"Gracie." Martin is the first to recover from surprise. "You got away after all."

"Welcome." Eric's voice is gentle as he hands her a flute of champagne. It's the voice Melissa's heard him use to quiet the animals, and the woman, Grace, is like an exquisite animal, a fine racehorse perhaps, strung tight and trembling. She doesn't reply. Eve deposits her son in Melissa's lap, damp and surprisingly heavy. Melissa bends her head to his, she feels a rush of warmth; she can't remember holding a child since Izzy was little.

"Hi, stranger." Eve holds her arms out as Grace advances. Her kisses, one for each cheek, are unreturned. "You smell wonderful, strawberries! That's so funny, it's exactly like Poppy . . . but gosh, your dress is soaking wet!"

Grace steps back, she doesn't reply. Melissa feels a pulse of admiration; she would have apologized, explained, made some awkward joke.

"Let's find you a towel." Eve gestures to the house. "There are heaps upstairs. Eric can—"

Grace frowns and shakes her head, the sort of woman who doesn't like a fuss.

"Well, at least take my wrap." Eve hands over a length of pink material from the back of her chair. "I'm so glad you made it after all," she continues easily. "You must be exhausted. There's plenty to eat. Do sit down."

She gestures to the chair next to Martin, but Grace sits by Melissa instead.

"Hi, I'm Melly." She smiles, feeling chosen. "Izzy's mother."

Grace says nothing; she is watching Martin and has started to shiver despite the warmth of the evening.

"Congratulations on the washing-machine repair." Martin raises his glass to his wife.

Eve laughs but Grace doesn't; she downs the contents of her glass in one swallow, standing to reach the wine for a refill. The neat outline of her buttocks is printed on the chair. Melissa bites back questions as

Grace sits down again; her hand is oozing blood from a graze along the side of her palm. Martin spots it at the same moment.

"Hey, Gracie, what have you done to your hand? Oh, Jesus, look at your face. Did you collide with the washing machine?"

"Exactly that." Grace's hands slide into her lap and she shakes her hair over her face. "Fucking clumsy of me."

Her words arrive in a little silence and deepen it; as if in response, Eric walks around the table, reaches over her shoulder, and puts the wine bottle by her elbow. Martin shakes his head; Paul is the first to speak. "Well done for surviving your accident." He raises his glass to the newcomer and smiles his most winning smile.

Grace looks away. Paul's face falls and he drains his glass. Melissa wants to smile; Grace seems immune to her husband's charm. She glances at her, at the glittering eyes, the sodden dress, and the seeping hand. The story about the washing machine is far-fetched; she recognizes trauma even if no one else does, something complicated that Grace is keeping to herself. Melissa passes salad, salmon, bread, none of which she has eaten herself. Grace might have had a minor car accident and, having damaged the car, be too frightened or embarrassed to confess, as she herself would be, though she's never seen anyone so unafraid, so little abashed.

"Well, I think you look amazing," she whispers, conscious that her words sound trivial, as if trauma could be erased by a compliment, but Grace's expression softens as she stares down into the garden. Melissa follows her gaze to the children dancing around the bonfire. Izzy's voice carries the loudest, she sounds happy. Melissa's mouth stretches into a smile so wide it feels dangerous. She puts her hands to her lips as if to hide her teeth while Grace turns her gaze to her. The assessment feels detached but not unkind.

"Izzy's having fun," Melissa confides. "She adores the younger ones. It's like she's turning back into a child herself."

"Mine don't tell me much. They're quieter if anything, a bit grumpy. Growing up, I'd hoped." She taps the table with her fingernails. Thin lines of dried blood are embedded in the folds of skin that border each nail; trauma as she'd thought. Melissa looks away.

"Which do you think, Eve?" Grace raises her voice. "Are our children growing up or getting younger? We can't decide."

Eve turns from Martin and glances around at the group as if confused; there is a pause while she visibly gathers her thoughts. Eric leans forward, watching.

"Both." She opens her hands. "Their thinking has become more complex, even in the time they've been with me; they're all very capable of quite abstract reasoning and questioning. They can be challenging at times."

"Is Izzy challenging?" Melissa asks, praying her daughter hasn't been rude.

"She might query the lesson plan a little, why a particular goal, for whose benefit, that sort of thing, pushing the boundaries. She doesn't always do what I ask, but that's good in its way; a sign of maturity."

"A bit of a rule breaker then." Paul looks pleased. "Like her dad."

Is that how you see yourself? Melissa stares across the table at her husband's flushed face—a bit of a rule breaker?

"On the other hand, they run down to the garden after the sessions like a bunch of little kids." Eve laughs. "Eric's hoping they'll use his new playground, nearer the house." She glances at the swing and the slide, the wooden cabin; stark shapes in contrast to the distant softness of the trees just visible against the sky. "We'll have to see."

They all look down into the garden then; the small figures of their children are silhouetted against the embers of the bonfire as if on a darkened stage. The scene recalls another: a group of performers at Glyndebourne with Paul's firm last year—*Faustus*. As the singers had gathered at the glowing entrance to hell, the music swelled and a sense of danger had billowed into the darkness. Ash stirs, the drool from his mouth seeps into Melissa's top. The barbecue has gone out; the evening feels colder. The candles are half burned down. She shivers, resisting the urge to get up and call the children back into their lit circle.

Down the table, Martin is shaking his head regretfully. ". . . no specific plans. A summer of boredom stretches ahead. How about you, Paul?" He looks across the table to where Paul is sitting a little slumped now, an empty glass in his hands.

"We usually opt for a villa." Paul waves the stub of his cigar. "We might try southern Italy this summer. Izzy likes her water sports. I'll probably hire a boat."

Izzy's turned thirteen; she's made all these new friends. She might not want to spend her holidays with her parents anymore, there could be battles ahead. Melissa's heart sinks.

Eve leans into the candlelight, her face is flushed. "I've just had the most brilliant idea." She has a dimple Melissa hasn't seen until now, a shadowy little pit on her right cheek. "Every August we stay in my father's old house in the Peloponnese." Eve's voice catches with excitement. "You could join us out there next month, all of you." She gazes around. Her eyes glitter; they look different somehow, larger perhaps. It may be the makeup, which Melissa has never seen her wear before tonight. "It's a paradise for kids, hundreds of olive trees to get lost among," Eve continues. "Why not come too?"

There is a gasp. Melissa isn't sure whose, was it her? She glances at Grace, who scarcely takes a day off, according to Martin. They obviously have no money to spare for holidays or travel. Grace is looking at her husband, her face is expressionless; perhaps she thinks the invitation is just one of those spur-of-the-moment things, well meant but unreal.

"That's so kind of you." Melissa touches Eve's hand. "But there must be heaps we can do in London without imposing—"

"It wouldn't be an imposition. We converted the outhouses over there specially for guests. We could all be as private as we wanted to be."

"Far too generous," Paul says. His words are a little slurred now. "We couldn't possibly accept."

"Our children would love the company," Eve continues, as though she hasn't heard him. She looks as eager as a child. "I could teach them in the mornings if you like. You can do whatever you want, read or sleep.

There's a pool that my father put in. It's very peaceful; ideal for writing," she adds, with a smiling glance at Martin.

"This is the kind of thing my wife does," Eric murmurs. "There will be no dissuading her. I think she feels guilty that we don't make more use of it."

"Guilt has nothing to do with it." The pink deepens. "You're always telling me to do what my heart tells me to; well, that's exactly what I'm doing now." She looks around, nodding seriously. "I really want you all to come."

Martin is watching closely; his eyes flick between husband and wife: Eric's tone, his glance, Eve's response; the silent exchange under the spoken one. Perhaps he's storing it all for a novel, perhaps he's been watching her and Paul too. She closes her eyes; she needs to think this through. Izzy would be happy, surrounded by the other children. Paul would spend time with Eric; she could relax for once, sit in the sun, swim, sleep. The warmth would be healing. There would be friends to talk to, Eve and maybe Grace. The offer bobs in front of her like a raft sent for rescue. No one speaks. Eve reaches for Ash and takes him back onto her lap, the dimple has vanished. The raft is bobbing by, soon it will be gone.

"It would be wonderful," Melissa hears herself saying a little breathlessly. "Izzy would love it, so would I, actually." She senses rather than sees Paul sit up in his chair; she looks at Eve instead, conscious she is accepting the offer without discussing it with him first.

"Astonishingly generous." Martin smiles at Eve. "Charley and Blake would never forgive us if we didn't accept." Then he glances at Grace. "We'll need to work it out, of course."

"You go. I can't, obviously." Grace's voice is very even. "I have to book time off months in advance."

"I've a ridiculous number of air miles saved up," Eve puts in swiftly. "I'll help with plane tickets."

"It all sounds too good to be true." Martin turns to Eve, grinning ruefully. "I confess I've been seduced by the thought of writing under those olive trees."

Melissa dares a glance at Paul; his face is bland, which means he's thinking fast. He's seen Izzy with her friends; if he wants her with him on holiday, he'll have realized he'll have to share.

"If you'll let me contribute, we'd be delighted to accept." Despite the slight slurring, he sounds sincere.

"Okay, thanks." Eric nods.

"We just have to persuade Grace now." Eve's eyes shine as if in triumph.

Melissa glances at Grace, but she is staring down into the garden again. If she feels unhappy, she's hiding it, but then it's easy to hide your feelings, she does it herself all the time. Perhaps Grace is wondering where her children are. The dancing figures have disappeared. The bonfire has almost gone out; a little breeze has come up. Eric walks around the table to stand behind Eve; his hand is on his wife's shoulder but he's looking at Grace. "You should come if you can. Is it too late to swap holidays at work?"

"Oh yes, please try." Eve leans forward. "You'd enjoy it so much."

"It's not a question of enjoyment." Grace's glittering warrior look has gone; she sounds exhausted. The things she isn't saying float between them, the stark, simple things. She earns the money; someone has to pay the bills.

"Let's hope you can manage to get some time off." Eve reaches across the table as if to touch her hand, but at that moment the light breeze strengthens and the candles flutter then extinguish. For a second everything vanishes, it's as though each is alone in the dark. Eric steps into the house, a switch is flicked, and lanterns on the wall light up. The table springs into view, cluttered with smeared plates and chunks of drying bread. There is a forest of empty wine bottles. The leftover meat on the barbecue is darkly charred. Melissa puts her hand to her growling stomach. It had been so easy to eat nothing this evening; Eve had been preoccupied and hadn't noticed. Now it's an effort not to seize a hunk of bread and cram it into her mouth. At that moment the children reappear. Sorrel first, dragging her feet, her eyes swollen. She is missing her skirt. Poppy is pale-faced and silent, hiccupping a little. They wind themselves around Eric.

"Goodness, darlings." Eve stares at her daughters. "You both look exhausted. Whatever happened to your skirt, Sorrel?"

Sorrel looks at her feet, sucking her thumb.

"The elastic must have snapped with all that running." Eve puts her arm around Sorrel. "Never mind, we'll buy you another." Sorrel leans against her and closes her eyes.

Charley stands close to Grace but Blake stares back into the trees. The garden looks even larger at night, a wilderness stretching out in front of them.

"Where's Izzy?" Melissa asks, trying to keep unease from her voice.

"She'll be along in a moment, don't fret." Paul sits back in his chair, pouring the last of a bottle of wine into a glass. "I know my little girl rather well. She loves to make an entrance."

Melissa gets out of her seat and walks to the edge of

the veranda; the stone balustrade is gritty under her fingers. She has already spoken out of turn this evening; if she says any more, he's likely to remember.

"It's time we got going." Grace stands up. "Thanks, Eve, thanks, Eric, great food." She takes Charley's hand. "I hope Ash enjoyed his birthday."

She nods her goodbyes to Melissa and the others and starts to make her way back to the car, Blake trailing in her wake.

"Perfect evening," Martin murmurs, and hurries to catch up with his family.

Eve puts Ash down on the little sofa by the door and begins to clear the table with Eric. At that moment Izzy appears, her slim figure running swiftly across the lawn and then up the steps; unlike the other children she doesn't seem tired at all.

"What did I say?" Paul's tone is triumphant. "Home-time, madam. It's late."

As if she hasn't heard him, Izzy walks over to Ash.

"Watch out, sweetie." Melissa puts out a hand to restrain her. "He's just gone to sleep."

She needn't have worried; Izzy merely leans over the sleeping child, giving him a gentle kiss. A new Izzy, tender, absorbed. Eve was right, she's growing up. Paul takes her arm and they say their farewells. Izzy looks pleased when he tells her about the holiday on their way home; Melissa listens to their exchange but doesn't join in. She is exhausted. Paul seems satisfied with the way things went this evening; she crosses her fingers tightly in the dark.

Sorrel is sucking her thumb. The house is quiet because everyone's asleep, but the fire is still roaring in her ears. Although she's pulled the duvet up over her head, flames burn in the darkness, red like the inside of an animal's mouth.

"The fire is a beast and needs feeding," Izzy had shouted. "It'll get you if you don't run fast enough." She'd told them to run faster and faster; they ran till it was difficult to breathe. The others ran too fast for Sorrel to catch up, her legs were aching. Her skirt came loose, it got tangled around her legs, and then she fell over, bang. Her skirt came right off. Izzy stopped and picked up the skirt, she hurled it into the fire as quick as quick, a sacrifice for the beast. He was hungry, Izzy said, her eyes glowing like the fire. Sorrel's skirt melted in the flames. She began to sob.

"Fuck off crying," Poppy said. Sorrel had never actually heard Poppy say "fuck off" so loudly before. "Fuck off crying." Poppy began to shout it out loudly like a kind of chant.

Blake had laughed about the skirt being thrown on the fire, which made her feel worse. He took off his shirt but he tied it around his waist; perhaps he didn't have many shirts and was scared Izzy would throw it into the fire as well. "This is the best party I've ever been to," he had shouted. "Fuck off crying."

Charley held Sorrel's hand and ran with her. They were so far away from the adults, no one could hear them screaming "fuck off" at the top of their voices. It began to have nothing to do with her anymore so Charley had joined in and then she did too. It had been sort of exciting and sort of scary.

5. August

Eve

Eve's knife slices through the okra stems with a crunch. Splashing noises from the pool merge with the bells from the church and the bees in the sage; holiday sounds, synonymous with happiness. Everyone has a place they love more than anywhere else and for Eve it is here: this little Greek village, this house, this very stone step outside the kitchen bathed in warm sunshine. The views soothe her mind, the wide sky behind the mountains and those fields of gleaming olive trees beyond the garden that slope toward the sea. She's promised they'd go to the beach tomorrow. Martin is writing in the shade of the trees to her left, his red shirt like a flag that draws her gaze despite herself. Papers are spread over the dry ground around his table. He says it's going well, that this is the most perfect place to write, that he can see his way into the story now. He's grateful. She puts the knife down. She can step back. It's not too late, they've hardly touched.

He arrived yesterday at noon with Charley, Blake, Melissa, and Izzy. It had taken them a couple of hours in the hired car from Kalamata Airport, and they were all sweating when they arrived. The children had raced with Poppy and Sorrel toward the swimming pool through the trees, shrieking like little animals. Melissa hurried after them, Eric following more slowly with Ash. Eve brought Martin into the kitchen for a drink. It was as dark and cool as a cave, the air scented by a bunch of wild thyme in a jug. She put ice in his glass and watched him drink, head tipped back, throat working. A drop had bulged, trembling at the lip of the tap by the sink. He put his glass down and looked at her. The only sound had been the wasps around a pot of honey on the table. She led him up the twisting wooden steps for the view, up to the bedroom at the top of the house, hers and Eric's. He'd glanced at the bed draped with mosquito nets. She pushed open the wooden shutters and hot light had streamed in, blindingly bright. The wide landscape stretched in front of them, baking in the sun, with the yellow-brown Taygetus mountains on the left and a glittering line of sea in the distance.

"I'm in love with this place already," he'd said.

Her eyes were level with the pulse at his neck, neither took a breath.

"Mum!" Poppy's voice tore into the room, as she came thumping up the stairs. "They need towels."

"They're in the chest on the landing," she'd called without moving.

"Show me!"

She'd drawn back, not quite daring to meet Martin's eyes, and left the room. He'd clattered down the stairs a few minutes later, whistling.

Eve waves away a bee that has strayed from the sage, picks up the knife again, and continues to slice the okra. Martin is their guest, on holiday with his kids. He is married, as she is—of course nothing's happened. They are playing, that's all, he knows that too, a delicious little game, as brief and harmless as any the children play.

"Eve!" It's Charley's voice this time, she sounds breathless.

"Here I am," Eve replies calmly. Grace is joining them in a few days; her children have been fine, playing with the others in the pool or crouching and running with them among the trees. Their voices thread through the day; she has hardly seen them since they arrived.

"Ash has been stung." Charley bursts through the olive trees, she looks scared. "Eric said to find you, you have to bring something, his arm's all puffy."

Eve puts the knife down, hurries into the kitchen, and burrows into the cupboard above the sink, pulling out a half-empty box of acetaminophen, bandages, a sticky bottle of Calpol, and a can of antihistamine spray. Eric is sitting on the stone wall by the pool, Ash hiccuping and whimpering in his arms. Sorrel stands next to him, sucking her thumb. Blake and Poppy are nearby, shivering. Izzy is floating in the center of the pool, eyes closed and arms out, her face relaxed.

"He'll live," Eric says. The small upper arm is bulging, a punctum at its center. Eve kisses the swollen flesh, tasting an echo of sweetness on the hot skin. She sprays antihistamine on the sting and Ash yells with surprise, then seeing a spoon of Calpol approach, clamps his mouth around it. She takes him from Eric, unbuttoning her shirt. Her breast spills out, white against the brown of her arm, the surface veins like blue-green tributaries flowing toward the dark nipple.

"Ugh." Poppy screws up her nose in disgust. She swerves away and jumps neatly into the pool followed by Charley and Blake. Eric stands up, shaking his head.

"It's time he grew out of that, Eve." He slides into the pool after the children.

Sorrel lingers, her breath warm on Eve's shoulder. "I thought he was going to die," she whispers, her eyes swimming with tears.

Eve puts an arm around Sorrel's stocky little body and pulls her close, kissing her damp forehead. "Ash isn't going to die, sweetheart, it's just a bee sting."

"Joely couldn't breathe when she was stung, she had to go to hospital in an ambulance."

"Joely is allergic to bee stings then; Ash isn't. You mustn't worry."

Ash's eyes are shut, his fingers starfish on her breast. A cool shadow falls on her skin and Martin smiles down at her, grasping a sheaf of papers in ink-stained fingers. He sits on the wall beside her, comforting and disconcerting at the same time.

"Go and swim with the others, darling." She pats Sorrel on her bottom. "Ash is fine now."

Sorrel walks slowly to the pool and hesitates at the edge, gazing at the others in the water, uncertain.

"It's the easiest way to make him better." Eve stares down at Ash, embarrassed to meet Martin's eyes.

"I'm in favor." He leans forward. "Grace stopped after six weeks; shame really. Actually . . ." He studies a little marbled butterfly hovering at his feet. "She's joining us in a couple of days, if that's okay; a colleague's holiday was postponed so she swapped her slot with Grace."

"I know, she emailed me," Eve replies. "I'm thrilled she can come."

Martin rests his hand lightly on Ash's head. "Has he said any more words?"

"A few—'Mum,' 'tractor,' 'dog'; words like that, but he says them properly as though they've been in his head all the time, just waiting to emerge."

"This is just the beginning, the trickle before the flood; there's everything to look forward to."

She meets his eyes and finds herself unable to look away; the moment stretches until Sorrel jumps in the pool, splashing water over Ash, who jerks off the nipple and starts to cry. Martin spreads a towel under the trees a few feet back. He waits for her to settle with Ash, then sits down so closely that his shoulder brushes hers. She can smell tobacco and ink; the pages of his manuscript rustle as he reads. The peace is hypnotic. Her eyes close but snap open again as icy drops of water fall on her breast.

"Swim?" Eric is leaning over her, addressing Martin, who scrambles to his feet.

"Sure, great."

"You'll find trunks in the shed." Eric tilts his head at the stone building.

"Brilliant, thanks." Martin walks away, smiling brightly.

Eric sits on the towel and ruffles Ash's hair, his tanned hand beaded with water. "How is he now?"

"All better. Did I tell you that Grace is joining us in a couple of days' time?"

Martin emerges from the shed; the shorts he is wearing are too small. His body is pale in the bright light, well built, surprisingly powerful. The broad chest is streaked with gray hair. Eric glances at her; she looks down at Ash.

"I'm glad," Eric says. "She must need a break."

"I expect she's revelling in the peace and quiet."

"Unlikely. She's stuck at a shit job, below her capabilities, so her family can have the things they think they need, including holidays." Eric's voice becomes quieter when he's angry.

She watches Martin dive into the pool and emerge, his face creased in a large grin. Sorrel squeals. Charley swims up, hugs her father, and climbs on his back; he is laughing so much he struggles to swim. Izzy climbs out and walks away; Poppy gets out and runs after her and, after a moment, Blake gets out too and follows.

"You know they have practically no money," Eric continues. "Martin hasn't sold a book for years."

"Shh." She glances at the pool. "He was a bestseller, a prizewinner. He works hard—"

"He's living off his wife."

"Oh?" Something new and hot wells up, burning her throat. She gestures at the pool, the house through the trees. "Where do you think all this comes from?" The words are out before she can stop them; they leave a quivering echo in the air.

"Your father." His voice is very quiet now. "I work hard, harder than you ever have."

They haven't talked like this before, new territory. She steps back, unsure of her ground.

"I'm grateful, you know I am."

"Do I?" He leans forward and kisses her on the lips, a brief kiss with no warmth. Over his shoulder she sees Martin looking at them from the pool.

"You taste distinctly of honey." Eric wipes his lips.

"That's what it was, the taste on Ash's arm; no wonder he was stung. The honey was out on the table earlier. He must have helped himself."

"Wicked child." Eric rumples his son's hair.

"I'm back," Melissa calls from the drive, her pink caftan visible through the trees; she is weighed down with plastic bags on either side.

"Coming, Melly." Eve slips her finger into Ash's mouth, disconnecting him from the nipple. He makes a small noise of protest but his eyes begin to close again. She hands him to Eric. "He'll sleep now," she says.

Melissa has tipped a pile of scarlet tomatoes into a bowl on the kitchen table; she unpacks wine, lettuce, cucumber, and pots of yogurt. "Let me do lunch."

The honey is still on the table. The lid has come loose; Eve screws it back on firmly. She wipes the pot and puts it back in the cupboard, high up out of harm's way. Ash gets himself into far more scrapes than the girls ever did, or perhaps she's more distracted these days. She wipes her face. It's especially hot in Greece this year; hotter than ever. So many insects everywhere: flies, bees, wasps. Outside the cicadas are at screaming pitch, the sound fills the air. They get louder at this time of day. If you listen, it's like thousands of tiny violins making that seesaw noise they use in films to signal unseen danger, fast approaching.

Melissa

"You forgot the wine," Eve tells Eric as she unpacks the picnic. "What a shame."

Melissa glances at her; she wouldn't dream of reproving Paul. It would be far too dangerous. She forgot that last week when she'd corrected him about some flight detail in front of Izzy.

"I wish you hadn't done that," he'd said later.

She had been brushing her hair in the mirror before bed when he came up close behind her. His voice had been quiet and very cold. "You made me look stupid in front of my daughter."

"I'm sorry." She had spoken quickly, though her mouth had dried up. "I didn't mean to, I just thought—"

"Stand up."

She had pushed the chair back and stood up, her legs had been trembling.

"Turn around."

He bent her forward over the dressing table, the glass edge cutting into her abdomen. He'd held her neck very tightly.

"Please," she'd managed to gasp out. "I can't breathe properly—"

If he heard, he didn't loosen his hold; he'd pushed up her nightgown, entered her, and taken his time. She had blacked out, coming to on the floor later. The bruises were worse than usual the next day; she still needs a scarf. Eve is lucky, far luckier than she knows.

"It's down the side of the basket," Eric tells his wife, calmly, settling a cotton hat on Ash's head and smearing cream on the tender little arms and shoulders. The red mark left by the bee sting has almost disappeared. "Ash and I are going for a swim. Coming, Blake?" He swings Ash up on his shoulders, Blake scrambles to his feet, and they run across the hot sand to the edge of the sea. Melissa watches them race each other, Blake shouting and Ash screaming with laughter. Paul would have done the same if he were here; no, he would have done even more. He would have found the wine and poured it out. He would have built an elaborate sand-castle for the boys and taken the girls for a swim, made flattering comments about how pretty they were in their swimsuits and the beautiful color their skin was turning in the sun. He's charming with children, ut-terly charming. They fall in love with him, as women do, as she did. When they were first married he used to carry her into the sea. He taught her the backstroke and how to fish from a boat; moments that shine in her memory, like jewels in the darkness.

Eve places the contents of the picnic basket onto the stripy blanket: bread, glistening black olives, a cheese-and-spinach pie, cucumber and lettuce, flat yellow peaches, a lemon cake. "The children will be starv-ing," she says, catching Melissa's stare. "They always are, by the sea."

"Where have they gone?" Melissa asks, tearing her gaze from the pie. The pastry looks crisp and shiny;

she can imagine how it would taste in her mouth. She has hardly exercised since she arrived apart from a few early-morning lengths in the pool before anyone else is up. She can't afford to eat anything for lunch.

"Swimming." Eve unearths the plates and glasses. Eric and Blake are sitting in the shallows with Ash but no one else is in the water.

"There's no sign of them out there."

"Behind us, then. Damn, the wine isn't here, it's the only thing I asked Eric to pack."

"He's protecting my health." Martin is lying on his back beside Eve, his voice muffled by the book on his face. "He knows I drink too much."

There's an imprint of four bodies on the sand behind them. The girls' heads had been close together, their bodies fanning out. Izzy made the largest shape, then Poppy, Charley, and Sorrel—eleven, nine, and six— smaller imprints, ghost petals of a flower. Behind the beach is an impenetrable line of bamboo, stretching for miles.

"Where can they be?" Melissa tries to keep the panic from her voice.

"Gone for ice creams?" Martin suggests from under his book.

"It's not that sort of beach." Eve empties a bag of

crimson cherries into a bowl. "We're miles from any shops. Don't worry, Melly, they'll be fine. Poppy knows this strand like the back of her hand."

No child knows the back of her hand, young hands are identical. The blood flows invisibly beneath the smooth skin. There are no twisting blue veins like hers; no scars from hospital IVs. "I'm going to look for them." Melissa sets off at a jog, her flip-flops twisting on the sand, her cotton beach dress flapping around her legs. She passes a family sitting down at a table set back from the sea in the shade of an awning; two little boys, a man at one end, a woman at the other serving food, an old lady in between. Melissa watches the man get up, take a plate from the woman, and touch her face before he returns to his seat. The woman catches her glance and gives a cheerful little wave; an ordinary woman having lunch with her family; there must be thousands like her, millions. On the way home in the car, she will rest her head on the man's shoulder, her eyes will close, and he will drive very carefully so as not to disturb her. Melissa jogs faster, it must be the sweat running into her eyes causing them to sting; her face is soaked with tears. After ten minutes she reaches a stretch of concrete at the far end of the beach; two cars bake in the sun, a trash bin stuffed with cans is buzzing with flies. A motorcycle lies on its side. There is silence apart from the noise of cicadas. Could the girls have come this far? She looks at the sandy path winding through the trees, the tracks of a car visible in the grit. The girls would know better than to get in a car with a stranger, but all the same, panic begins to beat with her pounding heart. She may need help. She runs back sweating, the Greek family are all eating, no one looks up this time.

Eve's call reaches her before she arrives. "They're here, Melly."

She sees Izzy first. Her daughter stands out most clearly; even her back view is defiant, the turn of her head, the hunched shoulder. Eric and Blake have returned from their dip and are chatting on the blanket; Izzy is tickling Ash's stomach with a length of dried seaweed, dragging it backward and forward across his soft little belly as he screams and squirms, the laughter turning desperate.

"Oh, poor you." Eve comes forward to greet her, hands outstretched. "They'd burrowed into the bamboo plantation, bad girls."

"Come and sit down." Martin pats the blanket. "You're all out of breath."

They are treating her as if she were a child, an ill child. Poppy and Charley are giggling together; there is a smothered hiccup then more laughter in small explosive bursts. Izzy is watching them with a smile. Sorrel is asleep, her mouth wide open, her cheeks a warm red. Eve passes around slices of spinach pie on plates; she is smiling at Martin and seems focused on the food. Perhaps that's why she doesn't realize that the girls are clearly drunk.

"Orange soda, anyone? Nothing else, sadly." She glances at Eric as she pours out sticky orange liquid into plastic cups. Poppy shakes her head, spluttering with laughter.

Martin helps himself to a large slice of pie, Eric distributes salad to the children.

"Eat this." Eve gives her a slice of pie and salad; she touches Melly's arm. "And enjoy, forget about calories for once."

Melissa takes a mouthful of lettuce, her molars crunch together; tiny grains of sand must have gotten into the leaves. She puts her plate down. She won't mention the wine. Why get the girls into trouble? They wouldn't have drunk it all, a couple of swigs each would have been enough; they must have hidden the bottle in the bamboo. Izzy is safe, the girls are safe; that's all that matters, she should be thankful. She takes five black grapes and settles in the shade of the umbrella.

She bought a postcard in the village today; a painted one with a view of the mountains. She takes a pen from her bag: *Dear Lina, I expect you're enjoying the peace.* She puts her pen down and stares at the sea. She could have brought Lina with them if only she'd thought of it. She would have relaxed in the sun, maybe swum in the sea. Eve would have been fine with her staying. Lina's face was tired on the morning they left, she doesn't hum her little tunes anymore, but she still listens, better than anyone. *I miss you,* she writes.

"I'm going for a swim." Eve stands up, stripping off her dress. She is wearing a red bikini bottom, nothing else.

"You can't," Melissa whispers. "The children."

"It's fine, Melly." Eve looks down at her, amused. "The kids are unconscious. It's a holiday. No one cares."

She's wrong, the children will care. Children don't like adult bodies, especially their parents', but Eve turns and strides over the pebbles. Melissa glances along the beach. The old lady has left the table and is holding hands with the little boys, one at each side, by the edge of the sea. Eve walks into the water and turns on her back. Her white breasts float as though separate from her body. The cicadas from the plantation screech at high volume, the heat beats down from the white sky, rivulets of sweat collect at Melissa's waist. She longs for the cool water, but she'd have to take off her scarf and the bruises are still faintly visible around her neck.

Martin gets to his feet, stretching. "I need to swim off all that food," he murmurs as he sets off trotting toward the sea.

"If he can do it, Melly, I'm sure you can," Eric murmurs, facedown on the blanket. "Take my goggles."

The girls and Blake are asleep. Ash is heaping pebbles on Eric's back in little piles. She walks to the edge of the sea wrapped in a towel to her neck, the goggles in her hand. Martin and Eve are separate dots in the sea, far out. She puts on the goggles and discards the towel and then the scarf. The cold water is shocking then quickly delicious. A red fishing boat is moored on a buoy at least four pool lengths away. She swims as fast as she can, touches the splintery side, and then dives, glimpsing a jellyfish moving slowly through the water. The pebbles at the bottom are very clear. She surfaces, swimming toward Eve and Martin who have now moved close together and are floating on their backs. She dives down again. As she swims nearer she sees that they are joined together under the surface by a knot of fingers that look as if strange sea animals have become tangled together by accident.

Grace

Paul walks toward Grace in baggage claim at Kalamata Airport, the plump face creased in a grin. He looks cool in a cream designer suit and sunglasses; she is conscious of her frayed jeans and the ink stain on her T-shirt. He takes off his Panama hat and bows.

"Eve just texted to tell me you'd be here; apparently we were on the same plane. I'd have swapped seats, if I'd known." His eyes linger on hers.

She'd known, though. She'd spotted him immediately in the departure lounge at Heathrow. His height and then that handsome face at odds with its disdainful expression. She had waited at the back as he worked his way to the front of every line. On the plane she had slipped past him, head lowered, as he assembled an office of papers on the tray in front of him. She needed quiet, these hours of travel had been hoarded in advance. She was writing by the time the plane roared into the air. She ignored the clinking drinks cart and the offers of food. This was the space she had craved, alone but surrounded by people, safe in the way their flat no longer seemed to be, especially on her own. As the plane descended, she'd come back to herself as though from the depths of a river, the story coating her skin like silt.

"I've booked a car." Paul smiles, inclining his head. "Come along."

She edges away. She doesn't want to be forced into conversation with Melly's husband. She had planned to take the bus.

"Don't wait for me, I need to buy a present for Eve. I'll meet you there."

"I sent them a case of wine. We can say it's from you as well. Let's go." He slides his fingers over hers on the handle of her case, a trick that works. She removes her hand.

"A light traveler, my kind of woman." His teeth gleam. He leads the way through the airport, head held high, oblivious to the surroundings, the dense flow of language, and the overpowering heat.

The low-slung sports car is waiting for them in the baking parking lot; she is forced to sprawl backward into the bucket-shaped seat. He stretches across her to lock the door, his arm accidentally brushing her breast. She stifles a cry as a wave of panic washes her back to the dumpsters, the leash around her neck, those scrabbling hands. Paul glances at her curiously as the car surges forward. Sweat trickles down her back and she breathes slowly, forcing herself to relax. It's Paul, for God's sake, Melissa's husband, she's met him before.

He begins to talk as though to an attentive audience. His life is busy: projects, travel, a contract he's just won from Paris. She tunes out his words. Shops and people slide past, unfinished concrete houses string along the road. Dogs sleep on sidewalks. He accelerates when they leave the town, the yellow hills and motorway blur. The car finds its pace and the engine hums quietly. Paul continues to talk but her eyes close, exhaustion has caught up with her. Since Martin's been away, she has slept in fitful bursts, missing his warmth; terrified that the gang of boys could burst in, seeking revenge for the guy she stabbed. She hasn't seen them since but they might be biding their time, waiting to catch her out when she's alone and asleep. She's told no one yet, even Martin has no idea, still. In his absence, she's taken to pushing the kitchen table against the door at night and dozing on the sofa, lights left on, her sleep broken. Her fatigue is overwhelming; lulled by motion, she lets herself sink into sleep.

She is woken by stillness; the light is softer, the noise of the engine ticks to silence. Paul opens the door and glances around at an empty village square; he exhales sharply as if disappointed. "Well, this is it, according to the GPS. Eve said we should park by the café; the track leading to their house is too narrow. We have to turn left by a fig tree that's down a lane opposite the church. I'll lead the way."

Outside he hands over her case; she is to carry it this time. He has worked out some equation to do with time and effort and has come to the conclusion she's not worth the pursuit. She takes the case, relieved. Above them, the branches of a large plane tree spread out in a great canopy. Swallows skim like arrowheads above the outside tables of the café and disappear under the rafters. A couple of thin donkeys stand in front of an olive oil co-op across the road; an old man is sitting on the curb, jars of honey and olives on the ground around him. Grace sees the week ahead spreading out in the sun, a whole week. There will be time with the children, she and Martin might draw closer again. She'll tell him that she's missed him. She'll ask about his work; she might even share her own. Her heart lifts. Paul has crossed the road with long strides and has vanished into a narrow gap between two houses. She hurries to catch up with him. Her case bumps over paving as she passes pink geraniums in pots and a tortoiseshell cat dozing on a wall.

"Fig tree," Paul shouts, and turns left. She is close enough to see that he twists his feet when he treads on the fallen figs, crushing the flesh into stone as if enjoying the sensation. She picks up a fig that has fallen onto a wall; beneath the warm green skin, the pippy interior is sweet.

No one comes to Paul's knock on the gray wooden gate; he tries again, thumping hard. A scatter of small birds fly up from the fig tree. The gate opens after another wait. Poppy is on the other side in a red swimsuit, her braids sodden, the freckles standing out on her pale face. She steps back silently then turns and runs down a path, leaving wet footprints that disappear in the heat. She vanishes between the olive trees.

"Anyone would think we were robbers," Paul says, breaking the silence, "come to plunder." They walk through the gate into a paved space roofed with trees. To the left a straightedged building towers above them; a white awning like a sail is stretched over a table and chairs on a patio, behind which a doorway leads into darkness. In front of the house is a browning lawn. Rows of olive trees extend as far as she can see; there's a table covered in papers in their shade, a clothesline hung with towels and, farther back, stone buildings roofed with tiles. Eric appears from around the side of the building.

"Hi there. Sorry, we're by the pool, luckily Poppy heard you."

He shakes Paul's hand then Grace's. "I hope you weren't waiting too long. The door's unlocked, you could have just pushed it open."

Unlocked? Why is it that people with money leave so much untended? Eric smiles down at her, nodding as if in reply to something she hasn't said. "So glad you could make it." He walks to the gate and slides the bolt shut.

"It's great to see you in your natural habitat at last. What a place." Paul gazes up at the tall stone building. "Lucky old you."

"It was Eve's father's," Eric replies. "Dates from the Ottoman Empire. They hurled cannonfire at each other across the street, sworn enemies. It's safer nowadays, of course."

Is it? Nowadays it's more difficult to tell where your enemies are, harder to defeat them. It would be easier to live in a tower, and then Grace remembers she does. She fought a battle and won. She mustn't forget that, when she runs to the parking lot in the morning and back again in the evening, dreading the tap of following feet, or as she locks herself in at night, then lies awake, sweating with terror. The enemy has been vanquished, at least for now. She must remember she's a winner. She catches Eric's eyes on her and realizes her teeth are clenched. She turns away to look at the view.

"Come with me." Eric sets off down the path through the trees. "Your quarters are through there." He gestures at the cluster of stone buildings. "Everyone hangs by the pool or on the patio. I'm not sure how much schoolwork is being done."

The sounds of splashing become louder. Listening, Grace almost stumbles into Martin, who is on a sunbed facing toward Eve in a little clearing in the trees. She is lying on an opposite bed, Ash tucked into her back. Her face is intent, she's unaware of their arrival.

"Eve," Eric says quietly, "our guests are here."

She's immediately on her feet; Ash rolls into the space her body has left, his eyes still closed in sleep. Martin twists around, then pushes himself off his bed. His bare feet tip a glass of wine, which spills onto the ground. The earth is so hard that it stays on the surface, a pool of shining red, like blood, she thinks, staring at the way the olive leaves are reflected, a little pool of fresh blood. She looks up, meeting Eve's smiling gaze.

"Darling." Martin's face is flushed; he puts an arm around her. He doesn't usually call her "darling." He has put on weight and, despite the fluster, looks relaxed and amused, as if pleased with life. It occurs to her that he hasn't missed her at all.

"It's lovely to see you." He kisses the top of her head.

"Are the kids behaving?" Not the greeting she'd planned, but she feels off-balance, as though she's intruding. It's the best she can manage.

"Of course they are." Eve steps forward to kiss both her cheeks.

"Where are they?"

"Just over there." Eve points through the trees. "In the pool."

"On their own?"

"It's okay, Gracie." Martin pats her arm. "Melly's with them. You'll have to let go a little now you're here."

Grace pulls her arm away.

"Martin tells me you want to be a writer one day, like him." Eve smiles. "We must find you a table."

Grace doesn't allow herself to look at Martin. Her writing ambitions are private, he knew that. She won't tell him any of the details, she's changed her mind. It's not Eve's fault, she's trying to be kind.

"Shall we move on?" Paul asks pleasantly. "I'm longing to see my daughter."

Eric leads the way through the undergrowth. The small bushes snag on Grace's jeans; freeing herself, her head collides with a plate hanging from a tree. It falls to the ground, smashing into pieces.

"Okay?" Eric turns back.

"Of course." Grace begins to pick up the fragments. "Sorry."

"There's plenty more, don't worry." Eve gestures to other plates suspended in little groups, each painted with a black circle, a dark dot in the center. Grace hadn't noticed them before but now she sees there are dozens of them, swinging by strings threaded through small holes that have been carefully drilled in the glass. "Greek superstitions," Eve says, smiling at Martin as if at some private joke. Grace's head begins to throb. The heat is more intense than she'd imagined, hotter even than Zimbabwe; it must be the moisture in the air. She puts the shattered fragments on the wall.

They emerge onto the stone paving around a long, narrow pool surrounded by pine trees. Blades of shadow lie across the greenish water, swallows swoop to the moving cloud of insects hovering over the surface. The children are in a circle at the far end, the water up to their chests, chanting as they take turns to push a ball under the water. They wait until it bobs up, wait again, then after a few moments push it under once more. None of them have noticed the adults' arrival; they seem engrossed in the game. She counts them, you should always count children in the water: her two, their brown skin gleaming, Izzy's bright blond hair, Poppy's red braids—

"Ah, there you are." Melissa's voice comes from the deep shade of a pine tree; she stands up from her deck chair and puts her book down. Her pink caftan casts an upward glow to her pale face.

"How wonderful." She comes up to them, adjusting her sun hat. Paul leans forward to kiss her cheek, then he narrows his eyes at the children in the pool, searching for his daughter, smiling as he catches sight of her.

"I'm so glad you're here, not a moment too soon." Melissa smiles at Grace. "We missed her, didn't we, Martin?"

"We absolutely did." Martin looks toward the pool. "Though the kids have been fine."

"You should join them," Eric tells her. "You'll find everything you need . . . Christ." He begins pulling off his shirt as he sprints toward the shallow end, his shoulders moving as though there were animals beneath the skin. He dives into the pool, pushes aside Poppy, and pulls Sorrel from the center of the ring of children. A child, not a ball. Sorrel's face is streaming. Eric carries her out of the pool to Eve, who kneels to embrace her daughter. Martin kneels too; his mouth is turned down, he's shaking his head, looking helpless. Eric strides back to the shallow end, Grace follows, her mind blank with fury. He jumps in and hauls Poppy toward the steps by her arm.

"Let me go. It was a game," she shouts. "I had a turn so Sorrel wanted one."

"Out, Charley," Grace raps. "Blake, out. You will both apologize." They climb from the pool. Eve and Sorrel have vanished, along with Martin. Poppy wriggles free from Eric's grasp and disappears swiftly through the trees.

"Don't worry." Melissa indicates Paul who is sitting by the edge of the pool talking to Izzy, now floating in the shallow end. "He'll find out exactly what happened."

"You spoiled the game." Blake wrenches his hand from Grace's. "Sorrel was enjoying it. We were taking it in turns. Jesus."

"Don't swear."

"You do, all the time."

"Who thought this game up?"

He shrugs.

Grace turns to Charley, who is shivering by the edge of the pool.

"We all did, I think." She looks unhappy. "Sorry. We didn't mean to scare Sorrel; it was my go next."

"Go to your rooms." Grace keeps her voice calm with effort. "We'll talk when you've had a chance to think what it must have been like for Sorrel, who is only little, much littler than the rest of you."

Blake and Charley glance at each other as they walk off; when they reach the trees they start running. She hears a spurt of laughter; it sounds like Blake's.

"I'm sorry." Eric is behind her, water streaming off his shoulders.

"Hardly your fault." She looks at the disappearing figures of her children. They have changed in the few days since she saw them. They seem unfamiliar, sun-tanned, of course, a little thinner, but something else, hard to put her finger on, as if their loyalties have shifted and they are going by a different set of rules.

"Our pool." His brown eyes are clear as if rinsed by the water. "Our fault."

Paul walks past them. "We'll continue our little chat at the house." He sounds confident, relaxed even. Perhaps Izzy told him that the other children organized the game, that it had nothing to do with her. "See you all later." One large hand rests heavily on his daughter's neck. The heat of that palm must prickle uncomfortably against her skin, but her head is bent, it's difficult to see her expression. Melissa follows them, turning to raise her hands in a gesture of helplessness. What can we do—she seems to be asking—with such naughty children? Grace feels light-headed and enormously tired.

Eric glances at her. "You look exhausted, have a seat."

She lowers herself onto a stone wall that's covered with pink flowers shaped like little stars. Eric extracts a couple of beers from a cooler in the shade of the wall, flips off the tops, and hands her one. She holds the cold bottle against her neck. Eric seems kind—a kind, thoughtful man. She wonders if Eve sees that still; it's so easy to take things for granted, lose sight of what you have. Something is happening to her and Martin, a space opening between them that is widening all the time. It's hard to tell which one of them is moving away or how to close it up. Eric sits next to her with a little sigh.

"You'll have to forgive us," he says after a while. "We allow our kids a lot of freedom; it goes to their heads sometimes, especially here. Eve's very trusting. She thinks everyone is fundamentally good, that children are born moral, corrupted later."

"And you?"

"The opposite. Children are born barbarians and need to be tamed. My own are probably the worst." He leans forward to pick up a stone that has fallen from the wall then kneels to wedge it back. Was that a joke? She can't see his face; another stone falls out and a large beetle with horned antennae tumbles to the paving and scuttles into the shade.

"We're so lucky to have this place, the children love coming here; but there's always something to do.

Little things that don't seem important at the time but they add up." He forces the second stone back into place. "Eve says I fuss too much."

"It all looks perfect to me." Grace wipes her sweating face.

"That's because you can't see what's happening; we'll arrive one day to find the house is a heap of stones in the dust, and that the insects have taken over." He glances at her and smiles. "I'm joking, don't look so worried." He sits next to her again. "Blake's a good lad, by the way; he's been helping me prune the olive trees."

"That's wonderful; he'd love doing that." She smiles, feeling more cheerful. "Martin's been so focused on his writing recently, and I've been busy with long shifts." And sidetracked by fear; it's all she can do to survive, let alone concentrate on her children. "We haven't been there for him as much as we should."

"He reminds me a bit of myself at his age; it made all the difference to me when I discovered I was good with my hands. There are plenty more trees that need pruning at home if he wants." He smiles down at her. "Now, that swim. I'll grab your case." He disappears, jogging lightly through the trees. The glass plates chime in the silence. She looks at the water by her feet, seeing Sorrel's face with her eyes shut and mouth open, gasping for breath before she was pushed under again. How much longer would it have continued if Eric hadn't spotted them?

"I put your case in the shed where we change." Eric's voice makes her jump. He nods at a small building in the trees. "You should find a towel in there, watch out for the ants."

The green water is very cool. The stress of the past weeks seems to slide from her skin as she swims. She turns on her back, the white circle of sky between the pines is fringed with branches and crisscrossed by darting swallows. Small insects float by her face; a struggling wasp brushes her lips. Mosquitoes hum above her head. After a few more lengths she pulls herself from the water and sits on the edge. Eric hands her the towel from the chair.

"I'd forgotten how much I love swimming." She dries her face. "I used to swim a lot."

"Back home?"

Home. People often ask that, as if it's not possible for her to belong to more than one place or even to the country she moved to. "We couldn't swim in the dams because of schistosomiasis, but I snuck into the pool of the hotel where I worked."

"You met Martin out there?"

"I was working in the bar; he came in one evening when I was closing up."

"Of all the gin joints in all the towns in all the world . . ."

"Exactly." How random it must sound to him, how ridiculous. Another night, a different shift, and Martin wouldn't have found her, they wouldn't have fallen in love. They wouldn't have shared their dreams and she wouldn't have left her home. The smell in the garden reminds her of her grandparents' village in Zimbabwe: sun-warmed pine, wild sage, and the faint aroma of dung.

"How old were you?"

"Eighteen."

He nods as if he gets it, the things love makes you do when you're young, when you think life will let you make mistakes and there'll be time to come back from them. He reaches behind her for another beer and his skin brushes hers briefly, very lightly. She flinches.

"Sorry."

"No, it's okay."

It isn't okay. Her mouth has dried up and sweat prickles in her armpits. The memory has returned in a heartbeat, the mouth at her neck, the desperate struggle to breathe. She gets to her feet. "I should probably check on the kids." She turns away to hide her trembling lips.

"See you at supper," he calls after her; she senses him watching her leave, a little puzzled. The silvery green of the olive leaves blurs as she walks through them, as though the landscape itself were drenched in fear. She'd hoped the terror would diminish here, but if anything it's worse. Counseling is supposed to help, but everything she googled involves money; she'll just have to wait it out.

At supper, the children sit together at the end of the table; their sunburned faces float in the dark above the flickering candles. Ash is asleep in bed upstairs. Sorrel is sucking her thumb. Izzy has her arm around Poppy's neck; she passes the fingers of her other hand through a candle flame, back and forth, again and again. The children watch, mesmerized, until Eric moves the candle away. He chats quietly to Blake who sits next to him, glancing up at him often, nodding in agreement. Charley is unusually subdued. The incident in the pool seems to have taken its toll. Paul is yawning over his wine, Melissa crumbles bread on her plate, neither has noticed their daughter playing with fire. Eve glows next to Melissa's pallor, a smiling earth mother, serving out spoonfuls of flaky fish and curled tentacles in a tomato sauce. Her breasts swing freely in a yellow halter-neck top; the nipples stand out like little tubes. Martin is watching her from beneath lowered lids; Izzy's eyes flicker between the two of them. Grace puts down her fork. Her appetite has vanished. Melissa hasn't touched her food, but then she hardly eats, her cheeks are hollowed as if with hunger. Eric pours glasses of water for the children. He looks preoccupied; worried about the house maybe, the fight to maintain it all. Grace closes her eyes; behind the lids she sees stones falling, walls crumbling, a house becoming dust.

Then Paul calls out and her eyes open; he is waving a bottle of wine, offering it about. Martin holds out his glass then turns to chat to Melissa about the beach they visited the day before. The moment passes. Grace picks up her fork; Martin is allowed to look at another woman, everyone flirts on holiday. He loves her and their children. He's far too lazy to pursue anyone seriously. She can't help smiling at the way his shirt strains across his belly; too fat and too lazy. Martin catches her smile and returns it; she feels better. He can flirt all he likes; he belongs to her. Soon they will be in bed, together, but then her mind darkens at the thought of hands on her body, even his. They haven't made love in a month, maybe more. She looks at those familiar hands on the tablecloth, tanned now, the index still ink-stained; perhaps it will be different tonight.

Poppy nudges Sorrel. "It's your turn this evening."

Sorrel looks around the table then down at her plate, shaking her head.

"The kids have been taking it in turns to choose a myth," Eve tells Grace. "Then Martin makes it into a story; so clever of him." She turns to Martin, her eyes shining. "I expect Sorrel would like one with a dog in it. Can you do that?"

"Of course." Martin smiles at Sorrel. "Let's see, a dog. Can you tell me the name of a dog in your favorite story, little Sorrel?"

"Spot," Sorrel whispers.

There is a quiet snort, Poppy or Izzy, ignored by Martin.

"Once upon a time there was a dog named Cerberus—or Spot for short—who had three heads. One ate breakfast, the second lunch, the third gobbled down supper."

Sorrel giggles. Grace smiles; this is Martin at his best, telling stories, being funny, being kind. This is how he is with their kids, how he was when she met him.

"He belonged to Hades, a big old guy with a long ginger beard. Hades lived in a special place called the underworld."

"That's where people go when they die, right?" Izzy puts a tanned elbow on the table.

Martin nods and continues. "One day, Hades took Spot up to the world for a walk in the sunshine, where they met a pretty girl, picking flowers. She began playing with Spot, and they were having such a lovely time that Hades decided to take her back to his home."

"Oh, why?" Izzy asks.

"For Spot to play with, of course." Martin glances at her. "But then all the flowers in the garden began to die."

Sorrel slips her thumb into her mouth, her eyes are very wide.

"It turned out okay, though," Grace puts in. "Because—"

"Her mummy took her home!" Martin beams. "And the flowers started blooming again. The end." He bows to Sorrel, she smiles, and Eve claps loudly.

Paul laughs. "It's different from the version I remember. Didn't he—?"

"Bedtime." Eric scoops up Sorrel and heads for the stairs.

"Bedtime for us too." Grace rises. "Come on, kids." She kisses Martin. "Great adaptation," she whispers. "Don't be too long."

Outside the moon is shining on the olive trees; there is a dense scatter of stars in the sky. The bushes rustle quietly as they brush past them. When a dark catlike shape bounds across the path Grace stops, shocked. It vanishes up a tree, the wide tail disappearing into the leaves.

"What was that?"

"A pine marten," Charley whispers. "There are tons of them here, Izzy's been watching them for days. She says the fathers eat their own babies." She sounds disbelieving.

Blake is hitting the bushes with a branch from an olive tree; he looks absorbed.

"Careful, you might hurt something," Grace tells him; he glances up, surprised, as if he hadn't realized what he was doing.

She shepherds the children into the stone building and shuts the door. The bedrooms are whitewashed, each with a view of the garden, a shower, and a wide, soft bed. Martin comes in after an hour; he starts snoring as soon as he lies down. Grace lies awake, disappointed and relieved at the same time. The scent of sage and thyme drifts through the open shutters; from somewhere in the garden the glass plates clash together gently, making discordant music in the dark.

Izzy can't believe how ugly pine martens are. They look as though they can't decide whether to be badgers or cats or some kind of weasel. There are lots around here, they have beady eyes and lumpy bodies and scrabbly paws. They hide up in the pine trees so you're not sure if they're there and whether one might fall on you at any moment. Sometimes they creep along the walls like giant rats. No one else knows where the den is; it's her secret, hers alone. She saw the mother pine marten going into a hole near the bottom of a dried-up tree. It came out again later with a smaller one following it and they went scuttling off together. They didn't come back, that was yesterday. Izzy is pretty sure there's still one left inside the hole, though; when she went close up she could hear scuffling noises. Now she's watch-

ing from behind another tree. There's a new big pine marten who's arrived and is waiting outside the hole, probably a male one, the father maybe. He's crouching near the hole and keeping really, really still. It's boiling hot and the crickets are loud. There are ants crawling all over her feet and sweat is trickling down her back. She tries to breathe in and out very slowly so the daddy pine marten won't see any movement. There is a lizard on a stone near her left foot, like a plastic toy, green with little yellow bumps all down its back. She can hear Poppy's voice in the distance, calling her. She smiles, Poppy has no clue where she is. Then her father starts, his voice is much louder obviously, and she's worried it will scare the pine marten. "Darling," then a little later "Izzy Tizzy," which makes her want to vomit. Finally, he shuts up. She's safe. The only person who could possibly find her is Blake, who has started following her around like a little dog, but he's helping Eric cut stuff in the garden this afternoon. This is about the farthest away you can get from the house and still be inside the fence. After maybe half an hour the daddy pine marten crouches lower and goes stiff; a baby pine marten starts coming out of the hole and he pounces faster than you can see and the baby makes a noise like a rusty door opening. The daddy pine marten's jaws clench tight on the baby's tummy, which kind of bulges out then opens up, a bit like a purse with a red lining that's come un-zipped. The daddy pine marten runs off with it in its mouth; the baby is actually still moving though not much. When Izzy goes nearer to look at where they'd been, there is blood on the ground, it's still warm. The ants are at it already. The baby was powerless. It wasn't that interesting after all.

6. October

Eve

Eve hears footsteps. The scent of bonfire and apples drifts into the bedroom, the donkeys bray once from their paddock. Distant traffic hums against the quiet of the weekday afternoon. Her ring glints red from the bedside table; the old-fashioned settings leave scratches on skin. The footsteps are coming closer. Eve freezes, her lips on Martin's shoulder; her mind empties of pleasure.

"Martin, listen."

He opens his eyes, frowns at the unfamiliar ceiling, then sees her; the fan of wrinkles around his eyes deepens but she clutches his arm.

"Someone's coming."

He looks about as if for a place to hide and, pulling the duvet around him, rolls off the side of the bed farthest from the door; there is a muffled thump, a snort of laughter.

The girls are at school, Ash is at nursery for another two hours, and Eric is scoping out a project for a musician's garden near Brighton and not due back till evening. Igor was left in charge of the bonfire; might he be prowling around the house? What if Melly has walked over for coffee? It could even be Grace calling by before school pickup. Eve gets up and straightens the sheet, her mind scrabbling for words. *Sorry, I was in the shower*—that's what she'll say—*give me a few minutes. Yes, that's Martin's car in the drive. He took a notepad down to the garden, I think he was after some peace.* While she makes tea for her visitor, Martin could dress, sneak out by the front door, and reenter from the back. She kicks his clothes under the bed, tightens the belt of her dressing gown, and sweeps open the door.

"Sorry, I was in the shower . . ." Her gaze lowers, lowers farther. Not even a child, just the dog, half sitting, half lying against the wall, whining quietly. Her legs weaken with relief. She lets herself slide to the floor. "Noah! What are you doing here?"

She kisses his smooth head and he pads after her into the bedroom.

"I thought it was Eric coming to kill me." Martin begins to laugh.

"Not funny." She retrieves his clothes from under the bed but he catches her hand.

"Come back to bed."

"We can't."

"We have an hour at least."

"The poor dog—"

"He won't say a word." He pulls her down, narrowly missing Noah.

Later, he helps her change the sheets and leaves with a book ostentatiously tucked under his arm. She stands at the door to wave him off. Igor has dismantled some headlights and has spread them out on the forecourt by the garage; he looks up and stares at them both. She ignores him and turns back into the kitchen. Now that she is on her own, guilt begins to lap at her in small, cold waves. There is a little pile of vomit by Noah's basket; he'd come to find her like a child then, feeling ill. After she's cleaned up, she makes tea and lets Noah into the garden where he lies down on the grass. She sits on the swing and lifts her face to the sun. It's still warm, the dry summer has become a dry autumn; her eyes close.

The crunch of wheels on gravel startles her, she drops the cup, tea soaks into the bark chips. Eric's truck sweeps into the drive; he's returning earlier than planned. He emerges stretching and walks over to the shed. He hasn't noticed her on the swing; she watches his easy gait, the swing of his shoulders, the play of the muscles across his side, familiar anatomy. Guilt swells. She usually tells him the truth about everything: the children, of course, and the little things of every day, where she's been and how she feels, though she hasn't shared that for a while. She could slip off the swing right now, approach him, confess, but the risk would be too great; he might never forgive her. The punishment would be a deeper, lasting silence. She stares down the garden to the wood, wishing the children were around, running in and out of the trees as they did all summer, distant company.

"The shed's been ransacked."

"What?" She blinks up at Eric; she hadn't noticed him approach. His eyes are narrowed.

"It looks like Noah pushed the door open; the sack of fertilizer has been chewed. There are granules all over the floor."

Hence the vomiting. Distracted by Martin, it's possible she left the back door open after he arrived and the dog escaped.

"You know he must be kept in the house unless we're with him; he could get through the hedge to the road, if nothing else." He is lecturing her as if it's her fault and it probably is. "Did the kids let him out?"

"Of course not, they're at school."

He comes closer, his shadow cuts the sun. She slips off the swing and steps back. Her skin feels saturated with Martin; she probably smells of him.

"Why are you looking like that?" He takes her arm, staring closely at her face.

"Like what?"

"Guilty, amused. Was it you?"

"You are being ridiculous, Eric. I need to write up my notes, let me go." Beyond Eric's shoulder she glimpses Igor by the bonfire, half hidden by smoke. "Maybe Igor came into the kitchen for matches and forgot to shut the door."

Eric turns away, his face tight with anger. Her own begins to build; Eric believes the best of everyone, apart from her. It could easily have been Igor, but he's a trustworthy guy, according to her husband, he works his fingers to the bone for his family in Poland. He can do no wrong. Eric doesn't see the way he watches them, especially her, how resentful he seems, no matter how friendly she is. Eve retreats to the house and Noah follows her in, collapsing in a little heap on his cushion. Eric's chair is in its accustomed place at the head of the table; he made it himself out of oak. Solid, well crafted, the kind of furniture that will last a lifetime. She runs her fingers along the curve of its back, the smooth surface as familiar as his skin. The wood is darkened on the arms where his hands always rest. What is she doing? What madness to jeopardize everything she has; her marriage to Eric above all things. She's lying to her children as well, and to Grace, whom she likes very much. She has let her relationship with Martin slide from one thing to another, starstruck, flattered, careless. It must end now, before it's too late. She'll speak to Martin, bring it to a halt. He'll understand, he might not even mind very much; neither of them made promises they couldn't keep. They both knew it was a game and now it needs to stop.

The clock chimes two. Noah sneezes in his sleep. There's an hour left before she has to fetch Ash from nursery school. She flicks the kettle on, pulls out her files, and sits on the floor with her back against the stove, next to the dog. She thumbs through each child's work, making notes for her reports. Blake's writing is better, fewer reversals, his spelling has improved. Poppy has written a whole page. Izzy's handwriting is perfect but she has only completed two lines. Her drawings are disappointing as well, small, flat figures on the page, lifeless compared with Blake's swirling battles scenes or Poppy's vivid colors. While she is musing over the work, her cell phone rings, startling her.

"I just thought I'd see how you're doing." Melissa's voice echoes from the phone. "If you're worried about Poppy, don't be; Izzy says she looks out for her at break times."

"That's kind," Eve replies, feeling guilty. The afternoon with Martin has driven everything from her mind. Poppy started secondary school a few weeks ago; Eve thinks about her daughter all the time, sometimes she pictures her struggling in the classroom or sitting alone at lunchtime, but not this afternoon. This afternoon she forgot about Poppy completely. "You sound kind of hollow," she says quickly.

"That's because Paul's redone the kitchen; it's so minimal there's practically nothing in here now." Melissa laughs but the laughter sounds forced, it catches in her throat.

"You sound sad, my lovely."

"It's always lonely when Izzy goes back."

"I was just checking her work; her handwriting's very good. There's not much of it to judge by, but—"

"That's fantastic." Melly's voice brightens. "I knew it would improve."

Eve hasn't the heart to tell her that good writing might be a bad sign, that her daughter might not have dyslexia after all, but something more complicated, involving choice or defiance. It could take a psychologist to unravel the problem.

"Are you bringing Izzy on Sunday or is Paul dropping her off?"

"Paul's arranged to play golf with a friend, it'll be me."

"Let's chat about her work then." A talk could take time; Sunday will be perfect.

"Noah's poorly," Sorrel murmurs that evening, leaning her head on the dog.

"He's better than he was." Eve places glasses on the table, then napkins, knives, and forks. She sips wine as she moves about the kitchen, stirring the food, glancing at her children. These moments before supper are always the best of the day, warm with the presence of her children safely gathered in. Ash rolls his red tractor around the surfaces of the room, making engine noises; watching him, her tensions dissipate, her shoulders relax.

"I think Noah might have eaten something bad." Poppy draws a neat margin in her math book. "He's been sick and there are bits in it." She jerks her head at the small pile of vomit in his basket, dark pellets in it. Eve rinses the cushion in a bucket then puts it in the washing machine. It's lucky the dog survived.

"Noah got into the shed this afternoon." She ruffles Poppy's hair as she passes. "He ate some fertilizer but he's getting better now."

Poppy moves her head away. The braids are gone; her hair is almost shaved at the back. She'd insisted, before the start of secondary school. Eve had watched sorrowfully as the red hair fell in thick curls on the floor of the salon. Braids were babyish, Izzy had said. There are lines of blue across Poppy's eyelids, she looks older than eleven. Eve longs to touch her cheek, take her hand and kiss it, but what might have been fine six months ago isn't now.

Ash runs his truck lightly over Noah's back. Sorrel pushes her little brother away.

"Noah wants to sleep," she says.

Poppy looks up. "Izzy will think you're being mean to Ash, Sorrel. She doesn't like mean people."

Sorrel puts her thumb in her mouth; tears bulge then slide slowly down her cheeks.

"Jesus." Poppy rolls her eyes.

Eve needs to hurry supper, everyone's tired. "Wash hands, please, food's nearly ready."

The children jostle briefly at the sink and she washes

her hands afterward, noticing with a little jolt that her ruby ring isn't on her finger. And then she remembers, she left it on the bedside table this afternoon. She hurries upstairs and into their room, her hand outstretched, but she halts with a sick sense of shock; the ring is gone. She moves the pile of books and then the lamp to no avail; with growing panic she searches the floor under the table and then under the bed. Feeling breathless, she shakes out the duvet and the pillows. Nothing. Her precious ruby engagement ring that cost Eric all his savings twelve years ago has completely vanished.

"I'm starving." Sorrel's plaintive voice floats upstairs.

"Sit down at the table, sweetheart," she calls back. "I won't be long."

She straightens the bedcovers, heart thumping. Eric knows she removes the ring only before lovemaking; did he find it on the bedside table on his return? Has he guessed? He might have taken it to punish her and be waiting to gauge her response. She stands quite still, trembling, forcing herself to stay calm. It's far more likely it was knocked somewhere when Martin pulled the duvet off the bed; maybe he discovered it on the floor and put it somewhere safe, forgetting to tell her.

"Mum!"

She hurries downstairs. The children are sitting in their places; Sorrel looks unhappy, Poppy impatient, Ash is half-asleep. Eve puts the casserole on the table and lights candles with an unsteady hand. Eric enters and sits down silently, his expression serious. How can she ask him if he has her ring? If he doesn't, his suspicions will be aroused; if he does, what then? He might begin to question her; what would she say? She needs an excuse, something convincing; her thoughts spin. She cuts the baked potatoes and slides in butter, then serves everyone the casserole, fragrant with wine, dark mushrooms, and onions.

"So how did it go today, Pops?" She forces herself to sound bright.

Poppy shrugs, pushing her food around her plate. It might be wiser not to pursue her with questions tonight. She looks tired, her face is closed; tomorrow would be better. Sorrel glances at Noah as she eats, she looks worried. Ash's eyelids droop with tiredness. Eric smiles at the children; the kitchen seems as peaceful as it always does at supper, but below the table her hands twist in her lap.

"More food, anyone?"

"I'll help myself," Eric tells her.

She watches his face, trying to see if he is angry or upset; he seems preoccupied—what does he know? He looks up and meets her gaze calmly; she lowers her eyes, feeling helpless.

"Homework," Poppy mumbles, and slips from her place, leaving the room without helping to clear the table as she used to do. Eric picks up Ash and puts him on his shoulders. "Bedtime," he announces as he walks across the kitchen, calling for Sorrel to follow. No, his voice is too cheerful, he'd sound different if he was harboring her ring, suspecting her of having an affair; all the same her stomach churns with worry. Alone in the kitchen she texts Martin. *Have you seen my ring?*

Sorry, the answer pings back. *On the floor somewhere?*

As she clears the table, Poppy's angry shouts filter down; Sorrel begins to cry. The girls, quarreling again. They have been on edge since Greece. Poppy is better behaved when her friends are around. Eve runs water into the empty casserole dish. Sunday seems a long way off; the week could be broken up. She removes the last dishes from the table; in the end no one ate very much. She could offer a short session tomorrow, supervising homework, maybe a word game if there is time. Supper as well. It can be a regular event every Wednesday from now on; she won't charge. Melly can come for supper this first time, Martin too. She blows out the candles. She'll find a quiet moment to tell him their affair is over; it will end on a civilized note, an event to look back on. She texts the offer to Izzy, Melly, and Martin and feels better. She'll find her ring, of course she will. She can search their room in the morning after Eric has left for work, move the bed and the chests of drawers, turn back the carpet, look under the radiator. If it's not there, she'll search the house. It's bound to turn up, it has to; a ring like that doesn't vanish into thin air.

Melissa

A door slams in the night. Melissa wakes, her mouth dry with fear. Paul is in Paris, she locked all the doors before bed. She gets up, heart thudding, and runs to Izzy's room, wrenching the door open. Her daughter is sleeping peacefully, her bright hair spread out over the pillow. Melissa leans against the door, weak with relief. After a few minutes, she gathers her courage and tiptoes downstairs, her legs trembling. The silent kitchen is softly illuminated by concealed lights; it looks empty but the stench of alcohol invades her nose, a vodka bottle lies on the floor by the sink. Her breath catches in her throat. Intruders? Paul returning early? Then she freezes. Muted sobbing is coming from the pantry. She opens the door cautiously. Lina is sitting beneath the shelves, her hands around her knees, tears pouring down her cheeks. The kitten cowers by her side. Lina looks up then pushes herself to her feet, still sobbing.

"Lina! I thought we'd had a break-in! Are you all right? What happened?"

"My boyfriend, Hassan," Lina says through her tears. "We argued." She puts her hand over her stomach, pressing in.

"Are you hurt?"

Lina shakes her head quickly, too quickly. Is she telling the truth? Hassan was probably drunk; he might have hit her or harmed her in some way. Melissa puts a hand on her shoulder.

"Do you want to tell me about it?"

"I said it was finished between us; he threw the bottle . . ." She lowers her gaze as if ashamed.

Her boyfriend sounds like a man whose anger turns quickly to something else, something more. Melissa begins carefully. "There are men who like to scare women. They get angry and then they lash out; they say they are sorry and promise to stop but they don't." Her voice is rising despite herself and the words begin to spill out in a stream. "It gets worse and they aren't sorry anymore, but you're trapped because they could take the most precious thing you have—" She pauses, gasping for breath. What is she saying? It won't make any sense to Lina, in fact she could be frightening her. She takes both of Lina's hands in hers, speaking more gently. "Promise you'll tell me if he ever comes back."

Lina nods, she looks miserable.

"Let me make you some tea."

Lina shakes her head.

"Okay, sweetheart." She tries to smile. "I'm sorry if I've scared you; you've been scared enough for one night. Try to sleep now and take the day off tomorrow."

Lina disappears up the stairs, silent as a shadow. Melissa throws the vodka bottle away; she fills a bucket and starts to wash the floor to remove the spilled alcohol, scrubbing hard as if to scrub away deeper stains that she can't even see. She scrubs until her hands are raw. By the time she has finished she is trembling with fatigue, her feet are icy. She goes to bed, exhausted. A few seconds later, the cat leaps onto the pillow next to her. "You're not allowed up here, little Venus," Melissa whispers, "but I won't tell if you don't."

The cat curls up, purring loudly, a small, comforting presence.

The face that stares back at her from the mirror the next morning is papery white, the lines in the skin like fine cracks. Too much sun on holiday, too much salt water. She rubs in cream, but it makes no difference. Her skin looks tired, unlike Grace's, which glows, or Eve's, which seems lit from within, the skin of a woman with a lover. She puts the jar back on the shelf. That thing with Martin must be over. There's been no more touching, no glances, no holding hands, unless—she smooths foundation down her neck—it has changed into something else, something more. They wouldn't need to touch if they were sleeping together. Her thoughts jump and skitter like the cat when it's scared. Eve wouldn't do that surely, not to Grace. Everyone flirts; Paul more than most. It's simpler not to know. Melissa applies mascara carefully. She won't tell Grace, ever.

Izzy is sitting at the kitchen table writing in a note-book, the cat by her feet. The room looks as it usually does in the morning, the sun pooling on the shining floor. The smell of alcohol has vanished; last night's incident has the quality of a nightmare, disturbing but a little unreal. Lina is piling fruit into the NutriBullet.

"Okay?" Melissa asks her quietly. "I hoped you'd take the day off today. You look tired, you could do with a rest."

Lina shakes her head. She adds grated tamarind to the fruit and starts the machine. The noise fills the kitchen, drowning the possibility of speech. When she has finished making the smoothie, she tips it into two glasses and places one next to Izzy and the other at Melissa's place on the table.

"You drink it, Lina," Melissa offers. "It will do you good."

Lina shakes her head, her hand on her stomach. "Sick," she whispers.

"I'm not surprised. Go to bed then, sweetie. I'll clear up breakfast."

Lina nods and walks out of the kitchen.

"I need to go to Eve's this evening," Izzy says, sipping her smoothie.

"But it's Wednesday today."

"She's offering Wednesdays now, for homework. She texted you. She's doing food and stuff. You're supposed to come, why don't you for once?"

Melissa feels a pang of guilt. She forgot all about Eve's text, how stupid. Last night's events had driven it from her mind. She shakes her head. "I've already arranged to go to a client's house in the countryside. Sorry, sweetheart, I probably won't be back in time to take you. Maybe you could walk there? I'll join you later if I can."

"Grace can take me."

"Grace is on late shifts. Dad will pop you over if he's back in time. I'll ask him."

Blake and Charley are on the curb outside the flats when they arrive to take them to school; they clamber in. Poppy and Sorrel are picked up from the end of their drive. Poppy and Izzy start whispering together immediately. Melissa smiles; Izzy has made friends now, maybe friends for life. When she has dropped them all off, she phones Paul, who picks up on the fourth ring.

"So you're back!"

"What makes you say that?" He sounds irritated.

"Well, the ring tone—"

"So you've started spying on me now?"

"No, of course not, sorry. How did it go in Paris?"

"Well. It went well." He sounds impatient.

"When do you start?"

"Start what?"

She's phoned at the wrong moment; he's obviously exhausted.

"I'm going to Wiltshire to look at a client's house." She doesn't elaborate; he's not usually interested in the details of her work. "I'll be back tonight. Could you take Izzy to Eve's this evening? She's running another session on Wednesdays now."

"Sure." He sounds more cheerful. He never minds ferrying his daughter about. "How is she?"

"Izzy's fine but Lina's poorly. I've sent her to bed. Her boyfriend—"

"I'll head home," he cuts in. "I need a shower."

"Can you remember to be quiet? Lina might be sleeping . . ." But he's gone.

She stacks the car with samples: squares of paper in different colors to hold against the walls, swatches of fabric for the windows, plans for the lighting, the Stanley tape measure. She turns the radio up as she makes her way through Clapham Common, Wandsworth, and around the M25 until she joins the M3 at Junction 12. She picks up speed, turns the radio off, and thinks back to the Tuesday before. She had liked Jean-Claude on sight; he was different from other clients, thoughtful, kind, a little sad.

"Thank you for meeting me here, it was good of you to come." Jean-Claude had smiled over the silver teapot in the tea room at the Savoy. She'd smiled back. He had an intense brown gaze, white hair clipped close over a rounded head, and the South of France in his voice.

"The project intrigued me, of course I came."

"I've wanted to meet you ever since I saw what you did in my friend's flat in Chelsea. I hoped you might work the same magic on our house."

"I loved the images you sent me, have you any others?"

He reached into the briefcase by his feet and drew

out a bulging envelope, fanning the contents on the tablecloth between the plates of cucumber sandwiches and slices of fruit cake. The photos were of a Georgian house with faded brick; wide, empty rooms; exquisite windows; a long green view.

"I am trusting you with the whole restoration project, to do with the house as you please."

Melissa looked up, startled. The dark eyes were somber.

"My son is ill; the family is in France. We will be in Paris for a year at least, while he recovers."

He doesn't elaborate, he didn't need to, she understood. She would drop everything to be with Izzy if she was ill, nothing else would count.

"I'm so sorry."

Jean-Claude nodded, acknowledging her sympathy. "The house has been empty a long time." The brown eyes studied her closely. "It's in good shape structurally but it needs fresh air and light, heat, color, curtains, rugs, furniture; color most of all. I love the choices you made for my friend. Please, take the key." He passed a large iron key across the starched white tablecloth. It felt heavy in her hand, like an expensive gift. Her heart beat fast with excitement.

"I'll visit next week," she had promised. "I can't wait to get started."

After two hours, the gray spire of Salisbury Cathedral appears in a dip in the hills, so tall and finely wrought it seems to pierce the pale blue sky. She drives slowly through the winding streets of the city, past the gray stone walls of the Cathedral Close and the leaning, timbered houses. A few miles farther west toward the village of Broad Chalke, she takes a left turn and the country road narrows. She slows, opening her window; birdsong and the bitter scent of hedgerows enter the car. The white iron gate is where he'd described, a mile beyond a village of brick and flint. The house stands at the end of the long drive, tall, symmetrical, rose-bricked. Weeds straggle through the gravel; an old man pushes a mower across the lawn—the last cut of the year probably—the sound flares and fades as he walks toward her then away. A couple of thrushes peck at the grass. The walls are warm under her hand. A hidden England beneath the England she knows; calm falls like sunshine. Inside her feet tap on dusty boards pale with age. The kitchen has a dresser and an ancient ceramic sink, copper pans left behind hang by hooks above the range. There is a stage at one end of the room in front, a ballroom perhaps. The rooms in the attic smell of sun-warmed wood. She holds fabric up to the light, measures for curtains, paces distances, and returns to the view; there are sheep on the chalky slopes, beech trees in shadowy stands. The hours tick by, she doesn't want to leave; she makes a call.

"Hi, Melly." Eve's voice is brimming with warmth. "Why aren't you here?"

"I'm at work in Wiltshire, I haven't left yet. I'm sorry but I'll miss your supper. Paul's bringing Izzy."

"They've arrived already. Charley and Blake are here, with Martin. Join us when you get back if you can, I expect we'll go on till late. Bye-bye, lovely." A kiss down the phone, the tickle of a laugh.

It's less easy to disguise happiness in a voice than a face. Eve and Martin. She feels sick, poor Grace. They'll be careful, surely, the children are there, Izzy notices everything. Melissa revisits the rooms, walking around slowly, reluctant to leave. After another hour she locks the door, dropping the key through the letterbox. It lands with a little thud, the house is no longer hers. Rain begins when she reaches the motorway; Paul calls as she's passing Reading. She hears laughing in the background, music, and the noise of Ash wailing.

"We're staying over." Paul's voice is slightly slurred. "Eric insisted, I couldn't say no."

He must be drunk for Eric to have made that suggestion, drunk enough not to be able to walk back home.

"We're all having fun, except maybe little Ash," he

continues pleasantly. "Hang on a tick." She hears a door shutting, footsteps, a door opening then shutting again; he must have walked out of the kitchen and into another room for privacy. "He won't stop crying." Paul's voice has changed, darkened. "It's driving me insane."

Paul hates the noise of children crying. When Izzy cried as a baby, Melissa had to take her to another part of the house or out in the car. She bites back the offer she was going to make about collecting them. The anger and alcohol will make a potent mix; safer for her if he stays over there, Izzy will enjoy the night with her friends.

"What about Martin and the children?"

"His lady wife summoned them home."

Once back at home, Melissa takes her laptop to the kitchen for the warmth of the stove and looks up Salisbury, reading about the cathedral with its fourteenth-century clock and thick surrounding walls. The countryside nearby, the town itself, had a feeling of ancient peace, a place where one could escape. Women escape danger all the time, there are safe houses everywhere. She looked them up once; places run by Women's Aid where your partner can't rape you whenever he wants, because he'd have no idea where you are.

She closes her laptop with a sharp click. What is she thinking of? People would say she's lucky compared with most. She has a beautiful house, they'd say, money, a fantastic job, friends—though she's afraid if she tells them the truth, they would struggle to believe her. She wouldn't blame them; her marriage looks perfect from the outside and so does her husband. The truth would be humiliating and, worse, far too risky. Paul is clever. If he thought she was telling her friends, he'd hire a good lawyer, deny everything, and turn the tables on her. She'd be labeled anorexic, work obsessed, unfit to parent. He'd divorce her, gaining custody of Izzy.

She puts her laptop back on the desk with trembling hands; she can't afford to escape, ever. She picks up Venus and climbs slowly to her room. It's early to go to bed, far earlier than usual, but she can do what she wants tonight, and she's tired after the long drive, and very cold. She shivers as she passes Izzy's empty room. Strange how chilly their house feels tonight, despite the radiators everywhere, the windows that are sealed against the outside air. By contrast, the unheated house today had been warm, as though heat were stored inside the walls and seeping into the rooms. She stretches out in the empty bed, her hand on the purring cat. Sleep comes after a while and in her dreams there is a garden, children playing on a lawn, Izzy among them, and a house that's wide open to the sun.

Grace

Grace sits on her own in the dark flat, waiting for her family to come home from the party; they're very late. The children will be exhausted and so is she. A little drama unfolded two hours ago; it began midway through her evening shift. She sips tea as the story spools back through her mind; she can still hear the voice that started it all off, that lazy, entitled, male voice.

"Hey, you."

Guests had been entering the hotel from the dark street, shaking out their umbrellas, blinking in the bright lights of the foyer. The evening shift was only half done. She'd looked past the man leaning over the counter, to the lit-up sheets of water slanting onto the sidewalk outside. Rain at long last, rain on her skin would feel good. When you've spent a childhood in Zimbabwe, rain always feels good.

"Take my case to my room, will you?" The man had a long jaw like a horse and a huge frame. He looked strong enough to heft three cases.

"Let me call the porter for you," she replied. "Sir."

"Get a move on then, honey pie." The mouth twitched irritably.

She was too tired to find an appropriate reply; she lifted the phone, made the call to the porter.

"So where are you from, originally?"

Too tired for this.

"I asked you a question." Anger feathered the voice, he leaned farther over the desk. She could smell alcohol on his breath and averted her face, feeling sick, her heart banging with fear. If she left, she could get another kind of job closer to home, one where angry men didn't snarl in her face. There'd be less money but more time, much more time with the kids. The thought was irresistible, she smiled, she couldn't help it.

"Jesus Christ." Then more quietly, "Bitch."

She stared at the screen, keeping her face neutral. The man moved off, muttering to himself. There would be a complaint to management, she would be called in, again. She could have put her head down on the desk then and gone to sleep. Blake had a nightmare last night; something's worrying him, he's sensed her fear perhaps. She walks in a cloud of terror these days, hurrying the children to the car, lest at any moment one of the gang should appear. She daren't take the garbage out anymore. Those thugs could be hiding, watching from a doorway or huddled in the disused garage by the gate, waiting to pounce.

A male guffaw came from the bar, her hands started to shake, her vision blurred. She pulled a sheet from the pad in front of her and scrawled a few sentences. She signed her name and then phoned the manager, explaining he would need to come to reception, she was leaving in the next few minutes.

"How long will you be?" He sounded irritated.

"A while."

The doorman tipped his hat at her. He came from Jamaica a long time ago; she would miss his stories. She put out her hand and he took it, smiling warmly. He's seen staff come and go over the years, he could probably tell that she wouldn't be back.

The rain stopped on the drive home, the puddles shone in the streetlights. A sense of exhilaration began to grow. There was a job opening in the co-op around the corner from the flats, the notice had been in the window for weeks; it would take just minutes to get to work, there would be far more time in the evenings. She would be able to talk to the kids, find out about their day, eat supper with her family, all those ordinary things that she never gets to do. They could go to the park on weekends. She accelerated through the junction. There'd be more time with Martin. She'd be paid less but perhaps he could find some tutoring to make up the shortfall, he's talked about that before. He's been writing well recently, whistling in the shower, shaving with care, and ironing his shirts. It's as if something had been unlocked. They could take the day off tomorrow, go somewhere, walk hand in hand as they used to. He can tell her about his writing, she'll share hers. They'll talk about books; they haven't done that for years, not properly. She parked the car in the parking lot and called him, her heart beating fast with excitement.

And that's when it all changed. Grace unfolds her legs; her tea has gone cold. She walks into the kitchen and makes another cup. She'd been so happy just before she made that call. She pours boiling water onto the same teabag, stirs in the milk, adds sugar as a pick-me-up, and takes the cup back to the sofa. When Martin answered her excitement had quickly evaporated, which was ridiculous really; she hadn't given him a chance to hear her out.

"Can't hear you, Gracie," he had told her when he picked up; the rain had started again and she watched the drops colliding as they ran down the car windshield. "Speak up!"

She could hear Charley shouting in the background, Ash crying, and the throaty sound of a woman's laugh close to his phone. Eve's laugh.

"Where are you?" she asked.

"At Eve's. She's started Wednesday sessions now, she only told us yesterday. Sorry, I forgot to pass that on, but—"

"Martin, I left my job." The statement had emerged as a flat little line of words one after another, not at all as she'd imagined.

"It's like a zoo in here, what did you say?"

"When are you back?"

"The kids want to stay the night; they've done some homework and now they're having fun. Eve's made food."

"It's school tomorrow."

"Come on, Gracie."

"No."

His reply was lost in the noise and laughter. She'd ended the call and turned off the ignition. She sat in the car for a while; a young woman walked past in the downpour, with plastic bags of shopping and a toddler on either side. A teenager locked his bright orange bike to the railings. The landlady made a brief appearance, bulky in her padded anorak, her red hair hidden under the hood. She smoked a cigarette while her Pekingese urinated on the grass, then both disappeared back into her flat. Grace checked every shadowy doorway then got out, locked her car, and walked to the door—walked, not ran—staring straight ahead. When footsteps approached from behind, going fast, her head sang with panic. She cringed as a young bloke brushed by, jogging at speed. He was shorter than her attacker had been but wore a hoody like his. One of the four who used to hang out by the dumpsters, she was convinced. The boy vanished around the corner of the building. She hurried inside, checked the lift was unoccupied and, after it reached the thirteenth floor, that the narrow hallway was empty. She unlocked the front door, stepped inside, and slammed it behind her. She was safe.

The second cup of tea has now gone cold. She should get up, get on. Martin will be back soon. Once the children are in bed, they will curl close on the sofa as they used to do. She'll share her news properly and he'll put his arm around her and tell her that leaving her job was exactly the right thing to do. They'll start to make plans and then they'll go to bed together. They'll make love, she promises herself. The drama of the evening will finish on a happy note; the kind of ending dramas are supposed to have. The flat is very quiet. She walks to the kitchen and turns on the radio. She could have joined them at the party though he didn't suggest that. It's too late now, and besides, she might have blurted out her news when she'd prefer to tell him in private. She'll make the flat very tidy and then they can relax. She puts the breakfast cereal away and wipes down the appliances, polishing the surfaces till they shine; all the time, an image of the hooded boy who ran past her flickers in and out of her mind. It's time to share exactly what happened to her that night in July and how she's been feeling since. Martin will help, even if he simply listens with his arm around her; that will help.

It's only when she begins to sweep the kitchen that she notices the coins. Ten of them, pound coins, scattered all over the floor. The children, pinching cash for sweets? She takes the candy tin from its hiding place, realizing by the weight that it's empty. Her hands begin to shake and the tin rattles in her hand, just a little. When she opens it, the coins are gone. There'd been two hundred of them at the last count, Martin was going to take them to the bank. There's not one left. Instead there are a couple of keys: the key to the block of flats and the key to their own front door, the ones on the small ring with the little red tab, which she'd lost way back, just before the assault. For a while her head feels empty and thoughts refuse to come. Then she walks onto the balcony, craning her neck to see down to the parking lot. There's no one there, but the gang is back for sure; she's just seen one of them, after all. Her thoughts race. They must be acting out a plan that was hatched a while ago, maybe in the days following the attack as they watched their friend recover in the hospital with a policeman outside his room. They wanted vengeance for what she did and they've been prepared to wait for months. They must have pounced on those keys where she dropped them on the stairs perhaps, and not in the flat after all; a gift, but one they didn't use straightaway. They've been much cleverer than that. They've waited all this time and even then they didn't ransack the place, nothing so crude. She can see them strolling around the rooms, taking their time; they might have let themselves in before. The skin on her arms rises in little bumps; this isn't about robbery, it's about power. They have helped themselves casually, as if the flat was their territory to plunder at will. They've issued a warning; there's probably worse to come. She feels calm, as you do in an emergency. She calls security to schedule a lock change for their door, and then the co-op to arrange for an interview. She'll have to work longer hours than she'd hoped to make up the cash; she'll have less time with the children after all. She won't tell the kids about the robbery, just Martin. Where the hell is he? It's so late; what can he be thinking of?

She finishes sweeping the floor then hoovers the entire flat, removing every trace of their presence; it occurs to her she is removing evidence, but it's far too risky to involve the police; she'd have to start from the beginning and could be blamed for the break-in. What did she expect, they could ask, since she'd stabbed one of the gang?

One thing is very clear: they can't stay here much longer; it feels far too dangerous now.

*P*oppy is on the mattress, muttering in her sleep, her right arm resting on the outside cover. Izzy stares from the bed, narrowing her eyes, but Poppy's arm is still wrapped up and Izzy can't see the cut, so she turns to look out the window into the night. The evening worked out okay in the end in spite of the way it began, with Eve pretending that her stupid food and the music and everything were for the kids when it was completely fucking obvious who it was really for. Eve and Martin had been dancing and looking into each other's eyes and everyone was too drunk or too stupid to see what was going on, except maybe Eric, but it was totally clear he wasn't going to do anything about it. Dad was blitzed out of his mind; he tried to make her dance with him in front of everyone, as if she would.

That was when she decided to go upstairs and start the games. It was a party; everyone knows you are supposed to play games at a party. She pulled her little bag of dice from her pocket and led the way upstairs; the others had followed.

Blake hunches in the corner of the car on the way home as far away from Charley as he can get. Dad is singing so he blocks his ears. He wants to think about what happened: the feel of Izzy's breath on the side of his face and the way her hair tickled his cheek. He's been wanting to do something major to please her for ages, like rescuing her from a snarling dog or a burning building or drowning or something. Even though he didn't exactly rescue her, she must be pleased with him now. He did exactly what she asked; she'd said cut deeper and he had. She'd been holding Poppy's arm; Sorrel had been hanging on to Poppy's hand, whimpering. Charley looked like she was going to be sick. Blake's heart had been thudding in time with the music downstairs. He'd practiced on the tarpaulin covering Igor's bike, but skin's different, bouncier for a start. Warmer. He'd had to press harder on the blue handle and the skin on the underside of Poppy's arm bulged up on either side of the blade, then the tip sank in. He'd felt all sweaty. He pulled the knife along about four inches, keeping the blade quite deep like Izzy said. The blood welled up straightaway. It felt wrong and interesting at the same time. Wipe it, Izzy had said, so we can see.

Blake wiped the blood off Poppy's arm with the bottom of his T-shirt; the cut was straight as though he had drawn the blade along the edge of a ruler. He felt as if he'd passed a test. Poppy said it didn't hurt though she looked funny. Charley wrapped a shirt around her arm.

Blake squashes himself farther into the corner of the car. He's not going to start feeling sorry for Poppy. She'd thrown the dice with the fewest dots; what happened was fair, she knew the rules. They had been about to play it again but Dad called up and he and Charley had to go home and Eve said the others had to go to bed super quick because it was late. Poppy might have fallen asleep already but all the same he can't get her pale face out of his mind.

PART THREE

Watching the Grown-Ups

If the police had thought of comparing the video from the summer and the photos of that Wednesday night in October they would have seen the differences, wouldn't they? All the children were thinner by then and none of them were smiling. They were sitting in a row, keeping still. That's the interesting, no, heartbreaking thing: they weren't dancing. None of them. They weren't eating or talking either. They were watching the grown-ups dance. It should have been the other way around: children dancing, adults watching. Charley is with Sorrel and Noah on the small sofa; Charley looks bored, Sorrel, sleepy. Poppy and Izzy are on the big sofa, both frowning. They must have felt cheated. Blake is sitting on a chair, looking fed up. Eric is leaning against the wall, watching his wife. Paul is watching his daughter and Izzy is watching him back.

And let's not forget Ash. He's in his little seat, on the floor; he's bigger than at the start of the summer, of course. At the age he was then, a few months make all the difference. He was laughing in all the scenes back then, but here his face is shiny, which means tears, current or recently shed. His eyes are shut and his mouth is open. He might have been yawning at the very moment someone took the photo, but when I imagine the noise of the music and the shuffling of feet and Eve laughing, I can also hear very clearly the sound of a child crying.

7. October
The Night After the Party

Eve

Sorrel pushes in between Eve and Eric; her flesh is cold, clammy. Eve half wakes and puts her arm around her daughter's body; her nightie is soaked. Rain is spattering at the window. Eric is snoring.

"Have you been outside?" she asks sleepily, wondering if they locked the door last night, or even closed it. She can't remember. It had been so late by the time they went to bed, her head is still reeling from the wine and the dancing.

Sorrel shakes her head. She burrows farther, elbowing her way between her parents; a sour scent leaches out in the warmth.

"Let's get this off you." Eve pulls off the sodden

nightie and throws it over the side of the bed. Accidents happen. She kisses Sorrel's hair. "Better?"

Sorrel cuddles closer. "I'm worried," she whispers.

"About?" Eve's eyes are closing.

"Dying."

"Oh, sweetheart, you mustn't worry about that." Eve sinks deeper.

"I don't want to die." Sorrel's voice wobbles.

"You're not going to die." Eve forces her eyes open and kisses her daughter's nose. "I won't let you."

"Izzy says I am."

"She's right, in a way." Eric's sleepy voice joins in. "But not until you're a very, very old lady."

"I don't want to be a . . . old lady." Sorrel begins to sob.

Eve's head is thumping. She checks the little clock on her bedside table. Three A.M. "You're going to be a beautiful girl forever and ever," she whispers into her daughter's hair. "Let's all go to sleep now." She kisses Sorrel's warm cheek, touches a silky curl. Sorrel shuts her eyes. Eve hovers between waking and sleeping as she holds her daughter close and listens to her breathing gradually slow. Sorrel stopped wetting the bed years ago. Izzy was being truthful but she must ask her to be careful, Sorrel is easily scared. She strokes Sorrel's hair and slips into sleep again.

A fresh squall of rain hits the window; a door bangs from somewhere in the house. Eve wakes with a gasp from a nightmare that slides away before she can hold it. Her mouth has the sour taste of metal. Sorrel has disappeared, she must have gone back to her bed.

Eve props herself up on one elbow to study her sleeping husband. His looks still surprise her: the fine bones of his face and the set of his eyes, that well-shaped mouth. Her husband, the man she promised to have and to hold. She touches his hair lightly; how stupid she's been. She behaved badly last night; having decided to end things with Martin, she let herself dance and flirt with him. It must have been the alcohol. Paul kept filling their glasses, they all drank far too much, except for Eric. He'd watched her all evening. If he's noticed the ring's absence, he's kept it quiet. She'll search the room today once he's gone; there wasn't time yesterday, what with cooking and the party. She'll find it, she's bound to. She moves closer to him. In the cool morning light, with the warmth of her husband's body against hers, it's hard to believe she's been so reckless, stupidly reckless, since the summer. Well, it's over. Thank God she saw sense in time. There are no casualties; not Eric, not Grace, and not Martin. They got away with it, just. She kisses Eric on the cheek, he murmurs and half turns away. The watch on his wrist reads eight A.M. The traffic will be thick already. She kisses him again, on the mouth this time, and he opens his eyes. He registers the light and swings his legs out of bed without a word. He's late. He has a tree-clearing project in Hampstead today; he'll be caught in rush-hour traffic now. She gets up more slowly, her head banging with each step, and slips on Eric's checkered shirt, discarded from the night before. She pauses outside Ash's room. The door is open just wide enough to see his bed. It's dark in there and very quiet. She has a hazy memory of Ash crying and of taking him up to bed very late, she can hardly remember tucking him in. Poppy and Sorrel are getting dressed in their room. They had watched her dance last night while they sat in a solemn little row with the other kids. She probably made a complete fool of herself. She groans quietly and walks downstairs slowly to avoid jarring her head.

Izzy is sitting at the table, dressed in her uniform and writing in an exercise book. Eve had forgotten about Izzy—that she stayed the night.

"Hi there. We overslept, I'm afraid." Eve puts the kettle on, wincing at the watery light through the window.

"I know." Izzy doesn't look up; there are neat comb marks in her hair, still wet from the shower. She has made herself tea and is sipping it delicately. Noah climbs out of his basket, anticipating food. There is no trace of the limp he had in the summer—just as well, she forgot to have him checked by the vet.

"Could you ask your father if he can do the school run today, Izzy? I'd like Ash to sleep as long as possible, and Eric's leaving soon."

"Daddy left hours ago." Izzy makes a careful crossing out. "In a rush."

Paul rose early then, which is surprising. He'd been more drunk than anyone else; she has a vague memory of Eric helping him upstairs to bed.

"We'll just have to wake Ash then. We might be late for school this once, but it was a good party, wasn't it?"

Izzy doesn't reply. Eve drops bread in the toaster, takes milk and juice from the fridge, puts cereal on the table, and finds bowls and mugs. She digs out some acetaminophen capsules from the back of the cupboard, swallowing a couple down.

"Toast's burning," Izzy says as she rubs out and rewrites a word.

"Shit."

The toast is black. Eve puts more bread in the toaster and shakes dog food into the bowl. She hurries from the kitchen and calls up from the bottom of the stairs.

"Eric?"

No answer, he must still be in the shower.

"Poppy?"

"What?"

"Can you get Ash up for me?"

"Do I have to?"

"Yes, please. I'm getting breakfast; we need to leave in ten minutes."

In the kitchen Izzy is texting; she looks up as smoke plumes from the toaster again. Eve throws away the blackened slabs. Eight twenty. By now the traffic will be stationary. She calls the school but no one picks up; she is invited to leave a message. As she is talking, she notices Igor waiting for Eric by the truck in the rain, his hair plastered against his skull. She replaces the receiver and turns to call Eric at the same moment that Poppy appears at the kitchen door, shoeless, her hair uncombed. Izzy turns to look at Poppy too, her fair eyebrows raised.

"Ash isn't in his bed." Poppy looks very young. "I can't find him anywhere."

Melissa

No one is about; the weather has scared the usual runners away and the wet park feels peaceful. As she jogs around the pond for the second time, a message pings through on Melissa's phone.

Eve's busy, Dad's left. Can you take us in?

Eight sixteen. Melissa replaces her phone in her tracksuit pocket and runs home fast, rain stinging her face. She gets straight into the car, checking her Fitbit: 200 calories. Better than nothing, she can make up the rest later. She drums her fingers on the wheel as she waits for the traffic lights to change. The crowds swarm over the crosswalk, the downpour crackles against the windshield. In Wiltshire rain will be falling on that soft green lawn, the view across the valley will be shrouded in soft mist.

A horn blares behind her, the lights have changed, the traffic inches forward. She's scarcely a mile away but the roads are crowded. It's rush hour and everyone drives when it's raining. By the time she reaches Eve's house, she is panicking; they'll all be late for school. Izzy doesn't reply to her text, so she parks the car in the road and hurries up the drive. The back door is wide open and rain is pouring in. She can hear Poppy shouting and Sorrel crying somewhere. Eric greets her, his mouth set in a grim line. Melissa's thoughts dart to Eve's secret.

"Izzy asked me to do the school run today," she tells him. "Where's everyone?"

Eric is soaking wet. His eyes scan the garden beyond

her; something is wrong. He hasn't heard a word she's said.

"Are you okay, Eric?"

"We can't find Ash." His eyes are wild. "We've looked everywhere."

"He won't be far." She's never seen him like this before, she puts a hand on his sleeve. "What can I do to help?"

"Get in out of the rain, Melly. Eve's inside." He disappears through the door into the garden.

Eve is wearing a man's shirt, she is hunting through a tall cupboard, strewing thick coats on the floor. The dog rolls luxuriously in piles of heavy tweed and cashmere.

"Let me help you."

"Ash hid in here recently; they were playing a game and he was frightened." Eve pulls out a couple of Barbour jackets; her face is white, her voice trembling. The tracks of tears shine on her cheeks. "Martin rang when I didn't turn up for the school run; he said Ash has to be hiding somewhere."

Close up Eve smells faintly of stale alcohol. Her eyes are bloodshot and bright with fear.

"I'm sure Martin's right." Melissa tries to speak calmly. "Izzy used to do this on purpose to worry me, it drove me frantic."

"He's only three, Melly, he won't be doing anything on purpose." Eve wipes her eyes on her cuff with a savage gesture, smudging mascara.

Even at three Izzy knew how to make her suffer, but Melissa doesn't mention that. "He can't be far, he's not old enough to go very far."

"We've phoned the police. Can you ask Paul if he saw anything before he left? And check on the girls, they'll be worried." Eve disappears outside.

Paul doesn't pick up so she texts instead then walks through the kitchen into the hall. The house is quiet; her footsteps ring on the stone. She opens a door into a red-walled room with a large table, oil paintings, and the musty smell of ancient meals. There's a chintzy sofa and matching chairs in the next room, a dusty-looking carpet. It seems odd that she's never seen these rooms before. This part of the house feels neglected.

"Izzy?" Her voice sounds thin in the cavernous hall. "Poppy? Sorrel?"

There is no reply, only the tick of an unseen clock as it scrapes the hour and the stale scent of flowers left in water too long. Unease deepens. Eve's house has always seemed a sunny place filled with laughter, it's as though she's wandered into someone else's home by mistake. Melissa walks farther into the hall toward the stairs, calling for her daughter, for Eve's daughters. Her voice echoes back to her, but no one answers. This seems to be a house that swallows children. As she puts a foot on the first step, she catches a faint rhythmic creaking coming from a door that's half open, down a corridor she hadn't noticed at the back of the hall. When she pushes the door wider, the interior is indistinct, the curtains pulled halfway across, crooked as if someone tried to darken the room in a hurry. As her eyes become accustomed to the gloom, she sees Izzy astride a dapple-gray rocking horse, tilting backward and forward slowly. Sorrel and Poppy are squashed together in a large armchair sharing Izzy's laptop. Their faces are pale in the reflected light. Poppy is half dressed, Sorrel still in her pajamas. She has never seen Eve's children even glance at a screen before. Izzy spends all her time on her cell phone or laptop; staring at the children's faces, she's unsure now which is the more normal behavior. Charley and Blake aren't with them, there is a brief pulse of worry until she remembers that they didn't stay over last night.

"Hi." Her voice sounds overly cheerful, a little flimsy.

Izzy stares at her mother. Poppy glances up then back at the screen, frowning. Sorrel wriggles from the seat and runs to Melissa. "When's Ash coming back?"

Melissa takes her hand; the small fingers are icy. This

room is unheated; Eve must have no idea the children play in here. Ash will be colder than this if he's outside in the rain, dangerously cold. The body temperature in children falls much faster than in adults.

"Oh, it won't be long now," she says cheerfully. "Shall we get you ready to go to school?"

Sorrel runs back and squeezes into the chair beside her sister again. Melissa gazes at them helplessly; they look so small in that chair, so vulnerable. She tries once more, "By the time you come home, Ash will be here and everything will be all right again. Shall we get you dressed, sweetheart?"

A violent movement catches her eye through the gap in the curtains, a wild animal motion. She yanks aside the velvet-edged drape. This room faces directly onto the paddock; from here she can see the donkeys cantering around the field. Something has spooked them. She struggles to open the heavy sash, raising it by a few inches; the wind and rain blow in, bringing with them the high-pitched braying of the animals as they pound the enclosure. Beyond them, she can make out Igor and Eric at the edge of the wood. Eve is in the meadow walking through tall grass, head bent as she searches the ground. She looks smaller than usual, her hair wet and close to her skull. No one seems to have noticed the donkeys' behavior; their long ears are flat to their heads as they run, keeping pace with one another. She looks around their field in case there's a plastic bag caught on a branch or a stray umbrella tossed in by the wind, but everything looks the same as it always does: the trees at one side, the wildlife pond, the animal shelter, the gate. The pond. Her glance flicks back, it's too far to see more than the gleam of water from here. They were so lucky to have that pond on their land, Eric told her once, perfect for animals, being spring fed, cold, and very deep. Wild geese visit in winter; moorhens live at the edges. It's quite safe, he'd added, the paddock has a high fence, the gate's always kept locked. She looks up. A few birds are circling in the air above the pool as though displaced, waterbirds of some kind, she was never good at birds' names. Melissa lets go of the curtain and begins to run, through the hall, out the kitchen door, and across the veranda, meeting Eve jogging back. Eve is soaked through, her face a mask of mud and tears.

"Are the girls okay?" Then she grabs Melissa's hand. "What is it, Melly? What have you seen?"

"The pond." Melissa can hardly get her words out. "Have you checked it?"

"The gate's locked, a child couldn't possibly—" Eve begins but Melissa races past her and down the path. When she reaches the gate she starts to climb, but Eve catches up and, her bare leg swinging over the gate, knocks Melissa to the ground. When Eve starts screaming a few seconds later the donkeys thunder past her to the fence and stand together, tossing their heads. Eric vaults over the gate, runs across the grass, and wades into the pond, plunging deeper and deeper into the icy water, his arms outstretched to reach his son.

Grace

Martin swerves to avoid the screaming ambulance as it jolts from the drive to the road, blue light flashing. Grace is flung against the passenger door. Martin was wrong, Ash wasn't hiding, something terrible has happened.

"At least he's alive," she mutters. "He must be; you don't rush to hospital with a blue light if a child has died, or do you?"

Martin frowns but doesn't answer. They dropped their two off at school just now. Charley, the part in her hair crooked, had walked slowly into the playground, looking serious. Blake disappeared quickly, sneakers undone, lower lip protruding.

"When's your shift start?" Martin brakes and parks by the curb.

"I'm not working today." She hasn't told him she

left yet. She didn't tell him anything she'd planned to; he was too tired when he returned from Eve's last night. They were so late; he lost track of the kids, he'd explained; it turned out they'd been upstairs, playing games. Today there's been no time, obviously.

The drive is full of police cars. The front door of the house is wide open; Noah is drinking puddles in the middle of the road.

"Oh, Evie," Martin mutters.

Evie? That's new. Grace glances at him; she hasn't heard him call her that before.

"House left open all hours of the day and night." Martin pulls Noah off the road by his collar. Grace hurries up the drive and through the back door of the kitchen, Martin following. Melissa is by the sink, kneeling by Sorrel, who is crying into her shoulder, long, shuddering sobs that shake her body. Poppy leans against the wall staring into space, Izzy has her arm around her friend.

Grace bends over Melissa. "Can you please just tell me what's happened?"

Melissa straightens. Sorrel turns to fling her arms around Martin instead. Melissa follows Grace from the room. They sit together on the stairs in the hall, Melissa whispering with her eyes on the door in case the children emerge.

Grace stares at her in disbelief. "I don't understand. How did it happen?"

"They think he got up in the night and followed the dog into the garden. The paddock gate is locked but he must have squeezed underneath." Melissa's voice trembles. "He's wandered off before, but never at night. Eve was hysterical. Eric tried mouth to mouth, the ambulance came in minutes. They took over. Eve went with him, Eric followed in the car. We haven't heard anything since."

In Charley's biology book the lungs look like a sponge; if all those little holes were to fill up with water, how the hell would you ever get it out?

"We'll stay," Grace says. "We can help look after the girls."

"I'll stay too but I have no idea why the police are still here." Melissa sounds bewildered.

In case his parents hurt him, Grace thinks but doesn't say, then dumped him in the pond; it's how they've been trained to think.

"Can you assemble the children?" Martin pokes his head out of the kitchen doorway, making them both jump. "The police want to talk to them; they've talked to Igor already. They told me they have to speak to everyone who was around last night; routine, apparently. It's the children's turn now. Eric consented by phone." He turns to Melissa. "Can you get Paul back? They'll want to talk to him too as he stayed over. Information gathering, you know how they are."

Melissa texts rapidly, a reply pings back. "He's desperately sorry to hear what's happened. He's coming as soon as he can." Her face is tense with worry.

"You mustn't concern yourself." Martin pats Melissa's shoulder. "The police ask everyone questions if there's been an accident involving children."

Grace reaches for his hand. "Thanks," she whispers, glad of his presence, taking care of everyone, being kind. He nods, preoccupied.

Poppy is sitting on the sofa with the policewoman who introduces herself as Donna. After name and age checks, Donna moves a little closer. She has a heart-shaped face, thick fair hair, and a turned-up nose. Poppy inspects her carefully, she seems reassured. Donna is pretty, and pretty women are less threatening to children, though in fairy tales it's the pretty ones who are dangerous: Snow White's stepmother, Cruella, the Snow Queen. Grace catches Poppy's eye and gives her a thumbs-up.

"So, Poppy, did you hear anything unusual after you went upstairs last night?"

"We were playing games; I probably wouldn't have heard."

"What kind of games?" She is trying to relax Poppy but her voice has a wheedling quality that a child might find irritating.

"Just . . . you know." Poppy shrugs, glances at Izzy. "Games."

"And later?"

Poppy shrugs, shaking her head; her mouth tightens as if she is trying not to cry.

"Thanks, Poppy." Donna smiles. "That's all for now."

Sorrel doesn't reply to any of the questions. Her thumb is in her mouth and her eyes are full of tears. After a few minutes, Grace steps forward and picks her up.

Then it's Izzy's turn. She sits down and smiles at Donna. Donna smiles back, a little uncertainly.

"So you stayed last night, Isabelle?"

"Yes." Izzy sounds a little bored. Perhaps that's the way to deal with the police. Izzy might be clever, cleverer than Grace has given her credit for.

"I gather you live fairly close by; I can't help wondering why you didn't just go home after the party?"

"Dad was drunk."

"Right." Donna scrawls rapidly in her notebook and looks up again. "Did you hear anything in the night?"

Izzy stares at her.

"So you slept through until Poppy's mother called upstairs?" There's a hint of impatience in Donna's tone.

Izzy shakes her head. "Dad's car woke me earlier so I went downstairs to do homework."

"You're an early bird then, like me?"

Izzy shrugs. "I had homework to finish, it was too noisy the night before."

"Was that because Ash was making a noise?"

"The grown-ups were dancing; the music was really loud."

Donna writes fast. She is getting the story she needs, fitting the fragments together, like the first pieces of a jigsaw puzzle, which are always the easiest to place.

"What's Izzy up to?" Martin whispers to Grace, his eyes on Izzy. Grace glances at Melissa; her legs are twisted around each other, she is picking at her cuticles as she watches her daughter. She and Melly were the only ones who weren't here last night. Melly must have thought, as she had, that the children had been working, at least for part of the time.

"Saying what happened, I suppose," she snaps.

"She's making it sound worse than it was. There was music playing in the background and some dancing, not that much."

"And drinking," Grace mutters. "Paul was obviously plastered."

"Thanks, Isabelle, let's take a little break now." Donna signals to her colleagues and they leave the room.

"I'll make something for the kids. Sandwiches will have to do." Martin takes a knife from the block, pulls bread from the box, and peanut butter from the cupboard. He seems to know the kitchen well, but then it would be natural to help if he arrived early with the kids on a Sunday morning and Eve was busy getting ready. How foolish to let that niggling worry about Eve, about Martin and Eve, get the upper hand, especially now.

She glances at her watch. How much longer will they have to wait to hear anything?

Sorrel is tugging at her hand; the little girl is trembling. "I want Mummy," she says.

"Let's go outside and see if she's coming." Grace takes her hand, and at the moment of opening the door, a car pulls up on the drive. Eric gets out very slowly. He looks different, stooped; years older.

"Daddy!" Sorrel flies to her father.

Eric kneels to his daughter, clenching her to him, his face hidden as Eve emerges from the passenger seat. She is bent over, her hand on her abdomen as though protecting a wound. She begins to walk slowly to the house. She turns as Sorrel calls to her; her face is unrecognizable, so swollen and white it looks just as if she too had been immersed in water for a long time.

*S*orrel is in the playroom again with Poppy and Izzy
because the kitchen is crowded with people; Izzy's
dad has arrived; he isn't talking very much. Some of
the grown-ups are trying not to cry. Her daddy is actually crying, which makes her feel shaky. Mummy
doesn't look like Mummy. The playroom is dark because no one has turned on the light and she can't reach
the switch; the curtains are still half over the windows.
She can see the donkeys standing by the shed, their
heads hanging down; they look sad. No one is saying anything and it's scary. Ash normally makes little
noises in the background, like he's talking to himself.
They're not usually words but it doesn't matter because
you can tell what he means and, anyway, he's learning
words. Then it hits her all over again, like something

actually hitting her; he won't be able to learn any more words now. He won't ever actually talk in sentences. She starts crying and Poppy rolls her eyes but moves over and lets her sit in the chair with her. Noah pushes the door open wider and comes in and sits on the floor by the chair. She puts her bare feet on his warm back, which feels nice.

"Gross," Izzy says.

Sorrel takes her feet off again. "Ash was all right when he went to bed," she whispers.

"Shut up because he's not all right now, is he? He's dead." Poppy has started crying and that makes Sorrel feel worse. Izzy walks around the room looking at things like the china donkey and the spoon with Mummy's name on it and the little candles in candlesticks. She picks them up and stares at them, then she puts them back, like she is in a shop and she's thinking about buying them but deciding they aren't worth the money. She picks up Ash's red tractor and looks at it for a while, which makes Sorrel want to snatch it away, except she daren't. Noah licks Sorrel's hand.

"It's not because he likes you, it's for the salt and that's also pretty gross." Izzy makes a being-sick face.

Charley would hold Sorrel's hand if she were here and she would probably say something to Izzy about it not being gross if dogs lick your hand.

"I've got a good idea," Izzy says. It sounds like she's thought of something really nice. "We can play our special game. That'll take our minds off what's happened. I've got the dice."

"We can't," Poppy says quickly. "There's not enough of us. Blake and Charley aren't here."

"Oh, that's okay," Izzy says. "We don't need them for this one."

Sorrel's tummy hurts, she wants Charley to be here. Charley doesn't do whatever Izzy says and she makes her feel safe. Izzy gets up and takes the lighter thing from her pocket and lights one of the candles, it looks pretty, but Sorrel throws the wrong dice so she loses the game.

"She's too little," Poppy says.

"We can't change the rules," Izzy says; she holds Sorrel's hand gently at first but then really tightly because at the last minute Sorrel tries to pull away.

That night Poppy lets her sleep in her bed. She doesn't seem to mind that she's still crying; she can't help it because her hand hurts and she wants her mother so much her tummy hurts again—but her mother as she usually is, laughing and cooking and stroking her cheek, not silent and staring, like some sort of monster.

8. November
Three Weeks After
Ash's Death

Eve

The little seat, the stroller, and the carriage have disappeared; corners that were stuffed with toys are now sharp-angled with light. The teddy with the shiny waistcoat and the red tractor have gone to the loft. The children appear and disappear on the edge of Eve's vision, light-bodied and silent as ghosts. Eve walks slowly through the upstairs corridors from room to room, as if deep underwater. It's hard to make her limbs work, hard to breathe. She stands by the bags of clothes in Ash's room, puts in the green onesie, takes it out again, holds it to her heart. Eric wants to burn everything as if he could destroy grief that way. Ash was burned after the autopsy. Ashes to ashes. She had hoped no one would say it, but someone did, a woman she didn't know, clutching a prayer book and watching her face.

Eric carried the small coffin, red-rimmed eyes burning out of a blank face. A church warden helped. Eve watched as they made their way down the aisle. Poppy was by her side, Sorrel on her lap. Charley sat on her other side in order to hold Sorrel's hand. Charley is a soldier of a child, as it turns out, stalwart and kind, hurrying to help with the funeral leaflets and the hymn books. Melly and Paul sat behind them with Izzy, whose head was bent throughout. Martin was behind them with Grace and Blake. The thud of Blake's sandals hitting the pew threads her memories along with Eric's face, Grace's fierce hug, and the tears on Melly's cheeks. Sorrel was as tearful as she had been since Ash died, but she can only hold her; there are no magic words, or none that she can find. The girls will heal, Eric had muttered at some point in the day, their lives will go on. Ash's has ended, she'd replied.

"He is dead," Eve whispers to the yellow room, painted to match their golden-haired boy. She won't see him again. She won't feel his face against hers. The agony drenches her and then recedes before crashing again. She doesn't cry, she hasn't cried since the day it happened. She doesn't have the energy. She doesn't eat, and sleeps only when the sky pales outside, waking again an hour later with her arms aching as if from the weight of a child. Once she woke Eric to ask him if drowned children were heavier than sleeping ones. He shook his head and turned his face away. They've hardly talked since the funeral.

She sits down on the bed, still holding the onesie. Faint music floats up from the kitchen; she hasn't been downstairs in three weeks.

There was no water in the lungs according to the autopsy, the policewoman told them.

Eric had asked her, confused and stumbling over his words, if that meant Ash had died even before he fell in the water. It didn't, she'd explained gently. An absence of water in the lungs was common in drownings; the larynx spasms in cold water, no water therefore enters the lungs. The technical term was "dry drowning." It was a tragic truth that more children drown at their homes than anywhere else. Children get out of their beds and wander, she said, they fall into canals and rivers and swimming pools, even the sea sometimes; no one should feel guilty.

Eve feels guilty, though; she knows it was her fault. She didn't tell the police she'd been drunk. Drunk enough to leave the back door open, drunk enough to sleep through her son calling her and the sound of his footsteps as he stumbled his way downstairs. A tragic accident but one she could have prevented.

Grace and Melly come over most days, taking turns cooking. Charley and Blake and Izzy keep the girls company after school, returning to their homes after supper. Eve told her friends she would understand if they didn't want their kids visiting the house, considering what had happened. Melly hugged her and said nothing would stop them from coming over, Grace said the same.

Eric sits by the bed in the evenings, his head lowered, saying nothing. A tide of blame swells silently between them: he should have made a solid gate with no gap at the bottom; he ought to have drained the pond and diverted the spring. She shouldn't have held a party midweek or gotten drunk. The swell rises higher, but if she accuses him he'll accuse her back. They can't afford that now, not yet.

Martin tiptoes in when no one is about and places something down on the bedside table that makes a tiny metallic noise. She turns to look; her ring, her lost ruby ring.

"I found this in our bed at home, after our last afternoon together," he whispers. "Sorry. It must have got swept up in my clothes after all. I brought it over to give it back the night of the party, but I couldn't get you on your own; then, well, with everything that happened I clean forgot." He shakes his head. "You must have been so worried. I'm sorry."

She'd forgotten all about the ring; it had been lost, she remembers now, she'd been so anxious, panicked even. That worry seems part of a distant dream that's faded to nothing. She stares up at him silently; he could be a stranger. If she feels anything for him now, it's to wonder how she could have felt so much and then nothing at all.

Sorrel comes into the room later and climbs onto the bed. Eve holds her daughter very close; the warm little body is comforting.

"I'm scared."

"Don't be, darling. We've made everything safe now."

"Ash couldn't breathe." She is sobbing.

"I know."

"He couldn't take a breath. He was trying to . . ."

"Don't think about it, sweetheart." Eve touches Sorrel's wet cheek. "Think about the happy times. We had so many lovely times with him." She gasps between her words as if surfacing for air, but Sorrel cries harder; she tries to talk through her tears but then Izzy is there. It's a Sunday, she's been here since the morning.

"Let your mummy sleep." She holds out her hand. "We need you for the game, Sorrel."

"Game?" Eve echoes dully.

"In the woods, fresh air. Come on, Sorrel."

"Go on, darling, it'll help you feel better," Eve tells her.

Sorrel clings to her but Izzy is smiling and holding out her hand and they both leave. When they have gone, Eve gets up and leans her head against the glass. Her eyes go to the donkeys' field like a tongue to a painful tooth. Igor has rerouted the spring and filled in the pond; the fresh soil has a brown crust like a new scar. Everything in the landscape is dull brown: tan branches, brick-colored earth, and heavy beige clouds. Leaves lie on the ground in sodden russet layers. The children shun the little house that Eric made, preferring the wood as their playground. She can see them from the bedroom window, running in and out of the leafless trees. Sorrel's red anorak shows up against the dark trunks. She lags behind and falls over often; she is probably crying right now. Her daughter's pain feels deep but inaccessible, like an ache in your abdomen that keeps you awake but you can't quite locate.

Eve slips on the ring. It feels heavy on her finger, a little loose. She descends to the kitchen, holding tight to the banister, feeling her way as if in darkness. She hesitates at the kitchen door; Martin is chopping herbs. There is music, something jazzy. She's not up to this after all, but Martin looks up as she turns to go.

"Ah, so you've come downstairs at last." He reaches to switch off the radio and it's too late to escape; he smiles, but seen across the kitchen, he looks smaller than he used to be, obscurely disappointing.

"I thought we'd get ahead with supper," he says cheerfully. "The kids are outside; Melly's gone to fetch them in. It's mild now but they say it's all set to change. The wind's in the north, a big freeze is coming, snow maybe. Unusual for the time of year. Storm Adelina is approaching. God knows where they find these names." He's talking fast, as if scared of silence. Eve looks out the window to the sky, where gray clouds have massed; if the predicted weather had happened three weeks back, the pond might have frozen over. Ash would have fallen on ice. He'd be playing on the floor now, with a scab on his forehead. She might have worried there would be a scar when he grew up. A little white scar, the kind of thing a girlfriend would notice; he'd smile and tell her the story, about how he'd followed the dog outside on a cold morning when he was little . . .

"It's good to see you up and about." Martin puts a

cup of tea in front of her. "I wish to God there were words to make it easier, I feel so helpless."

She sips the bitter tea; he's forgotten she takes milk. What does she care about how he feels? Words aren't important after all. They wouldn't have saved Ash's life; they won't bring him back. It's hard to believe she once set so much store by words, especially his. She can't finish the tea and gets up. Martin steps forward to hold her, she endures the embrace, too exhausted to move away. When the children thud up the veranda steps she raises her head in time to see Izzy come in and stop short, a flicker of contempt on that smooth young face. Eve pulls away before the other children stream in. Poppy follows close on Izzy's heels, Blake, and then Charley; Sorrel comes last holding Noah close to her chest. He's much too big to be carried now, she is staggering under his weight. The children kick off boots and shed coats, scattering a shower of little stones that clatter to the floor. They walk silently across the kitchen and disappear. Melissa follows the children in and shuts the door. By then Martin is back chopping herbs. Melissa takes the dustpan and brush from under the sink and sweeps the floor clean.

"I thought I'd make a pudding for supper," she says brightly, straightening. "The children will be hungry."

Eve slips away upstairs again.

Melissa

Melissa is slicing apples at the sink when Sorrel returns to the kitchen a little later. Now she understands why Eve cooked so much, how soothing food preparation can be, how usefully thoughts are blocked. She looks down at Sorrel. Her thumb is in her mouth and she is wearing a tiara crookedly jammed on her tangled hair. Tears are seeping through her fingers.

Melissa kneels and puts her arm around her. Sorrel leans into her wordlessly.

"Can I stay with you?" she asks after a while.

"Of course you can. Are you being a princess?"

Sorrel nods gravely.

"Where are the others?"

Sorrel's glance slides to the door. There are children's voices coming from the playroom on the other side of the hall. Izzy's is the loudest, Poppy's chiming in.

Sorrel leans closer. "I want to see the donkeys."

Melissa takes her hand; the skin feels surprisingly rough. She turns it carefully, noting a small round area of dark crust on the palm. A healing graze, a burn?

"How did you do that, darling?"

Sorrel pulls her hand away. Messing around with candles, probably. Eve always has candles at supper; the children played with them in Greece. She'll take them off the table, out of harm's way. She leaves the apple slices under water and finds Sorrel's anorak from the jumble by the door.

The donkeys are bunched together under the trees; their long heads swing to watch every movement. Melissa and Sorrel walk around the outside of the paddock hand in hand. It occurs to Melissa she should be jogging; she hasn't exercised since the accident. She slides a hand around her waist then feels guilty. How could her body matter against the grief that presses down on all of them?

"Did they see it, do you think?" Sorrel asks, looking at the donkeys.

Melissa follows her gaze, imagining those large animal eyes turned toward the stumbling child, absorbing the flung-out arm, the fair head disappearing beneath the clear, cold water, watching impassively as the broken surface steadied itself again.

"Maybe they did, darling; it might have been nice for Ash to know that the donkeys were there with him." A lie—he would have been terrified of the looming faces and sharp hooves; perhaps that's why he fell.

Sorrel holds her hand more tightly. "He couldn't breathe. He was trying to breathe but he couldn't." She is crying in earnest. "He couldn't . . ." She starts hiccuping violently.

"I know." Melissa kneels to take the little girl in her arms. "I know, sweetie. Shall we go back in now?"

Sorrel shakes her head. "I want to say goodbye to them."

She lifts the child, surprised by her lightness. Sorrel waves at the donkeys, they stare back, and in the light of that calm gaze Melissa feels momentarily reprieved. At least Ash won't have to bear anxiety or bullying, he will never face fear or violence, never feel anguish over a beloved child. They return to the kitchen where Eric is sitting, staring at the floor. Sorrel clambers onto his lap.

"Time for a nap."

Melissa jolts to see Izzy staring at Sorrel; she must have come in very quietly without making a sound.

"Hurry up," Izzy says.

"Being mother?" Eric asks Izzy as Sorrel slips obediently from his lap; his voice sounds sharper than usual.

"Someone has to," Izzy replies in a reasonable tone, and taking Sorrel's hand, she leads her out of the room. Melissa watches them go; at least Sorrel is being included now.

"Eric, I'm sure Izzy didn't mean—"

"It's okay, she's right. A nap is a good idea, I'm exhausted. Maybe we should all have a little sleep."

Five minutes later the house is quiet. Melissa sits on

the sofa by the fire; as her eyelids drift together, she hears, or imagines, the quiet crunch of gravel outside, footsteps, arriving or leaving.

Grace

Grace leaves the co-op and jogs the few streets home. Sleet is falling, the air is turning colder, there's a chilly wind. A storm has been forecast, the shop manager told her, Storm Adelina. Hurry home, snow is on the way. She is icy by the time she reaches the flat, slamming the door behind her. Much of the day has been spent filling bags with mince pies and frozen stuffing, customers stocking up for Christmas in advance. Her face feels stiff from smiling. She stands in the kitchen boiling the kettle for tea, and downs it quickly. She must hurry. She promised Melly she would bring fresh laundry to Eve's and stay for supper, though it's time they stopped going over so often. Eve's family needs a chance to grieve in peace; she needs time with hers. She takes sheets from the airing cupboard and kneels down to fill a suitcase with them. She's hardly talked to Charley or Blake despite changing jobs; in fact, they've talked even less. The children have been tired at night and silent at mealtimes, evasive with their answers as if their real life was somewhere else. They are all grieving, but that should be a time to draw closer, not move further away. They didn't ask her to change jobs, but all the same, the disappointment stings; nothing has turned out as she'd expected. She collects towels, stuffing them into Martin's old backpack. They can talk tonight after they've all come home; she could make hot chocolate and sit on their beds for a while, listen to whatever they might want to say. Martin will be with her and afterward they'll be together, curled on the sofa. It seems a long time since they've done that. They're busy, she knows that: his tutorials, her hours, both of them supporting Eve's family. Tutoring turns out to suit him; the agency calls most days, he's earning decent money, but she's missed him, missed the old closeness. She wants to see him suddenly, fiercely. She needs to feel his arms around her. She throws the suitcase and backpack into the car and drives fast through the sleet. On arrival at Eve's, she hurries up the drive with her load, the gravel crunching under her feet. Sleet blows hard into her face; the evening has darkened. Igor's bulky figure is just visible, retreating down the path to his home.

Melissa is draining potatoes at the sink when she enters the kitchen, Charley banging down cutlery on the table. Poppy has a book in her lap but is staring into space, her back leaning against Izzy's. Izzy and Blake are playing cards; her legs, splayed on either side of him, are covered with mud. Blake is staring at Izzy as though transfixed. Grace puts the suitcase on the floor, drops the backpack on a chair, and peels off her coat.

"Hi there." Melly puts the potatoes on the table, adding a lump of butter and a scattering of parsley. She seems calm, as though fixing meals for a large group of people is something she does often. "Perfect timing. The children had a nap and I fell asleep, but we're ready to go now. Gosh, are you okay? You look a bit tired."

"It's been a long day. Where's Martin?"

"He's around. Paul had to call in to the office; he's coming back for supper."

"Where exactly is Martin, Melly?"

"Oh, writing somewhere, I expect." Melly sounds evasive.

"I'll search him out. We need to chat before supper, there's so much—"

"Martin's upstairs," Izzy says. "With Eve."

"I'm starving," Charley announces in the little silence. "Can we eat now?"

"Could you call your daddy down?" Melissa asks her.

"I'll get him." Grace walks out of the kitchen,

crosses the hall, and starts up the stairs, aware as she does of the swift patter of feet behind her, then Izzy brushes past, ascends a couple of steps ahead, and turns to face her.

"It might be better if you don't go upstairs right now." There is a mixture of sympathy and curiosity in her bright blue eyes.

Grace stares then laughs. "Excuse me, Izzy." She begins to walk past her but Izzy moves sideways to block her way.

"If this is a game, Izzy, it's a boring one; please let me pass."

"You've a right to know what's been happening. I'd better tell you." Izzy sighs. "No one else will, they're all too stupid to guess."

Grace feels cold. The house isn't heated, which is strange, because Eve can afford to turn the radiators on as high as they will go.

"I'm going upstairs to find Martin," she says as calmly as she can. "Perhaps you could help your mum with supper."

"They're sleeping together." Izzy's eyes flicker over Grace's face.

"Sorry, what?" The words don't make sense straight-away, though Grace's heart beats so fast she feels dizzy.

"They've been sleeping together since Greece, in the afternoons when he was supposed to be at the library; I heard them. They were making these noises, so—"

"I expect you made a mistake." Grace is gripping the banister tightly. "Eavesdroppers often do."

"I saw them." Izzy lifts her phone in front of Grace's eyes. Her movement is swift, there isn't time to look away. The image is startlingly clear; Izzy has been bought the best kind of phone available. The photo was taken from above and the side, but the shape of her husband's naked back and shoulders is unmistakable; his head is turned sideways, revealing the familiar profile of his nose. Eve is beneath him, instantly recognizable as well, although her eyes are closed; they are lying on the carpet.

". . . thought you have the right to know the truth." Izzy's voice has become softer and sweeter. She turns to go. Along with the sympathy there is a gleam of triumph in her eyes. She runs down the stairs, crosses the hall, opens the kitchen door, and disappears inside.

Grace's mind fills with boiling hurt and anger, she can hardly move; a message pings through from Izzy with another image, a different one this time, a different angle: Eve and Martin are facing each other in close-up, clearly blind to the child who must have been crouching nearby, her phone on silent. Fury crescendoes. Grace begins to ascend the stairs, shouting for Martin; she doesn't want to surprise him in bed with Eve. Martin comes out from Eve's room as she reaches the final flight.

"Shh." Martin hurries down the stairs to join her. "She's asleep."

"You fucking shit." She slams her phone against his chest. Martin staggers back against the banister, his hands automatically clasping the phone. "Look at the screen," she hisses.

He regains his balance and stares at the image. His face pales then flushes a dull red; for a moment she is disarmed. He looks like Blake does when she catches him in the cookie jar, wondering if it's too late to lie.

"How the hell—"

"Izzy."

"Jesus." He hands back the phone, his hand shaking. "Why would she do that?"

"God knows. Who cares? The important thing is that I know you're a cheating, lying bastard—"

"We can't do this now; the children will hear."

"How dare you bring the children into it," she whispers hoarsely, "when they must have heard you screwing Eve for months."

"Suppertime!" Melly calls from the kitchen.

"If it's any help, Gracie, it's been over for weeks."

Gracie. Evie. Why does he do that with their names? Does it make them sound younger or sweeter, less threatening? Let him be threatened.

"Do you actually think I'd believe anything you say?"

"We have to go down now; we'll talk about this later." He walks ahead stiffly, his face crimson. She follows him across the hall and into the kitchen, trying to breathe slowly and calmly.

Melissa's glance flicks between them as she puts a casserole on the table and takes off her apron. "Sit down," she says cheerfully, though her cheeks flame; so she knew, or at least suspected. The betrayal stings.

"I hope you're hungry," Melissa adds, smiling. "I've cooked a lot."

Eric has emerged and takes his place at the table, yawning. "Sorry, I nodded off in my study."

"That's fine. We all went to sleep, even the children," Melissa tells him. "I think everyone needed it. I know I did."

"I've been out of it for at least a couple of hours," Eric replies, rubbing his face.

You've been out of it for longer than that, Grace wants to tell him; otherwise Martin wouldn't be fucking your wife in your house, under your nose. She can't say this, though, or anything like it; Eric is holding on to sanity by a thread. Their eyes meet, he smiles a brief, unhappy smile. Does he know? She looks at the lines on his face and the way his mouth turns down; his wife's affair could seem unimportant compared to the loss of his son. He might have decided to wait and see what's left when that loss is more tolerable. Eric is wise and patient. Wiser than she is, far more patient. She returns the smile with an effort and sits down next to him. She passes him the wine. The children file into the kitchen and take their places.

"We'll start without Paul," Melly says. Grace glances at her, a new Melly, more decisive. At that moment the door opens and Paul comes in, sleet sticking to his hair. He takes off his coat and gloves.

"Smells good. It turns out my wife can cook, or did anyone help her?" No one replies and he sits down, pouring himself a large glass of wine. He downs it swiftly, then pours another and drinks that too. He sits back and sighs loudly.

Melly's bright expression doesn't falter; she doles out portions of chicken in an herb-scented sauce and the plates of food are passed around.

"One too many. Trying to fatten me up?" Paul passes the extra plate back.

Melissa scans the table. "Who isn't here?"

Eric glances around at the faces; he looks at Poppy. "Call your sister down."

"Why is it always me?" Poppy stares back at her father and doesn't budge.

"I'll go." Charley bounds from the room. She is gone for a surprisingly long time, and when she reappears, she looks scared. "She's not in the bedrooms. I've looked everywhere, in Eve's room too. Actually, I haven't seen her since we woke up."

In Zimbabwe, immediately before the rains, everything goes quiet. Animals flatten themselves against the earth, small ones disappear, even the trees seem to batten down. The deep hush appears to last for a while, though it's probably only moments, then the adults rise and begin to move. Eric shoves his chair back so quickly it thuds to the ground, then he disappears outside, Blake at his heels. Paul stands, forking another spoonful into his mouth, then he follows too. Melissa vanishes into the hall, Grace hears the sound of doors opening and closing. The girls bunch together in the kitchen like little animals in a storm, undecided which way to run.

"She might be with Eve. I'll double-check; meanwhile can you kids look in all the rooms again with

Melly?" Grace leaves the kitchen and begins to climb the stairs; Martin follows her.

"Don't say anything about Sorrel being missing yet." His voice is tight with anxiety. "You'll worry her needlessly."

"Fuck off."

She knocks at Eve's door; there's no answer so she opens it and walks in quietly. Eve is lying on her back with her eyes closed. Sorrel isn't with her. Grace hesitates, about to back away. Eve opens her eyes and turns her head slowly toward her.

"Hello, Grace." Her voice is dull. "You okay?"

Grace sees she might be wrong. The affair might be over as Martin said. Eve obviously wasn't fucking her husband this evening and probably hasn't been for a while; she is barely surviving. "Sorrel hasn't been with you this evening by any chance?"

It was that casual *any chance;* Eve rears up in bed, breathless as if surfacing from the depths. "Look outside. The pond—"

"There's no pond now, remember? I'm sure . . ." Grace doesn't finish, she doesn't feel sure of anything.

Eve pushes back the bedclothes. Her legs are thin, much thinner than they were. She wrenches down her nightgown, Grace takes her hand; it feels cold and bony. The glowing woman in Greece, the one her husband couldn't resist, has been replaced by a wraith. Grace finds herself helping her up at the same time that she wants to scream; she wants to scream and shake her. The image of Martin's body on top of Eve's grates alongside ones of Sorrel's gap-toothed, uncertain smile, of the child struggling in the grip of some monster, screaming for help. Sorrel needs them, all of them. She must focus on that for now. She slips an arm around Eve and, half lifting her, guides her to the door. They are walking down the stairs together when the children clatter down behind her.

"We've looked in all the attic rooms. We can't find her anywhere." Charley sounds scared. Poppy's pale face is streaked with tears. Izzy is gripping her hand tightly. Melissa follows them, shaking her head and looking frightened.

In the kitchen they meet Eric coming in through the garden door. "I'm getting Igor to search the woods now." He is speaking in gasps. "We need flashlights. Call the police."

*D*irt is wedged under Charley's fingernails. All their clothes are muddy from searching for Sorrel in the wood. Poppy says it's okay because they are sitting on floorboards so it's not like they are getting carpets dirty or anything. It's cold up in the attic. The floor is splintery. They can hardly see one another. It's getting late; they are hiding though no one seems to be looking for them.

"Which is pretty fucking incredible considering, and also typical. Jesus," Poppy says; she sounds angry. "My sister is missing and they still don't care where we are."

"It's like ten green bottles." Izzy's actually got green bottles, empty wine bottles, taken from the recycling box. She lines them up and pushes two over. "See? Two of us have gone now."

"Sorrel hasn't gone like Ash has gone," Charley says, and stands one of the bottles back up. "She's somewhere, obviously. We just need to find her."

Izzy stares at her and she stares straight back. Charley doesn't bother trying to be Izzy's best friend like Poppy, nor is she under some sort of stupid spell like her brother. Blake looks different from how he used to, smaller, though that's not possible—people don't shrink if they're unhappy, or do they?

Izzy reaches under the bed where they keep the dice and candles and stones and matches. "We are going to play another game. It'll take our minds off all this stuff." She doesn't light the candle, though; she pulls a packet of cigarettes from her pocket and lights one up. She offers them around but nobody takes one.

"We should carry on looking for Sorrel," Charley says.

"You playing?" Izzy asks Blake, without taking any notice of what Charley said. Blake scratches his scalp like he's got lice, though it's probably dried mud. He nods because he never says no to Izzy, but he looks worried—not that anyone would notice, except Charley.

"I'll go first." Izzy rattles the dice in the cup and throws them on the floor. She looks at the dice then she picks them up and writes down the numbers in her little book, which she keeps in the back pocket of her jeans. It's too difficult to remember them otherwise, she says.

"Are you completely sure you're writing them down right?" Charley asks, but Izzy doesn't answer. Charley doesn't want to play, but if she does that means there are more of them, which means Blake's less likely to lose. It doesn't help because Blake ends up losing anyway. He's brave, her brother, braver than her, because he doesn't make one sound. She is the one who ends up with tears streaming down her face.

9. November

Eve

Eve is no longer underwater. She can see more clearly; everything is bright as if floodlit. Voices are loud as though everyone is shouting; most people are shouting. It's been two hours since Sorrel went missing. Police officers have swarmed onto the property, accompanied by dogs, German shepherds moving fast, noses to the ground. A helicopter hovers above the garden, beams are directed onto the wood and the meadow and the surrounding streets. Men are searching the garage, the barns, Igor's bungalow, the garden shed, fanning out into the woods. Voices echo from between the trees. Sorrel is scared of shouting and bright lights and dogs she doesn't know; she could be too scared to come out.

An incident room is being set up in a van outside the gates. A police officer sits next to Eve in the kitchen, a dark-haired young Welsh woman called Brenda. The woman's lilting voice is warm with sympathy. "What was Sorrel wearing before she vanished?"

"A red anorak." The color had glowed against the trees when she was playing in the garden earlier; red for danger, no one thought of that.

"Where are her favorite places?"

"The wood down the garden." Is that still true? She'd looked unhappy out there today, it was obvious, even at a distance. "Or in the kitchen near me."

"So where were you when she went missing?"

Brenda's young, that's the trouble, far too young. Her face is unlined, untried. What experience would she have in looking for missing children? Does she have any of her own?

"Mrs. Kershaw?"

"Sorry, what—"

"Where were you when she vanished?"

"In bed."

Brenda is scribbling something in her notebook; she might be writing that Eve is lazy and careless, criminally careless twice over. Eve looks away from that fast-moving pen; snow has arrived as forecast, white flakes whirling in the brilliant searchlights of the helicopter. Sorrel has waited all year to play in the snow.

"I have to go; it's cold out there, she might be—"

"There are fifty men and women searching the grounds. Once they've finished they will start over again, in case she's returned in the meantime. If she's here, we will find her." Brenda puts her hand on Eve's; her nails are painted a translucent pink, as if painting your nails was something that mattered. "We need your help to build a timeline so we can work out what might have happened to her."

So Sorrel has shifted from being lost to something worse, a victim that something has happened to: an accident in the woods or on the railway line; Eve's thoughts plunge deeper, getting darker. An assault, an abduction, a murder, that kind of "happened to"? Why doesn't Brenda talk about that? Doesn't she know all the possibilities are already playing in her mind, twisting and tangling in a knot that's getting bigger all the time?

"Was Sorrel a happy little girl before your son's tragic accident? I suppose we are wondering if there was any reason at all for her to run away."

"Happy." It takes Eve a second to process the word. "Yes. Of course she was."

"Is she being bullied at school?"

"Everyone loves her, her family, her friends, the teachers. Everyone."

Brenda looks up. "Children can sometimes run away if their parents quarrel; were you two okay?"

"Fine." They never argue in front of the children; they hardly speak.

"A happy marriage then?"

"Yes." It was happy, for years, happy enough.

"And what about you?" The voice becomes warmer, more sympathetic. "Looking after kids can be stressful—"

"No; it's losing them that's stressful, more stressful than you could possibly imagine—" Eve stands up. "Sorry, I have to go."

They don't try to stop her; perhaps Brenda realizes she's asked enough questions, at least for now. Outside flashlights are bobbing in the wood; it looks like a party, a Halloween party where kids muck around with lights in woods and scare themselves for fun. The helicopter has moved away; she can hear it hovering over other gardens toward the village. She finds Eric searching under the trees, one by one. His face is muddy, he looks spent. The tall trunks surround them like a hostile army, he had been right all along. She had joked about jungles but he'd known better. He warned her about danger and she'd taken no notice. She kicks aside heaps of leaves, hauls away fallen branches, blinded by tears and gasping for breath. She's made so many mistakes. Is Sorrel's abduction, if that's what it is, the price her child's paid for the sake of freedom? How irrelevant that seems, how stupid she's been. Eric was right to put safety first; it seems so obvious now but it's too late. He can do what he wants, raze the trees to the ground if he thinks it would help, though there's little point. It won't make any difference. The wood, thronged with men and dogs, feels as empty as any desert.

Grace

Two policewomen walk through the rooms, searching the entire house again. They check cupboards, under beds, and behind chests of drawers. The younger Indian woman looks delicate beside her middle-aged colleague, a stout redhead whose rolling accent sounds as though she's in a play, pretending to be Scottish. Thankfully they both move quietly and carefully, in order not to scare a hidden child.

Grace leaves the policewomen and branches off on her own, climbing narrow stairs to the next floor. She has never been so deep in this house, so high. The rooms here are smaller, uncarpeted, and cold. Martin raved about this house, its size and warmth; he clearly got as far as Eve's room but no farther. She hurries down the corridor, her feet thudding on the floor, treading down fury.

"Sorrel? Are you here, sweetheart?"

There are curled flies on the floors of the rooms that open off the passageway, cobwebs at the windows; the lights are dim. The dusty air stings her throat. None of the children would come up here. Charley would hate the dead flies. Blake would be frightened by the gloom. She could have that wrong, though. These things might not matter in a group; they might seek out the half-light, the undisturbed air; her children might be different in a gang. There are cigarette butts in a corner of the last room along the corridor, the floor darkened by scorch marks, a lighter on the mantelpiece. A heap of little stones under the bed, flinty ones. She picks one up, muddy, red-stained on one side, and stares around, seeking an explanation. Perhaps these items belong to past inhabitants or guests long gone. It's unpleasant up here, gloomy, the air feels stale, no one has been here for a long time. She leaves the rooms and hurries downstairs, meeting Melly in the hall. She looks tired and anxious.

"The police have been questioning us all in turn: Eve, Eric, me, Paul, Igor; everyone who was around last night. They're having a break now; it'll be you and Martin next. Paul's had enough; he wants Izzy to come back with us but she's refused." Melly's voice is trembling. "She says Poppy needs her to stay the night. Paul's waiting outside, he's put my bag in the car. I'm not sure what to do." Her eyes are lowered, as if reluctant to look Grace in the eye.

"Go home with your husband, Melly." Melly clearly feels guilty for keeping quiet about Martin and Eve, but Grace has had time to think and now she understands. Melly meant well; if Paul had been unfaithful, she might not have told Melly either, out of compassion, and the hope the affair would burn itself out. "Tell Paul I'll keep an eye on Izzy. My kids can stay too, it's late. I'll sleep on the sofa."

"Thank you. I'll be back," Melly promises. "First thing tomorrow."

Grace nods. When disaster struck in her grandparents' village, family moved in, kept the children fed and the homestead alive; as long as it took. Eve doesn't have family; it's down to her now, her and Melly.

Paul is waiting in the car, staring ahead, grim-faced. He turns as the door opens, gives an unsmiling salute to Grace as Melly climbs in beside him then drives off quickly, gravel spraying from the wheels.

The wood burner has gone out in the main room. At the far end, Poppy, Izzy, and Blake sprawl over one another on the sofa like animals in a litter. Their faces are grimy from searching in the wood. Blake looks hollow-eyed. Charley is lying on the floor with the dog. Grace sees with a shock there is a dark mark on her forehead, the skin has been broken.

"Charley, you're hurt. Let me see—"

"It's nothing; I fell when we were outside." Charley turns her face away. "Don't fuss, Mum."

"Is anyone here hungry?" Grace forces herself to sound cheerful; she'll check Charley later, when her friends aren't there. She might get the full story then. "We didn't eat supper; you might want something now?"

They stare at her blankly.

"I'll heat something up."

Charley and Blake nod, but Poppy looks at her as if she scarcely knows her. Izzy doesn't reply. The forgotten food has congealed on the plates in the kitchen; it looks greasy and unappetizing. They need comfort food, something warming, easy to digest. There are three cans of tomato soup in the back of the cupboard, hidden away as if Eve was ashamed of keeping canned food. Grace opens them all, tipping the thick orange liquid into a pot and setting it on the stove to heat. She makes toast, glancing back at the silent group of children. Shouldn't they be asking questions? Demanding to know what the police are doing, how long it will take to find Sorrel? Aren't they frightened, as she is?

The door opens; Martin kicks off his boots and comes in, blowing on his fingers. "I've been in the barns and outhouses with the police." His teeth are chattering. "We've searched the garages and the shed, nothing."

She fills mugs with soup for the children, leaving them on the coffee table in front of them with a plate of buttered toast. As Blake stretches for a mug, his sleeve slips back, revealing a wound on his wrist, a round red mark, wet-looking and surprisingly deep.

"What's that?" She takes his arm.

He snatches it back and shakes his sleeve down.

"How did it happen?"

"Science."

"Can I see?"

"S'okay." He holds his wrist to his chest; the other children stare at her.

"It needs cleaning."

He shakes his head.

She rejoins Martin. "Blake's got what looks like a nasty burn on his wrist. He says it's from science; it might need treatment. Charley's got a mark on her forehead too. We ought to speak to our kids on their own, away from the group, and find out exactly what's been happening."

"I'll take a look." He moves a little closer to her. "I'm sorry, Gracie. I made a mistake."

She steps back, rage beginning to rise again. A mistake? Like a mistake in math that you erase so it looks as good as new; except that it doesn't. If you look closely the surface of the paper is roughened; closer still, the tiny fibers have been torn apart.

"It started in the summer," he continues. "Just a few times. My work was going badly; you couldn't bear to let me touch you."

"So it's my fault?"

"Of course not. Eve was lonely, I let myself be flattered."

"Ah, I see. It's Eve fault."

"Eve and I are done, Gracie."

"You really think it's that easy?"

"I don't know what to say. It should never have happened; I know that. I'm sorry."

"Shut the fuck up," Grace says under her breath, glancing at the sofa. "We'll talk about this later."

The door bangs open again. Eve comes in followed by Eric. Snow rims their hair and eyelashes and they are covered in mud as though they recently emerged from the ground. They walk through the kitchen without a word.

"Izzy isn't here." Poppy sounds alarmed. "She was next to me a minute ago."

"Where's Noah?" Charley looks around.

Martin puts his soup down. "Let's not panic now, I expect she's taken him for walk. Any minute—"

"It's snowing, Dad," Charley interrupts. She sounds patient, as though explaining something to a child. "Noah's too young to be out in the snow for long."

At that moment Izzy walks through the door from the garden, Noah following.

"The dog needed to go out." She kicks off her shoes. "He's been stuck inside all day."

They'd all forgotten about Noah until now. Izzy walks barefoot across the room and folds herself gracefully on the sofa; she puts an arm around Poppy, who has started to cry.

Grace shivers; Izzy has left the door open, and the cold smashes into the room like a fist.

Melissa

"Slow down, Paul." Melissa winces as the car lurches around a corner. They skid to a halt by a traffic light.

There is a dull thump from the trunk. "We'll have an accident." She holds the dashboard as though braced for serious pain. "The road is icy."

The car smells of alcohol; Paul has been drinking again. He knows he shouldn't be driving, though she daren't point it out. If she'd realized how intoxicated he was, she would never have gotten in the car. He moves forward before the light changes, wrenching the wheel to the left.

"I'm sick of being part of that crazy setup." He takes another left. "We should get Izzy out of there as soon as we can. They've lost two kids; can't you see that something weird is happening in that house?"

Izzy had insisted on staying; she refused to abandon her best friend. It can't possibly be true that she's in danger, that there's some peril lurking at Eve's, picking off children one by one. Ash drowned in a terrible accident, Sorrel is missing; separate tragedies. Melissa doesn't reply; in this mood, he'll argue with whatever she says.

"I've had enough of the police and their bloody questions."

She glances at him, the flushed face and dilated pupils. He must have been at the wine all afternoon; a glass at his elbow while working, frequently replenished. He'd had more when he arrived at Eve's. The alcohol has tipped him into paranoia; she's seen it before.

"The police were simply doing their job." She tries to speak soothingly though her voice trembles; when he's drunk like this he takes it out on her later. "I was questioned, everyone was. It wasn't just you."

The Mercedes shudders to a halt by a pedestrian crossing, allowing two old men to walk across the road, but Paul steps on the accelerator when they are only halfway, and their terrified faces flash white in the headlights.

"If you hit someone on a crossing, it's manslaughter."

He doesn't answer, he'll probably punish her for that remark too. He turns into their road and speeds toward the house, his fingers clenched on the wheel. Melissa grips the edge of her seat, sweating in fear. The electronic gates swing open just in time and the car screeches in. The security lights flash on, lighting up her car on the forecourt, but it's too late. The crash of metal against metal is deafening. Her body slams up against the seat belt.

"What a bloody stupid place to leave your car," he yells. "You can fucking well pay for it."

She gets out trembling. Thank God Izzy hadn't been with them. The side of her car is badly dented and the windows are smashed, though his seems unscathed.

She reaches in the back for her bag as he slams his door and comes around the car toward her. She backs out quickly but he doesn't give her long enough. He doesn't see that the strap of her bag has become tangled with the seat belt. When he kicks the door shut, it catches the side of her face and her shoulder, knocking her to the ground. She lies quite still. Bright skewers of pain penetrate the darkness. Her tongue probes salty tatters of flesh in her mouth, though her teeth feel unbroken. She turns her head to watch Paul lurch into the house. She rolls on her side trying not to cry. Crying doesn't make any difference, it simply makes you more tired. She gets up slowly. The world spins and she steadies herself by holding on to the car. After a while she follows Paul into the house and shuts the door behind her.

"What does she think she's doing?" Poppy asks nobody in particular. It's as though Sorrel has done this on purpose to pay her back; she's pushed her away enough times. She bites her nails, spitting out the stuff underneath. Everyone's in bed but no one is sleeping.

"We could track her down," Blake says, "in the woods."

Charley sits up. "Let's try now."

"How would that work?" Izzy asks. "Your mum's downstairs, she'd never allow us out."

Izzy gets out of bed and onto Poppy's mattress; she takes Poppy's hand. "We need to stay close to each other now, like sisters."

Sorrel's hands are small, her fingers are soft, the

nails are bitten. She smells of sweets. Izzy isn't anything like a sister. Poppy pulls her hand away.

"We're stronger if we stay together," Izzy says.

"Like Russell Crowe in Gladiator," Blake mutters. "You know, before they fight."

Charley laughs, a hopeful sound that fades quickly in the dark.

"Do your parents fight?" Blake asks Poppy.

She shakes her head. "They don't talk very much, well, hardly ever."

"That's fighting," Izzy says.

"Ours do, a bit," Blake says.

"Well, my father hurts my mother, he strangles her," Izzy says. She sounds different, angry. They all sit up and stare at her. "In sex," she adds.

"How do you know?" Blake asks.

"I've seen it," Izzy replies.

"That's so fucked up," Charley says.

"Not as fucked up as yours." Izzy laughs. "Your dad is screwing Eve."

"That's bullshit," Blake says furiously.

Poppy has never heard Blake talk like that to Izzy; normally he's sort of gentle. Now it sounds like he wants to hit her; she feels the same. Mum and Martin. She wants to be sick.

"How would you know?" Charley asks.

"I sneaked into the room while they were doing it," Izzy replies.

"What's the matter with you?" Charley sounds outraged and as if she wants to cry at the same time.

"Bet you knew," Izzy murmurs.

"Poor Dad." Poppy wants to cry too. "Do you think he knows?"

Izzy tries to take her hand again but Poppy snatches it back and gets up and walks over to Charley's bed. Charley moves to make room for her and she slides in beside her. Izzy stays where she is, on her own on the mattress; she doesn't say anything. The last thing that Poppy remembers of that evening is how warm it is lying next to Charley and the sight of Izzy sitting upright as still as a little statue carved in stone. For the first time ever, Izzy looks lonely.

PART FOUR

Damage

I've thought of all the times when we could have forestalled damage to the children, but the truth is we were damaged ourselves. Even if we had worked that out, it wouldn't have been much use. Those early wounds run deep.

Eve had been ignored as a child, controlled but neglected; longing for freedom and longing for affection, she was ridiculously generous with both, and I don't just mean Martin. She trusted everyone. How would she have recognized cruelty when she was determined to love everyone she met?

Melly swapped one tyrant for another, her father for her husband; it's hard to know who caused the most damage, especially as she was hell-bent on damaging herself. When you are anorexic, it actually does something to your vision; you can't properly assess what you see. I heard that on the radio yesterday and I wanted to tell her, but I'm not sure if that would help; not now.

I was damaged by greed: my own. My grandfather told me that anything was possible; it wasn't his fault that I believed him. I thought I could manage it all—work, marriage, kids, writing, being scared. That was wrong, or worse, half right. He forgot to add that anything is possible, but not on your own. He might have thought that was completely obvious; I grew up in an African village, after all. I should have asked for help when I needed it. He told me to walk slowly and he was right. I might have noticed what was there in front of me. You can't blame Melly for not seeing things properly, when I wasn't watching either.

10. November

Melissa

Melissa wakes in the early morning, it's still dark. She doesn't move, moving seems impossible. Her face throbs with pain. Paul is snoring on his side, a meaty hand clenched even in sleep. What happened last night seeps back. She'd crawled upstairs, swallowing acetaminophen and ibuprofen from the packets in the bathroom cabinet. Then Ambien, which worked, though the blows, starting later, shocked her from sleep, hard punches landing on her face and body. She'd tried to shield herself but that only made it worse. Eventually he stopped. She can't remember anything else.

She gets up slowly, gasping with pain, still in yesterday's clothes, though her pants and jeans are around her ankles. She pulls them up and stumbles into the bathroom; walking hurts, her hip joints are stiff. The damage is much worse than usual; a bruise lies along her left jaw like mauve paint, clumsily applied. Her cheeks are swollen. There is a split in her skin like a tear that runs from the edge of her left eye to her mouth. It is possible to open her mouth. She unzips her top; a deep red splash of blood under the skin extends across her chest. She rotates her shoulder, also possible. She slips her hand down between her legs; blood on her fingers, her vulva is tender. No wonder it hurts to walk.

He'll avoid her for a while, though he won't apologize. He used to give her jewelry after episodes like this but he doesn't do that anymore. She turns away from the mirror and limps to the stairs. She needs tea, hot, sweet tea, and then she might sleep again.

The kitchen is shadowy in the early light; the luminous clockface reads six thirty. An empty vodka bottle lies on its side by the sink. She walks slowly to the kettle, trying not to jar her face; she switches it on, reaches for a cup, then stops. She can hear the soft sounds of breathing coming from the open door of the pantry. Lina's boyfriend back again? A different intruder? She feels very calm; there is little anyone can do to make things worse. She doesn't care. Paul has pushed her somewhere beyond caring: beyond anger, beyond sadness, and so far from happiness that nothing matters at all; though she is grateful, as she slides a knife from the rack, that Izzy isn't in the house. Her daughter is safe. Whatever happens to her own body now seems irrelevant. She walks to the pantry, clutching the knife, and opens the door.

A girl is curled in sleep on the floor, long hair covering her face, her dark limbs loose. Melissa is shocked to stillness. Her thoughts skate to another girl, a younger child—Sorrel curled in an attic cupboard or underground. This girl's arms are thin, she has a sparkling bangle around her wrist, her hair is tangled. Someone's daughter. She might be a friend of Izzy's or Lina's, given temporary shelter. Melissa puts the knife on the shelf, kneels beside the sleeping form, and gently touches her hand. The girl jolts awake with a gasp, lifts her head, and puts an arm across her stomach. Dark eyes scan hers, Lina's eyes. Melissa's bewilderment changes, deepens. Without the hijab, the thick makeup, and her disguising robes, Lina is a teenager, staring up in terror, her cheeks streaked with tears.

"Lina?"

Shame and fear struggle in those dark eyes. Melissa's thoughts fly to Izzy sleeping peacefully, unaware of what is happening at home. Safe. She smiles at Lina as reassuringly as she can.

"Let's get you up." She puts an arm around Lina and lifts her to her feet, bringing her into the kitchen. She sees a bruise on her temple, another on her arm, and something else, just as chilling, more perhaps. Lina is cupping her abdomen, but clearly outlined in her thin slip beneath the protective arm, the unmistakable swelling of a pregnancy that has only just begun to show. Melissa might have missed it if Lina wasn't so slim. Melissa's mind quietens as though the noise of years has faded away. Things do matter after all. She does care. She picks up the blanket from the sofa and wraps it around Lina as carefully as if she were another daughter.

"Sit with me, Lina, please." She touches the sofa beside her and Lina lowers herself gradually.

"What happened?" She makes her voice as gentle as she can but Lina seems frozen with fear.

"Did someone hurt you?"

The dark eyes lower, she nods.

"Who was it? Can you tell me?"

Lina lifts her head and stares at her; in the shame of that gaze, Melissa understands. The truth had been waiting for her all along; she had only to look, she had only to listen. She puts her hand on top of Lina's. The truth was hiding in sounds: the office door closing quietly each Saturday on pay day, the weeping in the pantry

when the boyfriend was blamed; it had been in the way
Lina's gaze never met her own; it's here, in the bracelet
on Lina's arm. A sorry present from Paul, like the ones
she used to get. There are moments in life, not many,
when you know with clarity that something has started
or come to its end. At this moment she knows her marriage is over, that she will leave Paul, taking Izzy, and
that her responsibility for Lina has begun.

"We need to leave. It's too dangerous for you here."
She can take Lina to safety and come back for Izzy
within hours. Lina looks at her; her eyes are unfathom-
able.

"We need to find somewhere safe for you until I can
find a home for all of us, you, me, and Izzy." A house
of some kind or a flat, they'll rent somewhere first. She
could find a different school for Izzy if necessary. Anything is possible once you make up your mind.

The dark eyes flare, hope or mistrust, she isn't sure
which. How much can Lina understand? It's ridiculous
that she doesn't know still exactly how well they can
really communicate. The kettle has boiled. Melissa
makes a cup of tea, adds honey, then gives it to Lina.
She sits next to her again, watching her sip and the
color creep into her cheeks.

All the questions she can't ask jumble in her mind:
How often did he hit you? How many times were you

raped? Why didn't you tell me? But she knows the answer to the last one: Lina didn't tell her because she was ashamed, as she herself has been, for years. Lina's hand is trembling, the tea almost slopping over. Melissa takes the cup and puts it on the table. Someone else will have to ask her those questions. She'll give answers more easily to a counselor than to the wife of the man who hurt her.

"Should we tell anyone that we are going? I know you split up with your boyfriend, but maybe there's someone—?"

At the mention of the boyfriend Lina shakes her head so violently that her hair flies about her face; perhaps he hadn't been a boyfriend after all, but just the last in a line of criminals who handed her over to men like Paul. They might still be around, keeping watch, ready to track her down if she tries to leave. Lina needs to go somewhere safe, but has she the right to take her away from the place she knows, as if Lina were her property? Has she the right not to?

"If I can find a place for you to go, would you allow me to take you there?"

Lina stares at her, her eyes narrowed with concentration, the effort of taking it in.

"There are places, houses, where women go when they've been hurt, where they couldn't find you." She can take her right now and return for Izzy later. "I'll need to make a phone call, but if you're okay with it, we should leave pretty soon. What do you think?"

Lina looks around the kitchen, the cupboards, the sink, the stove where she cooked, the window she'd gazed from, as if she's saying goodbye. Her focus settles on the little cat, curled now in her basket. Melissa waits, her heart beating fast.

"Lina?"

Lina looks up at her. "Okay." She nods slowly. "Okay."

"We may have to drive for a while. Can you put what you need in a bag, your passport and something warm to wear?"

"Passport." Lina shakes her head. "Your husband has."

Paul must have taken it for safekeeping, or more likely, to prevent her escape. "I'll find it. In the meantime, would you like me to tell the police what's happened?"

Lina stares. Her eyes are full of fear; she might have no visa and no official permission to work here.

"No police, okay. I understand. I'll knock on your door in ten minutes."

Lina stands up, still wrapped in the blanket, and disappears swiftly up the stairs.

The National Domestic Violence helpline springs up on the screen in Paul's study when Melissa taps Women's Aid into the keyboard. She jabs the number into her phone with fingers that fumble with haste. A brisk voice answers. She explains she is calling on behalf of her maid, giving an account of how she found Lina, what she saw.

"Yes, the perpetrator has access to her."

Unwise to name her husband, they might suspect an agenda. Lina can fill them in.

"Sixteen, maybe younger."

No one could have guessed; Lina was never without makeup and obscuring clothes.

"Syria. My husband said we were doing a favor for a friend by taking her on."

I never suspected he was lying, which was stupid; he's lied to me so often.

"Bruising. She's pregnant."

Paul would want to get rid of it, remove the incriminating evidence.

"I haven't asked specifically about rape."

I'm certain, though. He raped me, for years.

"She doesn't want me to involve the police."

I wish I hadn't mentioned the police to her, she was frightened.

"Can I bring her now?"

The woman explains that Lina would be welcome to seek immediate refuge but that she will need more details from Lina and she must ask for refuge herself. That's crucial. They have translators if language is a problem—women in many shelters speak Arabic, though it will depend which dialect she speaks: Levantine, Bedawi, or Mesopotamian, for instance; there are many others. Funding will be necessary; normally there's a process of application for money.

"I can pay, whatever it costs."

She's advised it's best to travel a distance from the abuser, out of London if possible; is there anywhere that she might like? Melissa stares at the map on the wall above Paul's desk, scanning cities at speed: Oxford, Brighton, Guildford, Chichester. The little red circles blur and jump: Reading, Swindon, Bath, Salisbury. The circle steadies.

"Would Salisbury be possible? I'll be working nearby, so I can visit. Yes, of course; I'll wait."

Melissa puts her phone on silent and creeps into her bedroom. Paul's mouth is open, his arms flung wide. He looks unconscious. She retrieves his keys from the floor by his side of the bed where he dropped them. When her phone vibrates, she tiptoes from the room to answer. Lina will be welcome in the Salisbury shelter, she is told, provided she asks for herself. One of the clients is Arabic—she speaks in Mesopotamian dialect but is familiar with some others—hopefully they will be able to communicate. She is given the number, which she puts into her phone.

"Lina will call on the way; we need to leave now. Thank you, thank you."

The clock on Paul's desk reads seven A.M. They'll reach Salisbury by nine depending on traffic. By the time she returns, Paul will be at work. She'll pack then, and collect Izzy from Eve's after school; their new life will start.

The large white filing cabinet in Paul's study is locked. She opens his desk drawers in turn, leafing fast through papers, documents, bills, envelopes. In the bottom drawer she pushes two empty whisky bottles aside, finding the red woolen pouch Izzy knitted him when she was a child for his most important, secret things. The keys to the filing cabinet are inside as she thought they would be; he always does what Izzy tells him to.

The passport is in the third drawer down in the filing cabinet. Dark blue, a phoenix stamped in gold on the cover, Lina Lahood. A young, hopeful face stares up at her. Fifteen years old. Fifteen. Melissa hunts through the other drawers, feeling sick. There's no sign of a visa or a permit of any kind. She locks the drawers and replaces the key in the pouch and the pouch in the drawer, rearranges the desk as it was and turns off the light. Passport in hand, she tiptoes up the stairs to the third floor. The door to Lina's room is closed.

She knocks softly.

No answer. Lina must be hunting through drawers as well, trying to decide what to take, what to leave behind.

"I've found you a place to stay," Melissa whispers.

She waits for the sound of a drawer closing, footsteps approaching the door, but the room is quiet.

She knocks once more, whispers more urgently, "We have to leave right now."

Silence.

"May I come in?"

She pushes the door open.

The bed is neatly made, the blanket from the sofa folded at the bottom.

Lina has gone.

Eve

Eve's head jerks from the kitchen table as the sound of banging grows louder. She must have fallen asleep for a few minutes though she didn't mean to, hadn't thought it would be possible.

Eric crosses the room to the door, stumbling a little as he hurries. He hasn't slept properly either. She hears his footsteps in the hall, the bolt sliding back, and the door opening, then voices, low-pitched, serious, female. Eric enters the kitchen again, looking about the room as if lost and finding his bearings in an unfamiliar place.

"Igor's refusing to open his door to the police; they want him for questioning again. They've asked me to go and calm him down."

"Igor?"

The shock is sickening, like a blow to her face. Igor. A second later she is surprised by her surprise; it makes terrible sense. The man who had watched her, or seemed to, must have been watching Sorrel all along. He must have looked at her from behind the trees in the garden, or through the lit windows of the house in the dark, waiting for the moment when the family was distracted. What better distraction could he have hoped for than the death of her little brother?

She follows Eric to the hall. Four policemen are waiting by the door, two men, two women.

"Why do you need Igor?" she asks the Indian woman. "What's he done?"

"I'm afraid we can't share that information yet." She looks genuinely sorry. Eve feels her own face tighten. She pulls on a coat with clumsy hands as Eric shoves his feet into boots. She watched Igor put Sorrel on his shoulders after a fall; those small legs dangling on either side of the bull neck; even then she'd felt uneasy. If Igor has hurt her daughter she will kill him. She fastens her coat and runs to join the others, her slippers slithering on the icy ground. The dark air seems tinged with red. If he is guilty, she will find a gun and fire it at him. The bullet would make a neat wound in that vast chest. She would fire twice, no, many times, and walk away without a second glance. She follows the little group, hardly aware of the direction. The bungalow is beyond the barns; the place is screened from the house by a strip of pines, the lower branches shaggy and brown. She has walked past without looking for months, years even. The policeman holds the gate open; once inside the trees, the quiet deepens, as though they have stepped underground. The lawn is cut, the path looks swept, even the soil in the beds is as evenly granulated as cake crumbs. The order is menacing, like a prison yard enforced by some obsessive guard; what obsessions drive Igor?

Eric knocks at the door. "Igor, it's me, Eric. Don't be scared."

The door is opened a few inches; Igor's frowning face appears. It's all Eve can do not to shove him aside and run past him, screaming her daughter's name.

"It's all right," Eric says quickly. "There's been a mistake."

"Igor Kowalski," the largest policeman intones, "we ask you to accompany us to the station to answer some questions in connection with the disappearance of Sorrel Kershaw."

Igor opens the door a little farther, still frowning. He looks fatter in his pajamas, his paunch revealed by the soft cloth. His stubble is orange against the pallid white of his skin.

"I'm sure we can clear this up quickly." Eric steps in front of the policeman and puts a hand on Igor's shoulder. "I'll come to the station with you."

Igor takes in the group on his doorstep; his bulldog face sags. He looks uneasy, guilty even. Eric places his own jacket carefully around his great shoulders. Eve shudders at the thought of those muscles, their brute capability. Eric clearly believes in his innocence; a man is innocent until proved guilty, he would tell her in his measured tone, but it wouldn't make any difference to the way she feels—Igor looks guilty because he probably is.

"I'm coming too." She steps forward, puts her hand on Eric's arm. "I have to be there; I want to know the instant he tells them—"

"You need to be here for Poppy, keep things steady for her," Eric replies quietly. "I'll phone as soon as I find out anything."

He's right, she knows that. She must stay here. Poppy will need to know her mother's at home, not where she'd rather be, beating on doors in the police station, begging for information. She watches Eric hurry after Igor as he is led away by the policemen, stumbling in his loose slippers. She might have known. It's what people always say, that the criminal is someone close to you, someone who has been there from the start, inside your home or nearby. She attempts to enter the bungalow, but the Scottish policewoman steps in front of her, shuts the door, and stands with her back to it. "I regret you are not permitted to enter."

"What's he done with my daughter?"

"A statement will be released later. I'm sorry not to be able to tell you more at the present time." Her face is sympathetic but she doesn't move, not even an inch. Eve steps back, panting. She must use her wits. Grace will help, she'll know what to do. Eve hurries down the path, passing the smaller policewoman stationed at the gate. Back in the kitchen, her handbag is lying on the table, the contents spilling out: her coin purse, hairbrush, car keys. Three happy children smile up from the photograph in her wallet. She stares at all the objects on the table as if unearthed from the rubble of a dig, relics of a vanished life.

Igor's words return to her in the silence: ". . . so that's why I couldn't find him under the hood"—his idea of a joke on a warm day back in the spring, when life was full and she was happy. She grabs the keys and runs to the cars, releases the hoods in turn, heaves them up. Only the engine, water tank, and greasy wires, dark tubes that twist like guts. She slams both hoods shut. On the way back to the house she bends to vomit in the flower bed. She gropes her way upstairs.

It might not have been Igor, it might be worse. Sorrel might have gone to the road to look for her, forgetting that her mother was in bed. Her fluttering skirt would have shone in the gloom like a flag. Who knows what monster might have slowed as he passed, what truck she might be in, what cellar, what boat? An adult can last thirty days without food—she googles this with trembling fingers—much less without water. She can't find any information about a child. Fear settles closely over her, a great bird with hooded wings and talons that tear. She forces herself to shower, then puts on her clothes as though she were dressing someone else, someone old with stiff limbs that refuse to bend. When the phone rings her heart lurches. She leans against the window to take the call, out of breath as if she has been hurrying.

"Difficult news, unexpected." Eric pauses.

"What d'you mean, unexpected?" she gasps out. "What's he done?"

"Some of Sorrel's clothes were found under Igor's bed—a few of them, in a tidy little pile."

She holds the windowsill, afraid her legs will give way. "Which ones?" Her mouth is dry, her head clamoring with the kind of questions no mother should have to ask. Was it the little red anorak? Her skirt? Her underwear? Were they muddy or torn? Bloodstained?

"Not the ones she was wearing when she vanished," Eric replies quickly. "That's all they told me. They're still questioning him. I'll phone back soon when I know more." Beneath her in the house, the front door opens and shuts. From the window she sees the children file out: Blake, Poppy, who turns to look up at her, Izzy, Charley, then Martin. Grace follows, watching from the steps as they file into the car.

Poppy must have been persuaded to go to school by Izzy, who doubtless thought she needed the distraction, as if you can be distracted when your mind is full of grief and shouting with fear. Will she cope with today? She must call the teacher, tell her she'll come immediately if Poppy wants to come home. She sees Martin nod at Grace before he gets into the car. He looks different seen from above; his shoulders are rounded, his abdomen protrudes. She turns her head down toward the garden to where the pine trees cluster behind the barns. She's never looked at them properly before. Now she sees that they make a dark smudge in the landscape, like a mistake someone made then tried very hard to rub out.

Grace

Grace waits on the steps as the children settle themselves in the car. Blake gets out again, runs into the house, and reemerges with his backpack. Above them, she glimpses Eve's face hovering at her window, pale as a ghost. Does Eve know that she knows? Once the car has gone, she hurries into the house and up the stairs.

"Igor's at the police station," Eve tells her as soon as she enters her bedroom. "He had Sorrel's clothes under his bed." Her face looks frozen with fear. "There are two policewomen guarding his house right now."

"Shit." Grace sits next to her on the bed. She glimpsed Igor when she arrived last night; she could have called out to him, asked what he was doing. Would that have made a difference? Forestalled a plan?

In the silence, they hear footsteps rapidly crunching

down the gravel drive. Eve springs up and looks outside. "One of the policewomen is leaving," she whispers.

Grace joins her at the window. The Scottish policewoman is striding down the drive, talking into her cell phone, a frown distorting her features.

"I want to look in his house," Eve says. "In case there's something the police have overlooked, something else important."

"I'll come with you."

Outside the raw wind catches them and they bend against it; neither has thought to put on a coat. They become soaked by fine drizzle in moments. Their feet tap over the wet stone of the veranda. A few months ago they had all gathered here, there had been meadowsweet and buttercups on the table, the children leaping around a bonfire. Eve and Martin had been flirting even then.

"I slept with Martin." Eve's cheeks flame, she's come to the same memory; despair and hurry have jerked loose her secret. Is she asking for forgiveness?

"I know." Anger rises in her throat, hot and sharp. "I've known since yesterday."

"I can't remember why now." Eve doesn't ask how she knows; her bloodshot eyes search wildly about her, as if the dull greens and browns of the garden might provide some clue or reason. "He talked to me, he

seemed to listen. I wasn't used to that. I guess I was carried away by his words. I'm sorry, that sounds inadequate. I don't understand it now so I can hardly expect you to. Whatever I felt has vanished completely."

She's wrong, Grace understands. She knows exactly how Eve felt; she was seduced by his words as well. It doesn't make the pain any less, in fact it makes it worse—Martin has used the same trick twice. Grace glances at the hurrying figure by her side. Eve had lovely kids, a kind husband, fabulous houses, beautiful jewels—every gift it was possible to possess—and yet she took someone else's husband, casually, lightly, as though entitled, like a child who helps herself to what she wants, without thought.

They are passing the empty paddock. The donkeys must be inside their stable, it's too cold for them outside. Their new metal trough gleams in the rain. Eve's most precious gifts have been torn from her. Compared to those brutal amputations, the affair with Martin is a flesh wound. She'll survive; Ash didn't, Sorrel might not. The little girl's flowerlike face, her trusting whisper, pull at Grace's heart; the decision to help isn't a decision after all, she has no choice.

Eve's words continue to pour out as she hurries. ". . . never trusted him. Eric thought he was great. He

liked the children, he resented me for some reason, but I never dreamed he was capable of this. My God, how blind we were; we had no idea, no inkling, though he practically lived with us. Why the hell didn't we look more closely?"

But it's the things that are close to you that are the most difficult to see, the things glimpsed beneath the surface. The boy who attacked her, you and Martin. The opaque green water of the swimming pool in Greece flashes across her inner eye, the shadows on its surface, the children in the shallow end, playing games.

Eve stops short as they approach the bungalow. "We have to be careful, there's another policewoman on guard at the front gate. We'll go round the back."

She pushes through a border of hydrangeas lining the path, their blowsy heads brown and soaked with rain, and then into the trees that encircle the property. The light darkens under the pines as they walk beneath them, the fallen needles cushioning their footsteps. Wet branches brush against her face; their minty scent is strong. They reach the wire fence at the back of the bungalow. Grace pulls up the bottom wire, Eve crawls beneath on all fours, then Grace rolls through after her. The small space outside the back door of the bungalow feels claustrophobic, a dark place where a child could be bundled into the house unseen. The frosted sash window to the right of the door is fastened with a sliding bolt between the panes.

"Have you a credit card?"

Eve fumbles in the pockets of her jeans and finds a battered plastic library card. "God knows how many times this has been through the wash."

Grace takes the card, slides it under the metal arm, shifts it aside, then lifts the window as far as she can; there is just enough space to maneuver her head and shoulders through. She tips forward, clasping the sides of the little sink beneath, and, twisting her hips clear, jumps to the floor. The door bolt slides back easily and she opens the door. Eve is gazing at the trees. Despite her comfortable home, her plentiful possessions, the food on her table, her face has that gaunt suffering look familiar from the television news, of desperate mothers on beaches, in camps, or up against barbed wire at a road block; women enduring grief, enduring loss. Grace pulls her inside quickly.

"Let's look in the bedroom first," Eve says hoarsely. "That's where they found her clothes."

There is a smoothly made bed in the tiny room, a couple of checkered shirts in the closet, an empty chair, nothing in the trash can or under the bed. There is little trace of the man himself, little to go on. They go back to the hall; the heat is suffocating.

"I haven't been in here for years, this was where our nanny lived." Eve laughs, an embarrassed, miserable sound. "It was icy cold back then. She locked us out of our house to keep it tidy till my parents returned and shut us in here instead. My brother got out; he climbed the fence behind the wood and ran along the railway to meet his friends in the village. I didn't dare. I can't think why we never told; she would have been sacked immediately."

Children don't tell, though, not even the most important things; her kids have told her nothing for weeks. Grace looks at Eve, seeing a small girl left on her own, a little girl who might grow up desperate for warmth, who might marry quickly, too quickly, and look again.

The surfaces are bare in the kitchen, the kettle is shining, even the floor looks newly washed. Eve opens cupboard doors revealing cups lined up, crockery neatly stacked. The handles of his saucepans are precisely aligned.

"It's so tidy." Eve is looking under the sink where the bottles of detergents are in height order, the dish towels in color-coded stacks. "Too tidy."

"Perhaps he needs order, some people are like that,"

Grace replies. I'm a bit like that. Maybe that's why the kids love Eve's place so much, for its disorder, the messy chaos, the opportunities it presents, freedom among them. The chance to break the rules, do things you wouldn't normally dream of; maybe that's what appealed to Martin. She gazes around at the barren surfaces of the kitchen, but Eve is hurrying past her, out of the kitchen and down the hall to the bathroom. When Grace catches up with her she is staring at the gleaming pink bath, the matching sink and toilet.

"I don't know what I was expecting," Eve whispers; a small shoe tossed in the corner perhaps, or drops of blood splashed on the shining tiles. They turn to the sitting room opposite. The curtains are pulled over the windows but light filters through the thin cloth onto a brown carpet, a sofa with plumped cushions pushed against the wall, a small television in the corner. The clock on the wall ticks noisily. There are a few books on the shelf in the alcove: a child's atlas, a dog-eared stack of *Reader's Digest*s, a paperback edition of *The Small Garden*. Eve kneels by the fireplace, moving aside logs, examining each one closely. Grace feels a downward lurch of horror; can she actually be searching for the charred remains of her child?

"Shouldn't we leave that to them?" Grace asks. "That policewoman could come in at any moment. We ought to leave." She helps Eve up, catching sight, as she does, of a small framed photo on the mantelpiece. A younger, slimmer Igor with his arm around a small blond, the couple encircled by three little girls, a dog at their feet, and a trailer in the background. As she holds it to the window, the photo slips in the frame, revealing the white edge of another behind it. She releases the catch at the back and pulls out the hidden picture, an auburn-haired child the same age as one of the girls in the photo, but it's not one of them. The gap-toothed smile is unmistakable. Eve takes it from her with trembling fingers. In the silence of that moment, loud footsteps sound on the path outside. Someone is walking up to the front door, someone is fumbling with a key and turning it in the lock.

*T*here's a horrible smell. Her throat hurts from screaming.

Something is trickling into her eyes and her mouth. It's warm and tastes like soup.

Mummy will come. Daddy will come. They will. They'll find her and they will take her away and she'll be safe.

She can pretend that Charley is holding her hand and that Noah is licking her face. That Poppy is really near, so she can go and get into bed with her if she wants. Poppy always lets her, even if she rolls her eyes.

It's dark. Not just ordinary dark but thick black, which is getting blacker though there are tiny bright green bits that fizz.

It's actually difficult to breathe. The panting noises

she makes are scary but that's better than shouting, which is really scary.

It feels like something is inside her chest, bumping around like an animal trying to get out.

She's done another wee, which is stupid and scary and it smells, but she couldn't help it.

She can't straighten out her arm because it hits against something.

She mustn't shout because it's way worse when she shouts, but then she does. She starts shouting and her head is full of noise so that she can't tell whether the noise is inside or outside because the air is screaming and her throat is screaming and the blackness has gotten inside her head. She's hitting at the roof. A blade of light like a knife cuts into the darkness, it hurts her eyes. The animal inside her chest is banging so hard it's going to come out through her skin, and something heavy is pressing down at the same time so she can't shout anymore or whisper or breathe properly and then she knows that the monster is in here with her. It's sitting on top of her and stopping her from breathing and very soon she's going to die.

11. November

Melissa

Melissa has no option but to take Paul's car; her own is too badly damaged.

Borrowed car for school run, she writes on a Post-it note. *Then shopping. Suggest you take a taxi to work.*

She leaves the note stuck to the kettle. He'll be angry when he wakes, furious, but it doesn't matter, she won't be here to suffer that. She slides slowly and awkwardly into the front seat; at least she can move her arm well enough to drive the car. Lina has a head start of about twenty minutes. She could be anywhere by now. How stupid to imagine that Lina trusted her. Why would she? She'd trusted Paul once, she'd hardly trust his wife who had never lifted a finger to help her, who had seemingly turned the other way. She should never have mentioned the police; Lina might think she is in even greater danger now.

The Mercedes glides quietly through the gates, then Melissa drives slowly through the empty roads searching the sidewalks and doorways. Eight A.M. The streets are becoming busy, children walking to school, people hurrying to North Dulwich station. Lina might already be on a train, disappearing into the city, leaving no trace. Melissa decides to circle around the streets twice then come back. She can sit in the car opposite the station entrance, watching in case Lina comes. This could all be a waste of time; Lina could just as easily be making her way to Herne Hill or Brixton station. She could be waiting for a bus or simply walking into London. She'll be unsafe. When Paul realizes she's missing he might make a call; the men who brought her here could track her down. There must be dark networks to catch girls like Lina, and then, a plunging thought, girls like Sorrel too. She grips the wheel tightly. She may tell the police after all, because of girls like Sorrel.

She drives straight past Lina the first time. The young girl has pressed herself into the corner of the bus shelter. She lifts her head briefly at the sound of the car, the hijab gives her away. Melissa pauses, reverses, and parks, braking quietly. Lina is looking down again as Melissa walks toward her, as if still hoping to escape notice. She stands up at the last minute, tensed for escape, but it's too late. Melissa puts her arms around her and holds her as closely and carefully as she would Sorrel.

"Thank God. Oh, thank God." Melissa starts weeping, weeping as she hasn't for years; for Lina, and for Ash, for Sorrel, for herself. Gradually the tension in Lina's body disappears as if Melissa's tears are melting her resolve. After a minute Melissa feels her back being gently patted; Lina is comforting her.

"Sorry." Melissa brushes away her tears and takes Lina's hand. "I'm sorry. Will you let me help you?" Her heart beats fast as she waits. Lina could refuse and walk away, there would be nothing she could do then. Lina looks at her and inclines her head minutely, making her choice. Melissa takes her hand and they hurry across the road to the car. She gives Lina her passport and it's Lina's turn to weep. She holds her passport close against her chest, murmuring as she might to a child, tears dripping off her chin.

The traffic is building up—it takes an hour before they reach the outskirts of London, going west. Lina seems absorbed by the small streets, the skyscrapers, factories, and bridges. Melissa is conscious she is driving away from Izzy who is probably in school assembly right now. I'll be back for you later, sweetheart, she tells her daughter silently, I won't be long. She glances at the clock on the dashboard. It's nine—nearly two hours have gone by since her phone call.

"There is a shelter in a town called Salisbury, a house where you will be safe, looked after. That's where we are heading right now."

Lina's eyes are on the car in front; she is still clasping her passport. Her head is tilted toward Melissa, listening.

"The people there need you to talk to them. I've already told them a little about your story but now they need to hear from you, to make sure you're okay with this plan." Melissa hands over the phone. "A woman there speaks Arabic, you can tell her what you want to. You'll be very private; I won't understand a word."

Lina speaks hesitantly at first but gradually the tone changes, becoming more animated. She speaks more confidently though there are tears in her voice. She listens then talks some more; after a while, she sounds calmer. The conversation lasts twenty minutes, and then she says goodbye.

"Okay." She hands the phone back; she sounds very tired. "Okay."

They are free of London now and speeding past fields fringed by shadowy woods and dusted with snow.

Lina's eyes have closed and her head rests against the window. The roads are busy but Melissa drives as fast and smoothly as she can. The tall spire of the cathedral takes her by surprise when it appears between the hills. The GPS guides her to the suburbs, an unremarkable street of terraced houses, damp sidewalks, box hedges, and trash bins. She pulls up outside the gate.

Lina struggles awake and looks around, taking in the houses and the road. Is she working out where her escape routes may lie?

"We have arrived, Lina. This is your shelter," Melissa tells her softly. "You'll be safe here." They get out of the car. She won't mention plans or promise visas; it's enough that they have arrived, that a different life is about to start for Lina. She digs in her handbag, tears out a page from her diary, scrawls her cell phone number and hands it over. Then she takes Lina's hand and together they walk through the wooden gate and up to the front door.

Eve

Eve and Grace cower behind the half-open door of the sitting room. Through its hinged gap they see Igor enter the bungalow, he is still wearing Eric's jacket over his pajamas. His body seems to fill the narrow hallway as he walks past. Eve's heart is beating wildly, Grace is silent beside her, scarcely breathing. The electric murmurings of a kettle reach them from the kitchen, then the clash of cups. He is getting ready for guests. Who can he be expecting, what accomplices?

Igor's footsteps come out of the kitchen, cross the lower part of the hall, and enter the little cloakroom. Eve holds her breath and then it comes, a bellow of surprise. He has seen the open window and surmised a break-in. They hear his footsteps coming closer as he heads back down the hall. Eve moves swiftly, ignoring the little ripping noise of fingernails on cloth as Grace tries to hold her back. She steps out, barring the front door. Igor comes to a halt in front of her, his face blank with shock. He looks familiar yet different, as if he had turned into his older brother or even his father. His cheeks are loose, the eyelids swollen as though he has been crying. He shoulders roughly past her and disappears out the door, shouting something in Polish. Eve fumbles for her phone while Grace starts after him before a policewoman appears, Eric at her shoulder, Igor hovering behind him. The policewoman is new to them, young and fierce-looking, her thick brows low as if angry. Eric's are raised in disbelief.

"What are you doing here?" His voice is furious. "This is Igor's house."

"You can't expect me to sit quietly at home, waiting for scraps of news," Eve snaps back. "I had to do something."

The hall feels cramped with bodies. Igor is breathing heavily, the policewoman watching him. Grace is standing close; Eric's face has turned red.

"You aren't allowed to enter someone's home like this, it's against the law. He has the right to privacy, like everyone else," he tells her.

"The right?" She spits the words. "Igor had our daughter's clothes under his bed and you're worried about his rights?"

"He has no idea where Sorrel is."

"We found this hidden behind a photo of his family." Eve thrusts the picture of Sorrel at him.

Igor moves toward her but the policewoman steps between them and steers him toward the kitchen.

"There's something you should know." Eric takes her arm while Grace turns toward the front door.

"Don't go," Eve says quickly.

"This is between you and Eric," Grace replies. "I'll see you back at the house."

Eve watches Grace walk down the path; guilt and gratitude jostle. She wants to run after her, thank her, tell her she needs her strength, beg her to return, but Eric is leading her into the sitting room.

"You'd better sit down." He closes the door behind them.

She watches Eric pace about the room, frowning at the floor as if planning his words.

"Sorrel came here often," he says after a couple of minutes. "She and Poppy gave Igor their own clothes for his family."

Eve stares at him, astonished. "That's utter rubbish. They hardly know him."

"They spent hours here."

"Who told you that? Igor?"

"They've been coming here for years." Eric's voice is flat. "They came to watch television. He made them jam sandwiches and gave them crisps, sweets, chocolate biscuits. Normal stuff that kids like, things we never allow them to have."

"He's making it up." Eve stands up but the room turns and she sits again quickly. "They would have told me."

"Poppy did tell me, today, in the police station."

"Poppy?"

"I took her out of school. It turns out they've been giving him their stuff for a long time."

"It's not true; I'd have seen things disappear."

"The girls dared each other to take more and more: jerseys, school uniforms, winter coats. Poppy said you never noticed."

Clothes go missing sometimes, it's impossible to keep track. When she can't find something, it usually turns out to be at the dry cleaners or stuck behind a radiator, perhaps on the floor of the car. If it fails to reveal itself in time, she buys a replacement; it's easier than hunting for hours.

". . . as often as they could," Eric is continuing. "They made sure it was when I was away from home so they wouldn't be noticed."

How is it possible that the girls spent so much time at Igor's? She'd kept an eye on them from the kitchen window, watched them running in the garden, playing among the trees. Admittedly she'd gotten on with cooking, studying, and looking after Ash, but they were safe and happy in the woods, making dens. They told her that, didn't they? They always came in for meals.

"They told him you were putting the clothes aside for charity anyway," Eric tells her. "They begged him not to say anything or they'd get into trouble." He picks up the framed photo. "They live in that trailer. His kids are the same ages as ours. They don't have enough warm things to wear. It's not surprising the girls wanted to help."

"It sounds like he was manipulating them; he probably sold it all for cash."

"Why is this so hard for you to understand?" Eric puts the photo down, his fists ball in his pockets. "Everything Igor says checks out with the police. It's not very complicated. Our children have more clothes than they need so they gave some to Igor for his kids. They like him, he's kind; he made them feel normal, like other kids."

"It's a pity we don't live in a trailer." She stands up. "Why don't you buy one? We might all feel more normal then." She can hardly believe she said that, a ridiculous, childish reply. It will infuriate him, but perhaps that's what she wants. Perhaps she wants to make him shout at her so she can scream back; they could fight for once. Everything could come out: Ash's death. Sorrel's disappearance. The affair. He could yell that it's all her fault. She would yell back about despair and loneliness, guilt and rage. She stares at him, panting slightly; the air seems to ring with all the words they haven't said.

Eric follows her from the room into the hall. "Igor's staying until Sorrel is found; he's going to leave us after that, he's decided." He leans against the wall looking tired. "The important thing is he's our friend and not a criminal."

She walks out the front door without replying and continues down the path. He's wrong; the important thing is Sorrel. Sorrel is the only thing that matters now. The impulse to fight has gone. She doesn't need Eric to make her feel guilty, she is crushed with guilt already.

When she reaches the kitchen it feels empty. Grace must have gone back home; it's her turn to fetch the children later. Eve looks around, shivering. The house is cold and messy, it's really far too big for them. There are dirty plates to load in the dishwasher, and the floor looks unwashed. Eve stares out the window, searching the garden as if to catch sight of her two precious daughters running away from her to the warm, tidy little bungalow hidden behind the trees.

Grace

The puddles on the road are bright with reflected lights, the streets packed with tired-faced shoppers carrying bags. Children tussle on the sidewalks. It's Christmas in a month's time, fervor in the air already.

"The search for missing six-year-old Sorrel Kershaw is now well into the second day. An estate worker who was helping police with inquiries has been re-

leased. The net has been widened to include nearby gardens and garden sheds, schools, parks, bus and train stations. Anyone who has any information—"

Grace switches off the car radio. The second day— children can be found sheltering in huts or doorways forty-eight hours after they run away. Survivors of avalanches or earthquakes last that long, babies are pulled from the wreckage days after the event. Another voice whispers that if Sorrel has been abducted she faces far more danger than if she'd been in an accident; the harm isn't random.

She swerves to avoid a car, distracted by a little girl with fair hair flying behind her as she skips along the sidewalk holding her mother's hand. Ash had three Christmases, that's all; Sorrel may not have another. Grace blots her eyes with her fingers as she draws up on the road opposite the Charter School.

Izzy and Poppy are waiting on the sidewalk. Izzy is standing near Poppy, leaning toward her and talking, but Poppy is staring blankly at all the other children who swirl about them in little groups as if they were inhabitants of a different planet. Grace gets out of the car and hurries across the road.

"Hi, you two."

Poppy stares at her, a question flaring in her face.

"Sorry, Poppy. No news yet, but—"

"Give us some credit," Izzy interrupts. "We knew there wasn't."

Poppy didn't, Grace wants to retort—she was hoping for something, for a piece of news that might just have arrived. The girls climb into the back seat, Izzy sitting close to Poppy, who stares out the window.

"Where's Blake?"

Izzy shrugs, Poppy doesn't answer. In the rearview mirror Grace sees a tear roll down her cheek.

"You don't have to go to school tomorrow, Poppy; I'll talk to your mum and dad."

"Like they'd care," Izzy mutters.

A message pings through from Blake. *You need to come to the assistant principal's office.*

"I'm going to find Blake," Grace tells them. "It could take a while, you could walk home if you like."

"Blake's done something wrong, I expect. We'll wait." Izzy sounds bored.

Grace calls Dulwich Hamlet to ask them to tell Charley it might be some time before she picks her up, then she walks quickly down the lane, past the bike rack, and across the forecourt to the school. Mr. Richards hurries across the large hall to shake her hand, a quick, firm clasp. She met him two terms ago to discuss Blake's dyslexia, he seems older already. A good-looking man, his dark hair going gray, a kind face creased with worry.

"Is Blake okay?"

"Let's talk in my office."

The stuffy room is crowded with piles of books and papers, a laden desk occupying half the space. Blake is hunched at a table; he looks smaller in these surroundings, much younger. He's staring at a pair of pruning shears on the table, medium-sized, with a worn-looking wooden handle and blades neatly curved together. The sharp edges shine in the harsh overhead light. Mr. Richards indicates a seat and she sits down slowly.

"I'll get straight to the point. Blake is here because a boy—let's call him Tim—saw these in Blake's backpack. Tim was going through the bag to borrow a ruler, or so he says. When he saw these he told his mum, and she phoned me. We called Blake in, searched the bag, found the shears. It's straightforward if disappointing." He pauses as if to give her a chance to reply, but there is nothing to say, though her heart is thudding with anxiety. There will be a plan or punishment of some kind. Blake's lips tighten; he's waiting too.

"Blake told us that he was lent them by a friend of the family, a landscaper for whom he does gardening jobs. Blake apparently used these to prune apple trees; he said he'd put them in his bag to keep safe over the weekend and forgot to take them out before returning to school." Mr. Richards, to his credit, doesn't sound skeptical, just tired. It has probably been a long day. Blake can't have been the only child to cause trouble. "Blake says he had no intention of using these shears for any other reason than to prune trees. I'd like to call his gardener friend to find out if what he says is true."

Grace gives him Eric's name and his cell phone number; luckily Eric never answers his phone, he doesn't need this distraction now. She'll find him herself, have a quiet word . . .

"Ah, Mr. Kershaw, sorry to trouble you, sir . . ."

Eric has answered after all; perhaps he thought this could be news of Sorrel. Grace pictures his face falling and feels a deep pang of guilt. At the end of the conversation Mr. Richards turns to face them both.

"Mr. Kershaw corroborates Blake's story. He says it's probably his fault that the shears are in the bag because he forgot to take them back."

Blake looks at Grace, a narrow-eyed glance that assesses her reaction. It carries guilt as well as relief; you would have to know him very well, as she does, to see he is still hiding something.

Mr. Richards is continuing. ". . . not complacent about weapons of any sort in school. The police classify bladed garden implements as weapons if found in an inappropriate place; school is an inappropriate place. Blake knows this. His good record of behavior, Mr. Kershaw's endorsement, and the fact that this is a gardening tool all work in his favor." He sighs briefly. "Blake will tell you we met with the school safety officer this afternoon. As a first offense and for the reasons I've just related, we will not be taking this further at the present time, beyond recording the incident in detail, of course." His tone sharpens. "However, you will know that knife crime is soaring—forty thousand knife-related crimes in Britain last year and counting. The police take even the possibility of such crimes extremely seriously. If Blake brings any instrument that carries a blade into school again the consequences will be significant." He stands briskly and opens the door. "I'll be sending you a letter."

They walk out to the car in silence. Blake climbs in the front, ignoring Poppy's questions.

Grace drives to Dulwich Hamlet and hurries in for Charley. Her daughter slides into the back seat next to Izzy and then leans forward eagerly. "Any news?"

"Not yet, but the police are searching, people are looking all over London—"

"Could you stop saying that?" Izzy interrupts. "You are upsetting Poppy. And Blake."

She leans forward and trails her fingers over Blake's

face. Blake is frozen; there is something about his immobility that reminds Grace of an animal caught in a trap.

"Poor Blakie," Izzy murmurs, then she leans back again.

A decision arrives in Grace's mind like a gift or directive. "Silly me. I forgot to go to the bookshop." She turns the car onto Eve's road and pulls up outside the gate. "You girls go in; Blake needs a couple of books. We'll have to pop back to the village."

"Can I come?" Charley asks. "I want a book."

"This is for school. Out you get now, girls, we won't be long."

The girls get out silently; she watches them walk slowly up the drive. Izzy has her arm around Poppy, who is hunched into herself. Charley follows, shouldering her backpack and glancing back at the car.

"Which books?" Blake asks.

"I've just had a better idea. Let's get some tea—the books can wait."

The café is packed—it's that time of day when energy runs low; people need a pick-me-up, something sweet in their mouths. They are jammed against three women eating macarons and some kids from the middle school stuffing their mouths with crumpets; questions about the shears will have to wait till they are back in the car after all. Grace orders tea with crumpets and chocolate cake. They'll chat instead, as she's wanted to do for weeks.

"So how's things in big school, in general, I mean?"

He shrugs.

"Mr. Richards seems okay."

He glances at her then away.

"What about the other teachers—who's the nicest?"

He shrugs again. The crumpets and cake arrive with the teapot and she pours them both tea. Blake eats his crumpet fast and then another, then the chocolate cake; he seems to relax.

"So what's it like, pruning trees?"

"It's all right."

"Eric really values your help; you know that, don't you?"

"Yeah." He sounds casual but his face flushes pink.

"I thought we might go somewhere this weekend, find a wood maybe. A family outing, what d'you reckon?"

"Okay." He sits up. "Dad too?"

She glances out the window; a couple walk by, arms entwined, each with a hand on the baby carriage, smiling at the unseen child. She shouldn't have used that word, "family." Blake thinks she and Martin are together but it's hard enough to be polite to Martin; an outing with him would be impossible.

"He'll be busy," she says, still looking through the window. "You know, tutorials." She glances back. Blake is staring at her; his expression contains contempt and something worse, like pity. She was wrong; he doesn't think they're together; he knows what's happened and probably why. Izzy must have filled him in.

"We should get back." She stands up, jolting the table. Her teacup tips over and the dregs spill, a dark stain spreading quickly on the white cloth. She pays at the register then they drive to Eve's road in silence. She parks a short distance from the entrance to Eve's drive.

"Now we're on our own, we need to talk properly about what the teacher didn't find," she begins, "because I know there's something you aren't telling me."

Beside her, Blake has become completely still. Only his fist moves, opening and closing, opening and closing.

12. November

Melissa

Melissa steers the car carefully into their driveway and switches off the ignition. She leans back, exhausted. The drive from Salisbury took longer than the journey there and now it's early afternoon. Paul will be safely at work, albeit fuming about the temporary absence of his car. She must find clothes for herself and some for Izzy, assemble the material for the Wiltshire project, call a real estate agent to arrange viewings of available flats to rent, and then leave by taxi to pick Izzy up from Eve's house, all before he comes home. She doesn't even want to get out of the car. If it hadn't been for Izzy, it would have been hard to leave the shelter this morning. It had felt safe, far safer than the home she is about to enter.

The heat had bellied out as the door had opened. They'd felt the warmth on their cold faces. They'd stepped inside, squeezing past strollers crammed in the narrow lobby. A teddy lay on the bottom step of the stairs. Faint strains of music floated down from higher in the house and the smell of toast came up the hall to meet them.

The woman who let them in was in her thirties with a thick braid of brown hair over her shoulder; her arms were looped around a pile of clothes. She looked tired though her smile was wide.

"I'm Karen," she introduced herself, dumping the clothes on the hall table; the flicker of concern in her eyes was quickly masked. "Come and have some coffee, you must be tired after your journey."

Melissa's reflection in the hall mirror surprised even her. The bruise had spread into her left eye socket and the cut across her cheek had widened; it might need stitches. There will be a scar. Karen tactfully refrained from asking questions and they sat together in the warm kitchen where a young girl was stacking dishes. The curly-haired toddler at her feet was attempting to pull the head off a Barbie doll. An older woman, her right arm in a cast, was reading the paper at the table; she ignored them at first. Karen gave them a plate of hot toast and mugs of coffee. Lina took a slice, ate it quickly, and took another. The woman with the cast looked up and flashed Lina a smile, then the toddler approached, holding out her doll for inspection. Melissa relaxed. Lina would be all right here; she would make friends. Karen talked about the house and how it was run, the mealtimes and washing-up routines. Lina's eyes tracked Karen's, listening and learning. They were taken to the bedroom she'd been allocated: a simple room with a bed, a wardrobe, and a chair. There was a view of other houses, neat gardens, the cathedral spire in the distance, and a door you could lock from inside. When Karen left them, Lina turned to her. Melissa had never seen Lina smile properly before, with a smile that reached her eyes. She hugged her; as she drove away, tears of relief and sadness stung the cut in her cheek. She'd miss her friend.

Now she unlocks her own front door quietly and stands in the hall, listening. The house is silent. She begins to climb the stairs, but as she nears the top, she hears the noise of the shower. Her heart sinks. Paul hasn't left for work after all. The empty vodka bottle by the sink last night flits into her mind; already intoxicated, he must have attacked Lina as well as her, then drunk himself into oblivion. He was lucky to survive that amount of alcohol; she might have guessed he would only be surfacing now. He's late for work, but she won't comment; he could hurt her again. She'll have to wait until he goes out to make her escape or put it off until tomorrow. She returns to the kitchen and destroys the note she left earlier before he sees it. She makes coffee and feeds the cat. Paul comes downstairs with heavy footsteps; he avoids the kitchen and goes straight to his study without a word.

She clears her desk in the studio, rapidly shredding old papers, conscious that she is shredding her old life, beginning anew. Her hands tremble with anticipation; all the time she is aware of Paul in the house beneath her. He bellows once for Lina and then she hears him swearing, tugging open the fridge. Soon it's quiet, he must have left. She begins to slot blueprints and designs into her large portfolio case and doesn't hear him enter the room. She jolts when his fingers slide around her arm.

"Take your hand off my arm, please," she says as calmly as she can, turning around.

At the sight of her face, Paul flinches and steps back.

"You shut the car door on me last night, it caught my face. Then you hit me, remember?"

He frowns and looks away. Whether he remembers or not, she's breaking a rule. He's not used to her telling him what he's done. "Where is she?"

She meets his eyes, playing for time. "Still no news. Eric is making a televised appeal today."

"I meant Lina. I need my new golf trousers; she was letting them out. Mike's collecting me for a round at the club."

"I gave her the day off—wear something else." Her heart is beating fast; normally she would never dare talk to him like that. She is feeling brave and terrified at the same time and continues to place sheets of drawings in her portfolio one by one, apparently unhurried.

"What are you doing?" he asks.

"Getting samples ready for a client to collect."

"Dressed like that?"

His antennae are out; her mind races to stay a step ahead. "Of course not. I'll change after the gym."

"What about your face?" He sounds worried, but not for her; he's never marked her so badly and is scared of the consequences.

"I've got excellent makeup, Paul. I've used it before." She glances at the window. "Shouldn't you be leaving? It'll be dark in an hour."

"The club's floodlit," he says, but he leaves the room and runs downstairs. She hears him rattling in the drawer in his study.

"Where are my keys?" he shouts.

As his feet thud upstairs again, she reaches for the keys where she left them on the chair and slides them into the back pockct of her jeans, just before he bursts back into the studio.

"Where are my sodding car keys, Melly?"

"How should I know?" She stands perfectly still, back against her desk, the keys wedged in her pocket. "I thought Mike was collecting you."

"My golf clubs are in the car."

"Your old ones are in the closet; you could take them instead. What time will you be back?"

He shrugs. "There's a thing at the clubhouse later." He walks to the window. "Mike's late." He taps his fingers on the sill. "Let me know if they find Sorrel."

In a minute he'll leave, then she will. They will never stand together in this house again. She will never lie next to him in bed. For a moment she feels dizzy, as if on a cliff top with endless space beyond the edge.

Outside, a horn sounds twice, then a car door shuts, footsteps approach the front door.

"Goodbye then." He disappears swiftly without waiting for a reply; she hears the front door open and Paul greeting Mike, the clatter of golf clubs being pulled from the closet, followed by the slamming of doors.

He never usually says goodbye.

She piles jeans and sweaters into a large suitcase. The dressing table is bare as usual apart from a few photos: Paul grinning on their wedding day, absurdly handsome; she looks so young beside him, her smile so uncertain. She leaves that photo on the table and chooses two others: Izzy and Paul on a snowy slope, another of them in the sea. She places them between her clothes. Izzy will want them. She'll want to spend time with Paul once the divorce comes through. "Divorce," she whispers to herself, her heart beating fast. She puts Izzy's clothes into a smaller suitcase, hurrying now, anxious to be off. What if Paul should return for something and catch her packing? She chooses a jar of face cream from her collection, abandoning the tubes of thick foundation. She puts the protesting cat in the carrier, then hesitates, looking around. The house is hard to leave after all. She hasn't been happy here but it has sheltered her and Izzy. Lina too. She writes another note, scrawling quickly:

Client invited me over to Brittany; Xmas shopping, taking Izzy and Lina. Borrowing car. M.

He will be furious but she won't be here to suffer that; the lie might buy a little time.

She places the carrier on the passenger seat of Paul's car, throws her bag in the back seat, slips her portfolio beside it, and drives off. Tears well and she lets them come. Tears of exhaustion, relief, sorrow. She should stop because she can hardly see and is skidding around corners, a hand on the carrier to steady it. She is aware, as the car lurches, that the weight in the trunk is shifting and rolling from side to side. She hadn't noticed it on the motorway today, but then she hadn't been skidding at speed. What if Paul was lying about the golf clubs? He lies about so many things; there might be something else rolling and sliding in the trunk, something he wanted to take out or hide. Melissa drives the remaining streets very slowly; it's hardly any distance but she needs to take great care. She steers the car around corners as her heart bangs against her ribs, her mouth dry with a new, deeper kind of fear.

Grace

Blake hunches down in the passenger seat, eyes lowered, brows drawn tight. This close she can smell his fear, man sweat already. His hands are larger, she looks closely, more muscled. She's missed this recent growth; he's on that cusp tilting toward puberty, hormones swirling, impelling recklessness.

"Your teacher believed the story about the shears but I don't, not completely." It was that glance in Mr. Richards's office, the way Blake checked her face to see if she'd been fooled as well. His hands clench tighter, he doesn't move or turn. He's so still he might not even be breathing, though she knows at any moment he could jump out and disappear into the dark street.

"It's okay, Blake. I'm not angry, just worried."

Terrified. There is something Blake is hiding, though the explanation of why the shears were in his bag seemed genuine. She turns farther toward him, trying for a reasonable tone.

"Eric supported your story, it's probably true. The teacher thought it was, but I'm your mum. There's something else."

His eyelids lower, shutting her out. Despite her intentions, her voice rises. "You're in danger, Blake, Dad talked to you about this months ago. If you carry weapons, it makes it more likely that weapons will be used against you."

He turns his face to the window, waiting this out. She leans over, rests her hands on top of his clenched fists.

"It's me. I'm on your side." She can feel the heat of his skin, imagine the sweating palms. He jerks his fists away. He might find it easier to tell the truth to Mar-

318 • JANE SHEMILT

tin than to her, but Martin would probably turn this into a joke. She leans closer. "When a child in a family goes missing, the suspects are the people closest to the family, relatives and trusted friends. When he works out our friendship with Eve's family, that safety officer Mr. Richards told me about could put two and two together and come up with an answer that'll do, even if it's wrong. You know what police do to us, people like us. They could make you out to be dangerous."

Blake looks away, bored by the speech or pretending to be.

Then she says it, she has to. "They might even think you've got something to do with Sorrel's disappearance."

She's lost him. She knows that as soon as he turns away and wrenches the door open. He scrambles out and starts running; for a moment it looks like he'll continue running down the street but at the last second he swerves into Eve's drive and disappears.

A minute later a car follows him in, Melly driving Paul's car very slowly.

It's cold now, but sweat is trickling down her back. Stupidly handled. Martin might have done better after all. Blake's school backpack is in the footwell where he dumped it; she picks it up, hesitates, then tips it out on the seat. The books tumble out first—a dog-eared workbook, a geography textbook—pens, then several empty packets of chips followed by a snowstorm of candy wrappers. The empty bag feels heavier than it normally does. She shakes again but nothing further falls out and then she remembers. Blake had been thrilled when he unwrapped this backpack four Christmases ago. It was the same as Martin's, made for camping expeditions, replete with flaps and hidden pockets. Martin had shown him the zipper under the rectangle of thick plastic lining the base of the bag; she'd been resigned to the thought of the candy he would stash in there. Now she pushes her fingers into the space, encountering, as she knew she would, a slim shape, roughly bundled in toilet paper to stop it from sliding around.

Mr. Richards would have found it if he'd known where to look. The shears were a decoy, as it turns out, intentional or not. This is the danger. She unwraps it with trembling fingers. A knife lies in her hands; a thing of beauty with a smooth indigo-blue handle and a long, shining blade. She turns on the light in the car. A line of red lies along the edge of the blade, separated into minute granules, thicker at the edge where it makes an uneven reddish stripe thinning to pale orange. If she looks hard enough she can convince herself there are little pieces of matter caught along the edge, dehydrated fragments, translucent like skin. She puts it down on the pile of candy wrappers, her head thumping to the rhythm of three questions: Whose blood, whose skin, who exactly has her son hurt?

Eve

"Sorrel!"

A crow rises from the ground, black wings flapping. Empty branches scrape the sky; the day is ticking fast toward its end. The police and their dogs have searched the wood again; Eve is still looking. There may be clues left on the ground, under the fallen leaves, or caught on a branch, something small the police might have missed.

"Sorrel, answer me, baby."

Her foot strikes unexpected softness. She moves the covering leaves with care and leans close to the ground, her heart tipping forward in her mouth. She sees a rounded shape, brown-gray fur, soft ears. A dead rabbit. She turns it with a foot and the guts spill out, mauve and gray against the amber leaves. She straightens, feeling sick, and walks away, halting at a leafless horse chestnut tree at the back of the wood by the fence. The children had been sitting in the dappled shade of a chestnut tree when she found them with Martin that afternoon in May, maybe the very same one. Babes in the wood, he had said; she should have taken that as a warning.

"Tell me where you are, my darling. Tell me you're alive."

She looks up at the birds in the sky above the wood, but the tilt of her head makes her dizzy and she puts a steadying hand on the wire. A certainty comes, as if from nowhere, that Sorrel is alive, she is waiting, she isn't far. It's as though she has left a trace in the air, touched the trees, or leaned against the fence. Eve closes her eyes; minutes go by, lost in prayer.

A car horn rips into the silence. Through the trees she can see the Mercedes pulling up in the drive. Paul's car, delivering Poppy from school. It was supposed to be Grace's turn, not his, and he is clearly annoyed. She must rescue Poppy from that impatience. Eve begins to run through the wood, across the meadow and toward the house, but it's Melly who gets out of the car, not Paul, and no one is with her. Something has happened to her face, it's a different shape and color. She is shouting and crying at the same time, though Eve can't make out the words. Eric comes out of the barn at a run, Igor following him. Melly is behind the car as Eve approaches.

". . . rolling from side to side. None of the keys seem to work." She rattles each in the lock. "I think I've seen him using his phone, he's probably got a special app; he's paranoid about security—"

Eric turns to Igor. "Crowbar. Length of steel. Anything."

For a big man Igor moves swiftly. He races to the barn and back again, handing a crowbar to Eric, who applies it like a lever. There is a wrenching noise and the trunk comes open, revealing a bag, a long black bag, zipped and bulging, the kind that's used for golf. Eve puts her hand to her chest while Eric leans in and pulls the zipper slowly, holding the bag so it doesn't jerk with the movement. He pushes the edges apart carefully.

Inside is a bundle of golf clubs, the expensive, heavy kind, wrapped around with thick cloth. The heads are different sizes, different shapes. Her father used to play golf but Eve has never understood what the different kinds of heads were used for. She can remember asking him but he never replied.

"I'm sorry." Melly can't seem to stop crying. "I thought, while I was driving over, I actually thought . . ." She doesn't finish, she doesn't need to. Tears are pouring down her face. Eve knows what she thought, she'd thought the same.

Eric puts an arm around her. "Okay, Melly, it's okay."

Melissa's mouth is moving awkwardly because of the swelling in her face. Eve knows with the stinging acuity of grief that it was Paul who hurt Melly; pity settles on top of grief and fear, another sliding layer. She glances down at the empty trunk but it isn't empty after all. In the corner there is a curved glittering shape. Eve reaches in and brings it out in her hand. She holds it so tightly that the glassy fragments dig into her palm. A tiara. A child's tiara.

PART FIVE

Disguises

The children dressed up all the time, pretending to be someone else, practicing for life, which is exactly why children play games. Poppy wore that little sequined jacket from the dress-up box—it went well with her hair; Blake pretended to be a soldier; Sorrel was a princess. Charley, well, Charley's always herself. Izzy was beautiful, and that was a disguise in itself.

It's quite funny to think that while we were admiring the children's disguises, we were busy making our own: Melly and her pretty scarves, Eve putting on makeup at the barbecue and becoming someone else. I wore glitter, disguising damage, like Melly. And all the time, Paul and Martin were disguising themselves as family men who loved their wives, though I'm not saying they were the same, I'm not saying that at all.

The children's motives were different. They weren't trying to hide; it was the opposite. Poppy was desperate for friends, she wanted to be noticed and it worked—Izzy noticed her. Blake wanted adventure, he found more than he bargained for. Sorrel? I think she craved power, she had so little; it breaks my heart that she dressed as a princess for her adventure when all the time she was walking into a trap. At least she left us a clue.

13. November

Melissa

Melissa's home isn't hers anymore; it's not even her kitchen. It feels different in here without Lina, who made it a gentler place. The police snap on every light and the shadows disappear.

"Normally we would ask these questions at the station but speed is crucial; anything you can tell us now could be put to immediate use." Detective Gordon gestures to the kitchen stool. Melissa sits down facing him across the island. Eve is next to her, Grace the other side; they're standing close as if on guard.

Detective Gordon sits too but remains taller than Melissa; one of those men whose upper body is disproportionately large compared to the leg length; his double chin bulges over his collar as he looks down at her. "Could your friends wait outside?" he asks, though it doesn't sound like a question. "Normally speaking—"

"Don't fucking normalize this." Grace leans forward, resting her hands on the island. Detective Gordon blinks up at her. "We don't care how many times you've dealt with a missing child. None of this is normal for us."

"I understand that you are close—"

"That's right." The stool scrapes loudly as Grace sits down next to Eve.

"In which case you can stay in a supportive capacity for now; there may be questions you can help with too. I will request your departure when appropriate; your cooperation at that point will not be optional." Detective Gordon looks down at his notes, then up again; his eyes find Eve's. "Let's start with Sorrel's tiara. Do you know when she wore it last?"

Eve's hand is open on her lap. The tiara has already been passed to forensics, but Melissa can see that its little paste stones have pressed blood-lined indentations into her palm. Eve shakes her head. "I've been trying to think if she was wearing it when she came to my room after lunch, but all I can remember is holding her, the warmth of her . . ."

"She was wearing it midafternoon." Melissa's hand

finds Eve's. "We went for a walk; she was wearing it then."

"Where was your husband at that time?" He turns his scrutiny to Melissa.

"He was in his office."

"Can you describe his behavior later that day?"

"He was angry."

"Why?"

"He'd been drinking." It feels dangerous to admit this in their house; she glances around swiftly as if terrified Paul were lounging against the wall of the kitchen, listening to her every word.

"So he took it out on you." He inspects her face; he doesn't need a reply. "You put your belongings and your cat in the car earlier today when you drove from this house," he continues.

Melissa feels Grace's hand slide into hers; now all three of them are linked together.

"That's right." Melissa lifts her chin, meeting his eyes. "I was leaving him."

"All marriages have their problems; despite this, they often continue for years, as yours had done. What were you escaping from today of all days, the second day of Sorrel Kershaw's disappearance? What exactly made you snap?"

He is implying she knows something about Sorrel, that she might have been running from something terrible; if there is something terrible to find, it has yet to be discovered.

"It had nothing to do with Sorrel," she replies, but the bulging eyes continue to stare; he looks unconvinced. The silence in the kitchen swells until she can't bear it anymore. "All right, I discovered he's been raping our live-in maid." The words sound worse in the kitchen than they did in her head, starker, more grim. Perhaps she shouldn't have said that. Eve's hands have started to tremble; she might be thinking that if Paul raped Lina and was behind Sorrel's disappearance, he could have raped her little girl too.

"Your maid told you this?" Detective Gordon raps out.

"She didn't need to, she is pregnant."

"That doesn't mean he raped her."

"It probably does." Melissa lowers her voice. "He has done exactly the same to me for years, I've been raped more times than I can count. Last night was worse than usual."

Grace's hand squeezes hers tightly. Detective Gordon assesses her with a narrowed gaze; she unzips the neck of her tracksuit top a few inches and his glance travels over the red stain on her neck and chest. The expression in his eyes grows opaque, judgments are being made behind them, impossible to guess at; her words wouldn't stand up in a court of law but she sees she is believed.

"How old is your maid?"

"Fifteen."

"Name?"

"Lina."

"Where is she?"

"She's safe. We need to find Sorrel—"

"That's why we need to speak to Lina; if she's been in contact, intimate contact, with your husband, it's possible she might have vital information that could lead us to Sorrel."

They'll send a car to Salisbury, it will screech to a halt outside that ordinary-seeming house. Lina will be taken from her room, maybe sent back to Syria. Melissa stares back saying nothing, as the seconds beat past. No one moves until Grace does; she leans forward so her face is close to Detective Gordon's.

"The person you need is Paul, surely. He raped Melly and Lina. Sorrel's tiara was in his car; why bother Lina when you should be questioning Paul?"

Detective Gordon doesn't flinch but there is a flicker in his eyes as if he recognizes power.

"Mr. Chorley-Smith is being questioned at the station as we speak," he replies.

Phone calls must have been made immediately after the tiara was found; the police would have approached Paul in the dining room at the golf club and led him away. The room must have buzzed with gossip behind his departing back.

Detective Gordon signals to the young policewoman who has been standing inside the door; she moves forward. "Please, could you wait outside now?" she asks Grace politely.

Grace's warm hand rests briefly on Melissa's shoulder; Melissa watches as Grace takes Eve's arm and then her friends leave the room, followed by the young policewoman.

Melissa is left alone with Detective Gordon, who walks around the island and sits down near her, whether to intimidate or calm her is impossible to judge. He gestures to the gleaming kitchen. "All new?"

"Paul keeps it updated." She nods, confused by the change in his line of questioning. "He brings his clients here, it's a showroom of sorts." Though he hasn't brought anyone here recently; in fact she can't remember the last time he did.

"And everything he doesn't want gets thrown away, I suppose?"

Garbage to be discarded for newer models, as she so often was, is that what he means?

"It's all stored," she says evenly. "To be sold on."

"He was an architect. Am I correct?"

"Paul is an architect, yes." He has at least twenty years to go before he retires. What game is Detective Gordon playing now?

He shakes his head. "Not anymore, not for a while."

"He's a senior partner, you can check with the practice: Chorley-Smith, Atkinson, and Humphreys."

"We did." He crosses his arms. "Two interns logged a complaint of harassment against him about seven months ago: inappropriate comments, text messages, that kind of thing. When we investigated that, we were told he had since been sacked for financial misconduct. He's been out of work for half a year."

"That's impossible. He goes to work; he has a steady income—"

"From your daughter's trust fund, of which, unusually, I gather he is the sole trustee." He removes his glasses, rubbing the small red patches on either side of his nose, and replaces them. "We found this out when we looked further into your husband's situation following his previous questioning; he claimed, you see, that he left the Kershaws' house early on the morning of their son's drowning to go to work. Although no blame attaches to him for that tragedy, we already knew he'd been sacked so it was clear he wasn't telling us the whole truth. Investigation into his financial affairs revealed the true situation."

"If I'm the only trustee, I can instantly invest on her behalf when the market looks good." Paul had smiled his most winning smile. *"You won't have the bother of signing, which could hold things up. I know about these things, Melly. You haven't a clue."*

No wonder he's been angry for months, drinking too much and taking it out on her. He'd been terrified of discovery. It's unsurprising he disliked being questioned by the police; he must have been scared they'd find out. He'd have thought himself safe, at least until the money ran out. Izzy's money, given by her parents. Rage begins to build.

"Tell me about his violence towards you."

This swift change is clever; he wants to use her anger. She knows this, even as her reservations are swept away, even as her face heats with fury.

"He's always been rough in bed, at least that's what he called it. I was only fifteen. I thought what he did was normal."

That's not quite true, she'd thought she deserved it. She's thought that for years, but not anymore. It's different now. She glances around the kitchen as if to remind herself she doesn't live here; she doesn't live with Paul. She's broken away, broken free.

"We married when I was twenty-one. The violence increased; it's been worse in the last year, much worse in the last few months." He'd seemed so stressed—little wonder, money must have been running out fast.

"You never thought of leaving him before now?"

"Often, but I put up with everything because of Izzy, our daughter. Everything. I was scared I'd lose her if it came to a custody battle. He had the money to ensure victory, or so I thought."

"What is his relationship like with Izzy?"

"He worships her, he always has." She is aware that her voice has softened, which must be confusing, but she can't help that. Paul's love for Izzy is his one redeeming feature. "He has terrible faults, but he loves her dearly."

"Can you think of any reason at all why he might have taken Sorrel Kershaw?"

"None at all, I honestly can't see him ever harming a child."

"I suppose that depends on your definition of a child. You were technically a child when he first had sex with you, your maid's technically a child."

Beneath his eye there is a little muscle that jumps; she can see it jumping as though he is hiding tension, as though while he is looking at her calmly he is also waiting for her to tell him something else. Then he leans back and his voice changes, becoming matter-of-fact once more.

"There is something we are missing; some little detail I haven't thought to ask. Let's start all over again."

Grace

There are no pictures on the wall, no ornaments or rugs, not even a book; Melissa's bedroom is bleak, as if it belongs to someone who is frightened to show who she is. Grace stares at the single photograph on the dressing table, trying to reconcile the young bride smiling hesitantly from the silver frame with the damaged woman in the kitchen below.

Eve is sitting on the hard little satin sofa by the window, catching her breath after the stairs; a month of lying in bed has weakened her. Grace sits down beside her while they watch three policemen in the courtyard below inspect the smashed windows and dented panels of Melissa's car. They walk to the garage, moving slowly, their leashed dogs beside them. The men are chatting a little, their shoulders hunched as if in disappointment. They've already looked around the house and garden, there's not much left to search.

What if Sorrel is never found? What if she is, but

in a shallow grave beside a woodland road? Time will give the answer, but time is running out. Grace has the sinking feeling she is keeping vigil with Eve, that this shared moment might be the first part of a mourning process. In Zimbabwe relatives crouch by the graveside where the spirit of the dead one hovers. They take earth from the grave in small bottles to encourage the spirit to return home with them. These rituals have comfort in them, a community coming together. Eve has no community, just her and Melly. Sorrel's spirit would only need a small bottle, Ash's a smaller one still. She moves closer to Eve and puts an arm around her.

The men are coming out of the garage, they confer. The tallest of them shrugs his shoulders, looking around. It's easy to see the whole plot from here; it seems there is nowhere else to search. The only color is the vivid green of ivy growing over a trellis at the back that separates this property from the next. The garden itself is made of a series of terraced walls topped by narrow platforms of raked gravel that mount to fencing at the back. Beyond the wire there are leafy branches, brambles, and bushes, seething growth that presses at the fence. Grace can just make out the same KEEP OFF notice in faded red she's glimpsed at the back of Eve's wood. The old railway comes past here too, a secret leafy way where nature flourishes unchecked. Perhaps Melissa listened to the cry of owls and foxes as she lay in bed at night, perhaps she imagined escape.

"Eve, I think it's time to go home. Shall we—"

"Wait."

The muscles in Eve's shoulders have tensed. Her gaze is now focused on the courtyard below. Detective Gordon has emerged from the house and is conferring with a little group of policemen, while pointing to the ivy-covered trellis. The men hurry toward it; a second later Grace sees them lift the entire trellis and move it aside. She could laugh if her heart wasn't pounding; the only green plant in the garden turns out to be artificial, she might have guessed. Now that it's been moved, the door to an old shed is revealed, the kind of dilapidated place you'd want to cover up, if only for appearances' sake. The shed door is opened and from here they can see a dark interior full of white machines. They watch as a dishwasher is trundled out, a washing machine, a stove. All look new or newish. Detective Gordon squeezes inside the shed, out of sight, two dogs are let off leash and follow, barking loudly. The remaining officers in the courtyard move forward as one.

Eve stands up, her hand to her throat. She runs from the room and Grace follows, hurrying down the stairs so quickly that afterward she doesn't remember that part at all. She will remember trying to push into the shed after Eve, though by the time she arrives, Eve has already disappeared into the shadowy interior. Two policemen move to stand shoulder to shoulder, barring Grace's entry. She tries to see past them because it's obvious that something bad, something very bad, has happened inside toward the back of the shed, where it's too dark to see properly. A hand grips hers tightly, Melissa's. They stand at the doorway together while the dogs bark in a deafening frenzy.

Eve

Detective Gordon has placed his hands at the edge of the lid of a large freezer chest, the kind you are not supposed to have anymore because of the risk to children, though this one is unplugged and, if you look closely, very slightly open, just enough space to slide a knife through. He is braced as if about to uncover horror. He doesn't notice Eve standing just behind him.

The men are waiting as well, also silent. Perhaps they think she has his permission to be there because no one has suggested she leave. Even the dogs have quieted. Detective Gordon is wearing gloves, transparent rubber ones like a surgeon's. A bad sign. All the signs are bad. He grips the edge of the lid and heaves, but the effort is unnecessary. The freezer lid opens smoothly and easily. The smell is atrocious. He reels back, bumping into her, though he doesn't turn around so he still doesn't realize she is just behind him.

"Fucking hell," he says loudly. His words hit her like shrapnel, the kind they use in a terrorist bomb, fragments designed to enter your body and then expand. Her mouth fills with warm fluid like blood but it has the sour taste of bile. She doesn't want to look in the chest after all, so she shuts her eyes and moves closer, then she forces them open quickly.

At first it's too dark to make out more than a curled shape at the bottom of the chest, thin legs twisted awkwardly together. She forces her glance to travel up the small, inert body. The face is the kind of stark white that happens after a major hemorrhage, though there is no blood to be seen apart from cuts on her legs and arms and dark crusting on her fingers and, yes, an enormous bruise on her forehead that looks like a painting of a flower, a deep mauve-and-red one with unfurling petals. She looks lovely. A lovely dead child, like Sleeping Beauty or Snow White, babes in the wood after all. Is there no end to the fairy tales that fit?

Detective Gordon turns his head, asking quietly for something. She doesn't catch his words but his glance falls on her and he looks aghast. She doesn't care. In that moment of his surprise she straddles the edge and is over, inside the freezer, half lying and half kneeling in the shit and the vomit and the broken glass, crying, at least she must be, someone is making that low groaning noise. She takes her daughter's body in her arms. She pushes her face against Sorrel's and wraps her arms around her. She was expecting her to be cold, icy cold, but she's still warm and her skin still smells of her. Detective Gordon reaches over the edge of the freezer.

"Fuck off," Eve whispers. "Leave us alone."

Detective Gordon doesn't take any notice. He slides his hand past Eve's face to place his fingers against Sorrel's neck.

"She's alive," he says.

14. November

Eve

The pediatric intensive care ward is hot and brightly lit. Eve is getting used to the background hum: nurses at the desk and the doctors on their rounds, the never-ending bleep of machines. She's learned to ignore the constant movement around the beds. From time to time there are muffled gasps of someone weeping. She focuses on Sorrel's fingers lying curved on the sheet; the crusted blood has been washed away. She holds her hand, the small palm lying motionless against hers, and watches the rise and fall of her chest under the sheet.

Sorrel's brain scan was normal. The blood tests showed early starvation and dehydration, nothing that can't be reversed, the nurse tells her. Her name is Annie.

Her voice is pleasant, the rhythm sings. She is from the south of Ireland and has creamy skin and black curly eyelashes, one of those kind, brisk girls whose quiet way of moving inspires confidence. Annie's glance plays constantly over the machines by Sorrel's bed, her fingers adjust the rate of the IV drip and the height of the pillows, she smooths strands of damp hair off her forehead. Eve watches to see if Annie is on shift, and once she is, Eve allows herself to doze.

Eric tells her to go home, but what if she misses the moment when Sorrel's eyes open? Eve has hardly moved from her bedside for three days, not even to brush her teeth. Eric holds Sorrel's hand; he is polite but more remote than ever. She wonders if Melly let slip about her relationship with Martin. She can't ask her; they haven't talked since Sorrel was found, she has no energy to cross the little gap that has opened between her and Melly.

The affair with Martin seems irrelevant now, like a film she saw long ago, with an actress taking her part, playing a character she hardly recognizes. It's impossible to tell what thoughts lurk behind Eric's brooding face opposite hers or whether he knows; only that he seems to have gone as far away from her as she has from him.

He brings Poppy to the ward after school; she's allowed ten minutes at a time. Her auburn hair and the bright splash of her freckles shine against the beige of walls and beds. Eve holds her, breathing in her health, her fresh-air scent. Poppy doesn't twist away anymore but her glance moves rapidly over the immobile bodies on the beds around them; it takes in the IVs, the catheters and machines, the electrodes placed on small chests.

"Can I bring Noah to see Sorrel?"

"I wish you could, darling, but things in here have to be very clean."

"Noah's clean."

"I mean sterile clean, in case of germs; some of these children are very sick."

"Is Sorrel very sick?"

"She's tired. Too tired to wake up properly yet; she didn't have anything to eat or drink for nearly two days, remember."

"Was she scared?" The tone shifts higher.

The thought of Sorrel's terror is like a flame that burns Eve's mind. Those soft fingers scrabbling at the lid above her face, the despair as she wet herself, how her voice must have sounded as she lay calling for her mother in the dark. The admitting team told her there was no sign of sexual abuse, a life jacket in a sea of horror.

"You know, Pops, I think she was asleep most of the time."

"You mean she was unconscious? Like now?"

"Yes."

"Why did he do it—Izzy's dad?"

"I don't know, darling." She looks at Poppy's hands stroking Sorrel's. Poppy's fingers are ink-stained and pink; Sorrel's skin is yellow next to her sister's, even her nails are pale. Eve touches Poppy's hair gently; it's longer now and falls forward as she leans over the bed. "We'll probably never understand completely," she tells Poppy, "though we might find out more in court."

"Izzy's still my friend, though," Poppy says, tucking her hair behind her ear. "It's not her fault. I feel sorry for her, actually."

She seems to have made up her mind in that generous way children often do, pity being better than anger, easier to bear. They can't abandon Paul's family, Poppy is saying, none of this is Izzy's fault. Eve watches Poppy root around in the bedside dresser for a hairbrush. She's right. It isn't Izzy's fault and it's not Melly's either, but she can't help wishing Melly had found the strength to stand up to Paul sooner. If she had escaped or even fought back, Paul wouldn't have been part of their lives; Sorrel would have been safe. If she'd shared what was happening with her friends earlier on, they could have helped her leave him behind. She watches Poppy brush her sister's hair off her face with gentle strokes and thinks of Melly's bruised face as she last saw her. Melly was Paul's victim too, she reminds herself, long before Sorrel was; she must have been terrified of defying him, what that would bring down on herself.

"Izzy wants to come and see Sorrel." Poppy leans forward over the bed to touch her mother's hand.

"The nurse said only family, my darling."

"Izzy's family."

"Let's wait and see."

In the end she misses the exact moment when Sorrel opens her eyes. Eric had taken Poppy home for supper by the time the specialist arrived on a late ward round. Dr. Ari comes every day, a small man with a rapid walk, a little bent, perhaps from the years of study and examining patients. There is a quietness about him that he carries into the room. Eve is watching his face as he listens to Sorrel's chest when the expression of pure delight breaks on his hawklike features, drawing her eyes instantly to her daughter. Sorrel is staring at the man in front of her, her eyes blank with surprise. Eve's tears come instantly. She takes Sorrel's hand and presses it to her cheek, her heart hammering with joy. "Sweetheart, you're awake!"

Sorrel turns to her; her eyes widen before the lids flutter shut again.

"A good sign?" Tears run down Eve's cheeks.

"An excellent sign." The skin around those dark eyes creases in a smile.

Eric is there when Sorrel opens her eyes again later that evening; she smiles at her father. His mouth tightens in an effort not to cry. When he leaves that evening he presses his lips against Sorrel's forehead. Eve stands up, thinking he will kiss her too, but he nods without smiling and leaves the ward.

Dr. Ari comes to the ward the next day; by then Eric has arrived. He ushers them both into a side room. Eve reaches for Eric's hand but he hunches forward to listen.

"So it seems our little Sorrel was lucky," Dr. Ari begins.

"Lucky?" Eric frowns.

"The oxygen deprivation was only partial. A small amount of air had continued to circulate in the chest."

She and Eric have read a copy of the police report: the magnetic seal in the freezer had become faulty in the damp shed over time. Sorrel, pushing desperately at the lid, must have managed to lift it a fraction. The thought of Sorrel struggling for her life is unbearable; beside her Eric shifts uncomfortably in his chair.

"Her speech?" Eve asks, dreading the answer.

"Speech should recover fully; memory might take longer. I should warn you some memories may never come back."

The specialist's face is set in tired lines despite his cheerful voice. He has two days' growth of beard; he might have been working all that time. He is watching their faces as he talks, as if to check how they feel about the information he's given them. He might have a little girl Sorrel's age at home; he seems to know exactly how they are feeling.

"The hippocampus is a small area of the brain responsible for processing memory. It's particularly sensitive to lack of oxygen."

"Are you saying that there's some microscopic damage to the brain despite her normal scan?" Eric glares at Dr. Ari as if he blames him for what has happened.

Eric's upset, Eve wants to explain to the specialist, angry at what's happened to his daughter, not with you, but Dr. Ari is experienced, he has probably seen this reaction before.

" 'Damage' is a misleading word," Dr. Ari says gently. "A child's brain has a great recovery capability. You should think in terms of months or a year. In the meantime, we'll be moving her to the general pediatric ward where she'll be for two or three weeks of rest and monitoring."

"Recovery capability," Eric repeats contemptuously in the hospital cafeteria later. "If he means she's really brain damaged he should just tell us."

"He didn't mean that at all." Eve sips the weak tea; it's late, they are the only people in the cafeteria. "He was telling us she's likely to recover. In the meantime, it's a blessing. Who'd want her to remember that hideous incident?"

"The police."

"Paul's in custody. They're not looking for anyone else."

"The police are bound to come sooner or later," he replies. "They'll want to talk to Sorrel. There was none of his DNA on her."

"Of course there wasn't. Paul's cleverer than that. Grace told me he was still wearing gloves when he arrived at the house the evening he took her. I thought you knew."

A day later Sorrel is moved from intensive care to the pediatric ward. Disney animals scamper over the yellow walls, the atmosphere is cheery, there are fewer machines. She is able to sit up and sip fluids. She has just taken a few mouthfuls of orange juice from a glass when the policewoman enters the ward, a pretty woman with a tilted nose and thick fair hair drawn off her face. She sits down and smiles at Sorrel. Eve takes the glass away gently.

"Hello there, Sorrel, my name's Donna. We've met before."

Eve glances at her, puzzled.

"You were in hospital when I talked to Sorrel the last time," Donna says softly.

The day Ash drowned; Eve takes Sorrel's hand. Sorrel stares at the policewoman without the slightest hint of recognition.

"Do you know why you are here?"

Sorrel's forehead wrinkles; it's as if Donna were talking in a different language, one she has never learned.

"We want to find out what happened to you before you were brought to hospital; is that all right with you?"

No answer.

"Do you remember going to Izzy's house recently?"

The blue eyes close.

"I was wondering how you got there."

Sorrel turns her head away.

"Who were you with, perhaps you can just tell us that?"

Eve wants to tell Donna to leave. There's no point in these questions right now. She must see that her daughter doesn't want to talk, doesn't want to remember anything at all.

"Well now, Sorrel." A light sigh. "Have you any questions for us?"

The eyelids flicker open. Sorrel's eyes meet Eve's.

"Where's Ash?" she whispers.

Grace

"Can we see her?"

"That's the tenth time you've asked me." Grace is squashed between Charley and Blake on the sofa. The television is on; they are watching the news. There are three pairs of bare feet on the table. They had sausages and beans for supper, the children's favorite. Grace is making an effort to be relaxed. It's easier than she thought it would be, up to a point.

"Please?" Charley takes another bite of her apple and turns beseeching eyes to her mother.

"Family only, I told you already."

"She's getting better; they've just said so." Charley gestures to the screen with the apple. "And the police are allowed, so why not us?"

Grace shakes her head. "The doctors say she needs lots of rest." She's explained all this before.

"When, then?"

"She'll be allowed home soon enough."

"In time for Christmas?"

"Maybe." Grace puts an arm around her daughter and pulls her in, kissing the crown of her head. It could have been Charley trapped in that freezer. Paul came so close to them all; thank God he's been apprehended now. "The main thing is she was found and she's recovering," she continues cheerfully. "Let's focus on that."

"Yeah, it's amazing." Charley rests her head on Grace's shoulder.

Blake gets off the sofa and bounds up onto the chair on the other side. His cheeks are bulging in a grin.

"Blake, how many times—"

"When's Dad back?" Charley interrupts.

Blake jumps to the floor and waits, poised for the answer.

"The tutorial ends at eight, so half an hour after that maybe?" Martin's in demand, the agency calls most days. He doesn't seem to mind. At least, he doesn't say that he minds, but he doesn't say much these days. He might even be relieved to escape.

"So, you and Dad . . ." But here Charley's bravery forsakes her.

"I'll text him to bring home a cake from the co-op; he passes it on his way back. We can celebrate Sorrel's recovery." Grace picks up the plates.

"Mum?" Charley follows her to the kitchen with the knives and forks.

"Yeah?" Bracing herself.

"You know those blokes who used to hang around by the bins?" Charley puts the cutlery in the sink.

"What about them?"

"The landlady said they've gone, she said to tell you."

"Since when have you been talking to the landlady?"

"She came out today when Melly dropped us off. She's nice, she's got a cute dog. She told me to say they won't be coming back. Can I watch *Neighbours*?"

Grace stares at her daughter. What else does the landlady know? What did she see?

"Mum?"

"Homework first."

She'll take the landlady a bunch of flowers tomorrow, maybe a box of chocolates as well. She feels warmed, the way you do when you realize you've got a friend you hadn't known was there, someone who's been on your side all this time.

There's a brief scuffle at the door as Charley leaves and Blake enters, pushing past his sister. He roots noisily in the cutlery drawer while Grace runs hot water over the plates.

"What are you looking for?"

"A knife."

"Jesus, Blake. What d'you want a knife for now?"

He bangs a jar of strawberry jam down on the counter and grins. "Lid's stuck."

She takes a coin from the few that have reaccumulated in the tin, slides it under the lid, which gives with a little pop. Blake laughs.

This is the chance you've been waiting for, she tells herself. Things have calmed down, Sorrel's out of danger. Go on, now, while he's in a good mood. She reaches into the cupboard behind the bucket and mop for the blue-handled knife she hid in her largest saucepan four days ago.

"I found this." The rusty stain along the edge of the blade is now a faint pinkish line. She can tell by the way his face has fallen that she has only a few seconds to talk. "Whose blood is this?"

"What were you doing in my backpack?" The tone is belligerent; the good mood has vanished.

"What if I showed this to the police?"

"You wouldn't."

"I would."

He tries to snatch the knife but her fingers close tightly around the handle. "I'd do anything to stop you from ending up like that lot in the parking lot."

His eyes darken with anger.

"What have you done, Blake?"

No answer. She picks up her phone. "I'm phoning the police, right now."

He watches in silence as she punches the keypad three times, then waits. They stare at each other across the kitchen.

"Police, please."

After a few seconds, his breathing becomes wheezy; she hands him the inhaler from the shelf as she waits.

"Ah, yes, good evening. I'm phoning to report possession of a bloodstained knife—"

"Rabbits," he mutters.

"What?" She lowers the phone.

"Rabbit blood."

"How come?"

No answer.

"How come, Blake?"

He grabs the jam and walks out of the kitchen without the knife. Rabbits, for God's sake. It's crazy enough to be true; there must be lots of rabbits in Eve's place. He might catch them and skin them for supper; she can see Eric teaching him, skillful, unsentimental. She hopes Charley didn't see. She puts the knife back in her saucepan; she'll give it to Eric next time she sees him;

it's probably his. She hadn't dialed the police, she'd punched three zeros instead and talked into a dead phone. She looks at the dirty plates in the sink. They can wait. She's tired, as if she's reached the end of a journey and she's somewhere better than the place she left, though she's still not sure where she is.

Martin comes back at nine with a large pack of chocolate mini-rolls, but by then the kids are asleep. They unwrap one each in the kitchen; he makes tea while she tells him about Sorrel's improvement.

"Thank God." He passes her a mug. "That terrible man. I thought I knew him. I suppose we naturally believe the best of people; he must have traded on that. He managed to fool us all."

I thought I knew you. Grace watches him over the rim of her mug. I believed the best of you as well, you fooled me too. She sips her tea. "Charley began to ask about us today."

"And?"

"She lost her nerve."

"What would you have said?"

"It would have been difficult." She puts her chocolate roll back in the silver paper and wraps it up again. "I'd hate to upset her."

Martin walks to the window. She looks at the familiar way his hair grows in a little whorl at the crown, thinner now than when they met, grayer; his shoulders are more hunched.

"A week ago, my publishers wrote to me about a teaching position in the creative writing masters course at Harare university. It would involve a year's tutoring, and the pay is excellent." He doesn't turn around. "They hope if I'm out there again, the same magic will work. I might even finish my book. The university offered to pay for flights and accommodation."

He comes back to the table, sits down next to her, and takes her wrist in his hand. "I've been mustering the courage to ask what you think and if you and the kids would come with me."

She could walk those streets blindfolded. She knows the people, the light and the jacaranda trees, the slums and the traffic, the noise, the fights, the dancing in the streets, the whole beautiful city. She can close her eyes and conjure her grandparents' village in a heartbeat; that smell of dry earth, of eucalyptus trees and roasting maize. She can see the sky. Her heart could open under that endless sky.

"You go, obviously."

"We could find good schools for the kids. They'd love it."

"They're at good schools already."

His grip on her wrist tightens. "I want to fix us,

Grace. We met in Africa. What better than a year out there, together?"

She pulls her wrist away. "A year apart."

Melissa

"I forbid it. Don't involve Izzy in the trial. It won't be for months yet." Paul's chin is peppered with gingery stubble, there's dirt under his fingernails. He looks small, sitting on the other side of the table, defeated. It's been four weeks but he looks a year older at least. Pentonville is another world, one he can't dominate. "Tell her I don't need her help."

Melissa hadn't wanted to come today, but she'd promised Izzy.

"She's planning the statement already. She's desperate for the chance to read it out, it's keeping her awake at night. Your permission is mandatory."

"I don't want her exposed to the media." He bangs his fist softly on the table. It isn't loud enough to attract the guard but she has to stop herself from flinching. "I don't trust them; they'll wreak havoc if they scent blood. It could rebound on her."

He's uneasy about this. Melissa hadn't wanted Izzy to be involved either but Izzy had insisted she ask, and she agreed in the end; when Paul's convicted, which he almost certainly will be, it will be important for Izzy to know she'd tried her best to help her father.

"It's an unusual request, but the lawyer's prepared to make an exception and she thinks the judge will grant permission; she just needs yours."

He's lost weight, his Adam's apple visibly jerks up and down when he swallows. "Will she be questioned?"

Melissa shakes her head. "She won't even be in court. She'll read it out by a video link then leave straightaway. She's happy with that."

He frowns, weighing it, working out the risks and benefits.

"I'll be released anyway, they won't find concrete evidence, because I didn't do it."

Melissa stares back silently; let him believe what he wants, it makes no difference.

Paul's stubbly face leans closer to hers across the prison table. "What actual evidence do they have, apart from Sorrel being found in our freezer and the tiara in my car?"

That's surely enough in itself, Melissa thinks but doesn't say. Sorrel might tell the police more given time, but Grace told her the little girl is hardly speaking yet and that she might not remember anyway. The prison warden checks his watch and glances at them; the bell is about to sound.

"Izzy just wants to help you, Paul," she tells him, standing up. "I'll tell her I tried; she'll be devastated to hear—"

"Just the statement then, nothing else," he interrupts harshly, staring up at her; it's strange how threatening he still sounds, even in prison.

She walks away after that; she's fulfilled her promise to Izzy, the only thing that matters. She won't see him again till the trial, but at least Izzy's mind will be put at ease.

That evening, she calls the shelter and Karen answers; she's excited, the news is good. The Home Office has agreed to let Lina stay in England. Lina's home in Syria is a conflict zone, she has no relatives there, both reasons for her to be allowed to remain in the UK.

"That's such great news." Melissa smiles for the first time that day.

"I'll find her for you; she's resting."

A few minutes later Lina's voice murmurs a shy hello.

"How are you?" Lina is twenty weeks pregnant but she rarely refers to the fact. Melly is cautious.

"Fine."

"Karen told me you are allowed to stay; it's wonderful news, Lina."

"Yes, thank you. I am happy."

"When we have a home, there will be a room specially for you, two rooms." Paul's child, but also Izzy's little half brother or sister. Lina's baby, someone to cherish.

"Thank you very much."

"Sorrel is still in hospital but she's getting better all the time."

"I'm very glad."

"Paul's in prison; I expect you know that. He's likely to stay there for a long time."

"I see."

"Whatever happens, you won't be hurt again."

Lina doesn't reply. They talk a little about Salisbury and the cathedral and the next visit Melissa will make when she comes to see how the work in the Wiltshire house is progressing.

After the call Melissa walks upstairs to Izzy's room but she has fallen asleep; her homework is in a tidy pile on her desk. Melissa strokes her hair lightly. She hasn't told her about Lina coming to live with them yet or about the pregnancy. There will be plenty of time. She watches her daughter breathing gently, relishing the peaceful moments that she never used to have with her, thankful Izzy is managing so well without the father she adores.

*P*oppy wants to laugh and cry at the same time. She wants to laugh because Sorrel's okay, and then she wants to cry because she doesn't look like Sorrel except for her eyes. The nurses cut her hair because it was all tangled. She looks yellow; she's got tubes going into her skin and she's covered with bruises. She looks tiny in the hospital bed. Was she that small before? Whoever took her must've just lifted her up and—no. She's not going to think about that. It's like Ash, she can bear to think about him only for little bits at a time. Izzy's being nice. She asks about Sorrel all the time, about how she is and her memory and everything. She's nicer than she used to be and Poppy gets that, because she is too. Mum says when you think you are going to lose something important it changes you; you concentrate on the things that really matter. Izzy hasn't said anything much about her dad. She probably feels embarrassed and guilty, but it's not Izzy's fault. If people at school say it's odd that Poppy's best friends with the girl whose father kidnapped her sister, then that's their problem. They don't know what Izzy's like—especially now. Izzy does her homework and she lends her clothes and everything. She actually feels sorry for Izzy, which she never thought she would. She feels sorry for Mum too. Dad never talks to her and you can tell she minds. It's her fault for having sex with Martin—if that's true—which is gross, but she's not thinking about that either.

Charley can't wait to see Sorrel. She turns out to be really important—much more than, say, Izzy. She hasn't seen Izzy for ages and it's been fine, but she's hated not seeing Sorrel. Perhaps she should feel sorry for Izzy like Poppy does, but she doesn't. It's not Izzy's fault about her dad but that doesn't make her nice. Actually, Poppy says Izzy's trying to be nicer, but people are what they are; you can change but not that much. You can pretend to be nice like Paul did, but it's hard to keep that up. Paul couldn't, obviously. Poppy is sure Izzy's really changed. Well, maybe she has.

15. March

Melissa

Paul looks different in court from the man Melissa saw in custody three months ago. He's well shaven and upright and wearing a suit that the attorney must have procured for him, an unfamiliar red tie. He's slimmer than he's been for years, lack of alcohol probably. He gives the appearance of a clear-eyed professional, a man who wouldn't dream of harming a child, who would be too busy to know any except, of course, for one beloved daughter.

Paul's attorney had met Melissa and Izzy at the door; a handsome Sri Lankan woman in her forties with a brisk delivery, hampered by a head cold. She had a tired face and a harried air. Her life might be tough—a full-time job, children, maybe a household to run, perhaps a difficult husband as well. Melissa caught herself looking for bruises. The attorney told them what they already knew—that exceptional permission had been given for a brief statement on the grounds that, according to the lawyer, there was nothing on record that specifically forbade it. The attorney introduced them to witness support, a pale young woman in a flowing skirt who took Izzy off to the video room to prepare her for reading her statement. Melissa lingered outside the door for forty minutes in case she was needed. She entered the court just as the prosecutor had finished speaking and made her way quietly to the back. She sat on the side where she could see the defense lawyer, the judge, and Paul.

The defense lawyer begins by explaining there will be, unusually, a short statement by live video link in support of the defendant by his daughter. They are directed to look at a large video screen at the side of the courtroom. There are a few quiet whispers, a little ripple of anticipation; a departure from routine is always exciting.

When Izzy appears on the screen she looks so beautiful that Melissa's eyes sting. Paul is staring too, frown-

368 · JANE SHEMILT

ing slightly. He agreed to this—is he still worried about her? About what she'll say?

"So, Isabelle." The defense lawyer is in her fifties, with a well-cut gray bob and an expensive-looking silk shirt. She smiles at the screen. An average child might not realize the smile is condescending. "As you know, we can see and hear you by the special video link we set up so the people in court today can hear what it is that you wanted to tell them about your father."

Izzy nods politely.

"So, when you're ready . . ."

"Where would you like me to start?"

"You have the statement in front of you, which I have had the benefit of reading. I suggest," she says gently, "that you start at the beginning."

Izzy looks down at the paper on her lap and then up again. "Start at the beginning?" She sounds worried. "It'll take ages. It began years ago."

"Just read out the first sentence then carry on," the lawyer repeats patiently. "Don't be nervous. It won't take long, so if you can kindly—"

"I was six when it began," Izzy cuts in.

When what began? Melly feels a pulse of anxiety; has it all been too much of a strain? This video appearance a step too far for a thirteen-year-old child? The lawyer looks puzzled, but to her credit she is still patient.

"I'm sorry, Isabelle, that's not what is on the paper. There may be lots of very helpful things you would like to tell us about your father, but we agreed you'd read out just what is written down in front of you."

"You suggested I start at the beginning. That's what I'm trying to do. I was six when he began to abuse me."

There's a soft noise in the court, a collective gasp, like the sound the sea makes on pebbles as the waves retreat. Melissa's hands go to her throat. She's not sure if she heard properly, or whether she imagined Izzy's words. She glances at Paul but he's looking at his daughter; his face is blank as if with shock.

"It's been going on since then. Seven years altogether. Like I said, it'll take ages if you want me to start from the very beginning."

The court is hushed, that deep quiet of an audience listening to a good story. The lawyer is staring at the screen, motionless. Paul is white-faced, his jaw is clenched. Melissa's world is veering out of control as it did years ago; she'd been a passenger in Paul's car when he lost control on a country road; she can feel that helpless slide toward the bank right now, see the frosted grass coming closer in the headlights. She grips the chair seat and takes slow breaths, digging her nails in her palms. Someone needs to stop Izzy; her claim is crazy, frightening. She wants to hold her daughter, call for an emergency doctor, maybe a psychiatrist.

"Isabelle." The lawyer has recovered, she speaks firmly. "You are here to read your witness statement. I suggest you immediately retract—"

"I am here for Sorrel. I retract nothing." Izzy's voice is clear; she sounds completely sane. "I want everyone to know that my father abused me and he's done exactly the same to my mother. He's a monster."

The lawyer's face changes, becomes expressionless; her lips tighten. She addresses the judge and her voice is much louder.

"Sir, I request a halt in proceedings. We have a hostile witness which we did not anticipate. I would like to confer with my client."

"Carry on." The judge's voice is measured, a necessary note of calm. He has a kind face; someone you need on your side, though judges don't take sides. It's about the truth, which is good, because at the moment Melissa has no idea what that word even means. She can't see Paul anymore; his head and the lawyer's are lowered in discussion. There is a buzz of whispers, glances are directed her way. Paul is violent, an alcoholic, deceitful certainly, but he loved Izzy. That was the star she steered by, the reason she endured all these years. Her daughter's happiness has been bought with her own suffering; it is inconceivable that all this time Izzy's been suffering as well. What she's saying can't be true. She's been stressed by her father's absence; the video has been the final straw. Melissa rises from her seat; she should take Izzy home now, insist that she rest.

The defense lawyer turns to the judge. "Your Honor, my client rejects these claims as utter nonsense. I request permission to cross-examine his daughter."

"Proceed with care. We know Isabelle has witness support with her but it's important to remember she is a child."

It's too late. Melissa sinks back into her seat, her legs trembling.

"Isabelle." The tone is measured. "You have written a statement which I will now read to the court, a statement that you swore at the time was the truth.

" 'My father has been close to me since I was little; we do homework together and he takes me away on holidays. I can't imagine life without him. I can't imagine him hurting another child.' "

The lawyer puts the paper down and addresses Izzy. "In light of these words, do you now retract the statement you made earlier?"

"I retract nothing," Izzy repeats; her face is pink. "He was with me when I was trying to do my homework, that's when the abuse happened."

"Your mother works from home, doesn't she?"

"Yes."

"It's rather difficult to imagine your father being able to act as you say while your mother was at home at the same time; can you explain how that was possible?"

"He locked the door, he told her he was helping me with homework. My mother's scared of him. She does what he tells her to."

Melissa closes her eyes, seeing the white door with its sparkly metal "I." She never once tried the door handle. Izzy was right, she hadn't dared. By obeying her husband, was she abetting her daughter's abuse? She pushes her hands to her mouth to stop herself from crying out.

"He took me away on trips, skiing and things like that. Mum wasn't allowed to come."

He had waved Melissa goodbye at airports, his arm tight around his special girl. Cheap, last-minute trips with shared bedrooms—*That's normal,* he said to Izzy when she objected once. *I have to keep you safe.* Safe. Melissa enjoyed the breaks too, if she's honest, pockets of calm in her life. She'd encouraged those breaks. It was their bonding time, she'd remind herself as she returned to the house and the calm of nights on her own. It seems so obvious now—how could she not have suspected, even for a moment?

"In your witness statement, you say you can't remember a time when you weren't close to him." The lawyer looks at the judge then Izzy. "Is that statement, in light of what you've now told us, a truthful one?"

"When he lay on top of me, I had to take off my clothes. That's pretty close, isn't it? And I can't remember anything further back than that. What he did to me has blocked it all out."

The picture is vivid. Melissa closes her eyes. The lawyer persists, though it must be obvious to her that she's losing the battle. "You also say that you can't imagine him hurting another child."

"That's true too. It's so awful to imagine what I went through actually happening to someone else that I don't. I just can't."

Paul's face is ashen, even his lips are pale.

"Why have you waited till now to come forward?" The lawyer's face is pale too. Her lipstick looks garish against the pallor.

"He said it was our special secret and that Mum would commit suicide if she knew." A tear trickles down Izzy's cheek—Izzy, who never cries. "He said I'd have to go to some special place for kids."

"But you're telling us now because . . . ?"

"He's tried to hurt Sorrel and he'll try again with someone else." Izzy leans forward, her face flushing a brighter pink. "He likes girls when they're little. Sorrel's six, like I was at the beginning." Her words tumble out fast as if she's been waiting a long time to deliver them.

Melissa can't see Paul's face anymore, it's buried in his hands.

"Do you have any actual evidence of your father's violence?" The lawyer's voice is quiet.

"My mum's sitting somewhere in court—look at her face. It probably doesn't count, but that's his doing too."

Heads turn. Melissa tries not to cringe. The bruises have faded by now but the line on her cheek where the skin was torn remains as an uneven pink scar. The repair was good but the puckering is obvious. She holds herself very still. She had tried to shield Izzy from what Paul did to her, but she must have known all the time. She wants to get up and run to her daughter, but she has to wait a few more minutes.

The lawyer is speaking again, heads swivel back. "Thank you, Isabelle," she says, then she turns and bows to the district judge. "I have no more questions."

She sits down; her silk shirt has become untucked, the immaculate gray bob a little disordered. The judge begins to talk—something about reconvening and more evidence—she doesn't catch most of what he says; her mind is so full of Izzy. After a few minutes he leaves the court. Then the whispers start and get louder, waves advancing up the pebbly beach with force. Melissa gathers her coat and her bag. She wants to go to her daughter as soon as she can, so she misses the moment when Paul might have looked for her, seeing only the door close behind him and the accompanying officer.

Izzy is standing just inside the room across the corridor. She looks different from the girl on the screen; in fact, Melly has never seen Izzy like this. She seems much younger suddenly, very lost. She is staring around in fear, as if she has found herself in the middle of the woods, having gone too far, and doesn't have a clue how to get out. She's no longer performing for the court; she isn't burning with anger. She's not a confident teenager anymore, but simply a frightened little girl who has suffered for years. This reality breaks against Melly with the force of an icy wave, but she mustn't drown; her daughter needs her more than ever now. The witness protection woman has her arm around Izzy and is murmuring something about her being very brave, but Izzy doesn't seem to be listening. When she catches sight of Melissa, her face relaxes; she runs to her mother and wraps her arms around her. Melissa lowers her head to her daughter's.

"Excuse me, Mrs. Chorley-Smith." The attorney has followed her from the court, the tired woman whom Melissa had felt sorry for.

Melissa looks up. "I have to take my daughter home now. This has been a huge strain for her."

"I'll be quick. In the next few days, Izzy will be called for an interview at a police station by female police officers in the forensics team." She lowers her voice. "She may need to undergo physical examination." Then she nods briskly. "The trial will be reconvened when all the evidence will be considered together."

"Will she have to attend that trial?"

"Fortunately not. The whole process could take many months; the kidnapping and abuse trials are likely to be joined. Izzy's presence at the resulting trial won't be required." She looks weary, there's more work for her to do now. She walks rapidly away.

Izzy lifts her head when the attorney is out of sight. Her eyes well. "I'm sorry, Mummy, I'm really sorry."

"It's me who should be sorry, my little sweetheart. If only I'd opened your door in the evenings, if only I'd come with you on your trips abroad . . ." She mustn't start crying, she has to be strong for Izzy. It's just her and Izzy now.

"At least he won't hurt you anymore," Izzy says through her tears.

"Or you, my darling girl." Melissa kisses her cheek.

As they begin to descend the steps, Melissa's arm around Izzy, a dark blue van sweeps past them with a small barred window at the back, high up. Paul could be inside. His head might be in his hands as he tries to comprehend the speed at which the world he knew has disappeared. She watches the van weave into the traffic, halt at the light, pull away, and vanish from sight around a corner. Melissa's arm tightens around Izzy. They walk down the rest of the steps, clasped tightly together and stumbling a little.

Eve

Sorrel is better, physically better; she has begun to speak a few words and she even smiles sometimes. Dr. Power, the young pediatrician in the outpatient clinic, is very pleased with her progress. She examines Sorrel with care, checking her reflexes and the back of her eyes. Eve watches the doctor, envious of her energy, her shining hair and luminous skin, conscious she has aged years in recent months. Her own hair is stringy, there are new lines on her face. Her nails are bitten down. She is tired all the time, even in the morning, even after sleep. The doctor smiles and pats Sorrel's hand.

"You are a brave girl, Sorrel; I don't need to see you for another three months."

"Thank you, Doctor." Eve wants to hug her.

"Call me Marian." The doctor has a wide smile, a scattering of freckles. "Sorrel has done better than we could have hoped." She leaves with a spring in her step, happy at this outcome, having no knowledge of the ripples of destruction that have spread outward or of the lives that have been twisted into different shapes.

Sorrel is exhausted after the appointment. Eve hurries her across the busy road in the rain to the car parked opposite and swiftly settles her into her car seat. Sorrel's eyes close almost immediately. Eve's cell phone rings as she is getting into the driver's seat.

"What did the doctor say?" Grace asks.

"She was pleased," Eve whispers. "Sorrel's making good progress, physically. The child psychologist is coming this afternoon." Eve watches an ambulance swerve into the hospital. It's lucky that you can't see into an ambulance from the outside; that desperate struggle to save a life should be private. She turns away from the flashing light, the phone tight to her ear. "Any news?"

"Melly phoned this morning." Grace leaves a little

pause like the one doctors give you before they break bad news.

"Go on."

"Are you somewhere you can sit down?"

"I'm sitting down already."

As Grace begins to speak, Eve watches the rain hit against the windshield and the traffic splash by but she doesn't hear any of it. The noises from the street have faded, everything has faded apart from the words she is hearing. Pedophiles make up 8 percent of the population, information gleaned from Google when Sorrel was missing, not easy to forget. A young bloke with a ponytail speeds by on his bike—could he be a pedophile? Or the guy in a suit hurrying past with a briefcase? That old man shuffling to the bus? Paul was a charmer, handsome, amusing, she had liked him; how could they have possibly known?

". . . then Izzy told the court he'd hurt Melly," Grace is continuing. "The scar on her face is still obvious; things like that can tip the balance."

Paul might have hit Sorrel too, at the very least he must have terrified her. A few moments pass while Eve clamps down horror. She glances in the rearview mirror; Sorrel is still fast asleep.

"How is Melly?" she manages. "I haven't seen her for weeks."

"Better than you'd think," Grace tells her. "She's stepped up, like you."

"Izzy?"

"That child's made of steel. I've had my issues with Izzy but I understand her better now. Melly's going to make sure she gets the help she needs."

There is another little pause; there's so much Eve wants to say to Grace, it's hard to know where to begin: her gratitude, the guilt, the lasting regret, the value of her friendship.

"Grace . . ."

"Take care." Then Grace is gone.

Sorrel's thumb has slipped from her mouth; she is snoring lightly. The thought of her daughter in Paul's hands is obscene. She had guessed the moment she saw the tiara in his car, but guessing is different from knowing; imagining is different from seeing, and she can see Paul clearly now, see the look on his face as he forced Sorrel into the trunk of his car, then into the chest in his shed. Eve shudders. The doctors had said there was no evidence of sexual abuse. Her gaze lingers on the sweet sleeping face of her daughter; she's been incredibly unlucky, and also lucky.

Eve starts the car. Grace was good to let her know; she couldn't have managed so much of this without her. Somewhere along the way Grace has found it in her heart to forgive her and save their friendship. She should reach out to Melly in turn, it's time she did. While Sorrel is playing with Noah after lunch she finds Melly's number on her phone; they talk for an hour until the child psychologist arrives midafternoon and she has to go.

Dr. Irving is a woman in her sixties with thick gray hair and eyes that tilt downward. Sorrel stares at her silently.

"I hope you'll tell me your favorite games and then we can play them together."

Sorrel moves closer to Eve; she doesn't reply to any of Dr. Irving's gentle suggestions. In the end Dr. Irving reads her a story, pointing out the pictures, though most of the time Sorrel's eyes are closed.

Afterward Eve walks with Dr. Irving to her car, listening intently to her quiet voice. "This will be a long road. At the moment Sorrel is repressing all memories. When she recovers mentally as well as physically, she may start to get odd flashes, triggered by something in the environment perhaps. That could be very frightening for her. Be alert and stay with her. It's always possible she could be overwhelmed by a sudden flood of memories, though in reality that's rare."

"What should we do to support her?"

"Give her space. Let the memories come if they do,

but don't seek them out." She pats Eve's arm. "She's doing as well as we could expect at this stage. I'll see you next week."

Later Eve tells Eric what Grace has relayed. Eric's face darkens; he gets up and stares out the window into the dark garden. "Sorrel would have been safe if I hadn't worked for Paul and introduced the family. It's my fault."

"Melly might have found me through Facebook like Grace did; Paul could have targeted us just the same. It's definitely not your fault." She pours a glass of beer and takes it to him. "It's not Melly's either. She has suffered too, more than we know. I was hoping you wouldn't mind if I ask her and Izzy to come and stay with us for a while."

"You can't be serious."

"Izzy told Poppy she can't sleep in her house, too many memories. I doubt if Melly can either." She touches his sleeve. "Sorrel's getting better. We can be kind, can't we?"

"Let's see what Sorrel says."

They're having supper in the kitchen later when Eve mentions the possibility of Izzy and her mother staying for a while. Something flickers across Sorrel's face.

"Izzy?" She sounds confused.

"She used to come here for lessons, my darling. She played with you and Poppy."

"She's my best friend," Poppy puts in, helping herself and Sorrel to more mashed potatoes.

"Oh." Sorrel's face clears, she nods. "Okay."

Eve catches Eric's eye across the table, he gives a little shrug. She nods and smiles at Poppy, who high-fives her sister.

"I'm glad we're able to do something that makes Poppy happy for once," she murmurs to Eric as they clear the table later. "It's been incredibly tough for her."

He doesn't reply but he seldom does these days; she takes his silence as agreement and texts Melly later. Her acceptance comes back swiftly.

Grace

"I don't have to go," Martin whispers, though they're outside and no one can hear. "There will be other sabbaticals, they come up all the time."

They've been over this; he wants her blessing. If this is a game he's playing, she's fed up with it.

"Of course you have to go. Go," Grace tells him.

"I haven't actually signed anything."

"You gave them your word."

"I guess the money will be useful."

"Useful?" Grace stares at him. "It'll be more than we've ever had."

"So take a few months off, you could write. You've always wanted to, we can afford it now." Martin smiles at her, the old melting smile. "Or better still, change your mind and come with me." He reaches to touch her hand but she tucks it under her arm. It's cold out here on Eve's veranda, away from listening ears. "You know the children would love it."

"If you need my permission to go, you've got it."

"That's not what I meant. I don't want to spend a year without you."

"We're staying put, you know that."

They look down at the playground below the veranda; the bright colors look garish in the weak March sunshine. The door of the little house has come off its hinges and someone has broken a window.

"Will you tell the kids?" he asks hopefully.

"It's your sabbatical, you do it."

"So I'm not forgiven?"

"Come on, you two." Melissa calls through the door. "Teatime."

There are seven candles on the cake. Sorrel sits in the chair at the head of the table, a paper hat on her head, a little crown of flimsy red tissue paper. The police kept the tiara, Eve didn't want it back. Sorrel is smiling, Noah's head resting on her lap; Charley is on one side, Poppy the other. Izzy next to Poppy. Charley has Venus on her lap.

Eric distributes tea and sits down next to Blake, who passes him a piece of cake.

"Thanks for your help," Eric says. "Nice work."

Blake's cheeks redden. He takes an enormous bite of cake.

"What help?" Martin asks.

"Blake's pruned a heck of a lot of trees," Eric says, smiling at Blake. "He's a great worker."

Poppy walks around the table, serving out more birthday cake. Melissa takes a bite; Grace wants to cheer though she knows she shouldn't.

Eve looks at her daughter. "Happy birthday, darling."

Sorrel looks around uncertainly as if searching for somebody who isn't there: Ash, maybe Paul as well, the ghosts of the dead and living seem to hover. Eve is a ghost too, thinner, paler. She sits completely still at the table, staring at her daughters, forgetting to eat. Eric is next to her but they don't talk to each other, another wounded couple who may not make it through.

"How's Izzy doing?" Grace asks Melly later as they load the dishwasher after tea. Izzy is playing cards with her friends out of earshot.

"Really well." Melly straightens, pushes her hair out of her eyes, and smiles.

"And the new trial?"

"That won't be for ages and she doesn't have to attend. She's had two interviews with the forensic team."

"I bet that was tough."

"Not as tough as an examination would have been." Melissa's voice sounds strained. "She refused that though and they didn't push. They said if they did, she might experience it as another, well, as another assault. Any findings would have been minimal anyway; it's been months since the last . . . incident took place."

"It's great they were prepared to accept her story."

"The story is all they get in lots of cases like Izzy's. And the school report helped; her grades were lower than expected and there's been some antisocial behavior which apparently fits; it's hardly surprising when you think about it."

"How is she now?" Grace glances across the room, where the children are playing together. Izzy's head is bent over the game.

"So much better. She's in counseling, we both are.

I'm not allowed to know much, but her counselor let slip she's quite defensive. I think that's good; in my mind that means she's a survivor."

"She gets that gene from you." Grace transfers the rest of the chocolate cake to the fridge but leaves one slice on a plate, nudging it along the draining board. "I think you're the strongest of all of us, Melly."

Melissa flushes with pleasure. She looks younger these days; her face is rounder and she keeps her hair loose. She doesn't wear those tight little scarves anymore.

"He says she needs peace, no upheavals." Melly begins to eat the cake.

You do too, Grace thinks to herself, that wretched man. "Have you found a buyer for the house yet?"

"Three. Eve says we can stay as long as we like, but I'm looking for somewhere nearby. It shouldn't take long."

Izzy is dealing out cards to the other children. Every movement she makes seems careful. It's as if someone is watching her or she is watching herself. That's what it must have felt like with Paul all the time. Izzy puts her cards down and claps her hands; she's won the round. She looks up and meets Grace's gaze with a triumphant little smile; Grace smiles back. Melly was right, Izzy is a survivor.

*C*harley tells her mum that it's been a really long time since there were any actual dyslexia lessons for Blake and the others, which is funny because that's why they all became friends in the first place. She wasn't even supposed to be there. Mum says they can't possibly ask. Ash died less than six months ago, which is nothing. According to Mum, some people are sad forever when their children die. Poppy says she misses Ash really badly but she doesn't want to talk to her parents in case it reminds them; Mum says they'll be thinking about it all the time anyway. They see them almost every day. Charley gets that it's been really hard for Izzy because of what her dad did and she can see that Izzy's trying to be nice, but it still doesn't make Charley like her much. She misses Dad, but not as much as she'd miss Mum to be honest. Dad slept with Eve, which puts her off both of them, though Blake says to get over it. He thinks Mum has. Charley doesn't think she has, quite.

Blake misses Dad all the time. Dad going to Africa makes about the sixth or seventh major bad thing this year. Ash dying was the worst, obviously. Then Sorrel being kidnapped and Paul turning out to be the one who kidnapped her. What happened to Izzy and what happened to her mum. The knife thing, obviously. He misses Dad in the mornings, mucking around with them and laughing, it made Mum's nagging bearable. And he misses him in the evenings watching TV. And going to soccer. He doesn't care if Dad made out with Eve, so what? He doesn't know if Izzy's one of the good things or one of the bad things. They play normal things like Monopoly now. She's nicer to Charley and Sorrel and Poppy. Well, to everyone really.

Izzy's proud of what she did and so is Mum. No one would have thought that because of her, Dad would end up in prison and Mum would be safe and so would she. Really safe. She did that on her own. Wow. She could have done it a long time ago, but she's not sure if any-one would have believed her, without what happened to Sorrel added in. It's great they're staying with Eve; she wants to see how Sorrel does, obviously. It's working out okay, living together. She can see Blake isn't sure about her now, Charley doesn't like her much, and Grace definitely doesn't since she told her about Eve and Martin. The important thing is that Mum, Poppy, Sorrel, and Eve are on her side. She's glad things have worked out as they have, mainly because Mum's completely different. She hasn't got any bruises, she even walks differently. It makes it all worthwhile. It's just her and Mum in their family from now on and Dad can't do one thing about it.

PART SIX
Friendship

I love the bit in *Winnie the Pooh* when Pooh says a friend is one of the nicest things you can have, and also that quote from Woodrow Wilson about friendship being the cement that holds the world together, which is a roundabout way of explaining to myself why I forgave Eve and why she forgave Melly. It's hard to understand otherwise, even for me. I mean, who would have thought I'd end up being close to the woman who had an affair with my husband? She was a friend first, then a sort of enemy, then someone I had to help, and, in the end, a best friend. I realized what she was made of the day they found Sorrel; you can see it in her face, which was on all the front covers of the papers. The journalists got there in time to capture it as she came out of the shed the day Sorrel was found. She was blazing with love. She'd been through things that would have destroyed some women—the loss of her son, the kidnap of her daughter—but that day she was on fire. She reminded me of my grandmother; the way she used to be for us. I forgave her; it seemed crazy to throw away our friendship because of Martin.

It took Eve a while to work it out with Melly— maybe she went down a similar line of reasoning: Why let a man destroy something as precious as friendship? It was different, of course, because Paul had destroyed so much, but that was hardly Melly's fault, and I think that's what Eve came around to thinking in the end.

We should have known by then, just when we thought it was all beginning to settle down, that something worse was coming our way.

16. April

Eve

Eve watches. She watches Sorrel and Poppy and even Izzy. She needs to keep everyone safe. There are rings under her eyes from getting up in the night to watch the children. Sometimes she slips into bed with Sorrel and holds her, watching the way her eyelashes cast shadows on her cheeks in the moonlight.

The whine of the power saw has become background noise in the daytime. She watches from the window as the trunks topple, the branches with their sprays of green descending slowly. Blake helps pull the undergrowth out after school and on weekends; Eric is tired after his long days, longer without Igor. He seems to have abandoned his former ideas about a Japanese garden. Evenings are silent, he goes to bed early, straight after supper sometimes.

Poppy is reading much more than she used to, old books Eve read to her a while ago: *Little House in the Big Woods*, *The Magic Faraway Tree*, Roald Dahl, *Beano* annuals; comfort reading like comfort eating or drinking. She doesn't talk about Ash much, nor does Sorrel. Sorrel has been told he has gone to heaven and isn't coming back. Fragments of memory have appeared, flotsam washed up from the deep: the glass plates in Greece, paddling in the sea, a doll she'd gotten for Christmas. Eve asked all the children not to push her for more and they listened, nodding.

The pain of losing Ash has returned with greater force, like a storm coming back across the sea, increasing in strength as it comes. In the day she can weather it but at night she is beaten to the ground. She can hardly crawl upstairs to bed at night. If it wasn't for Poppy and Sorrel or Melly and Grace, she'd have given up by now. Eric never refers to his son. She knows he is thinking about him when he stands at the window, his face drawn and fists in his pockets, gazing at the donkey field with the fence that extends right down to the ground.

The time to discuss the affair has passed; she doubts whether he cares one way or the other. The connection between them has thinned to the point that if it snapped, neither of them would notice; perhaps it's broken already.

Grace

Martin's letters are addressed to all three of them, Grace reads them out loud at supper.

". . . crowded classroom, listening as if their lives depended on it. I go to the park to write in the evenings; the little monkeys in the trees try to steal my sandwiches, they remind me of Charley."

"It's not fair," bursts out Charley. "How come he gets to have a holiday and we don't?"

"It's not a holiday," Grace reminds her. "He's teaching, earning us money."

"He sees these animals. He has picnics in the park."

Grace looks at Charley's resentful face. They could be there now, looking up at those monkeys, the sun hot on their faces and all the scents of Africa around them, if things had been different, if Martin had behaved differently.

"Well, we could have picnics in the park."

"Just us?" asks Blake.

"If you want," she replies, pleased.

"Nah."

The flat is untidy. They tidy it together and she tries not to do it again when they've gone to sleep. The co-op has promoted her to part-time manager but she's at home for meals and she writes alongside them when they do their homework.

"What happened to Ash?"

She is sitting by Charley, who is reading in bed. She smooths her hair off her forehead, the only time she's allowed to do that now.

"He drowned, you know that. It was a terrible, terrible accident."

"I know that's what everyone says happened, but no one knows if it's true."

"It may not have happened precisely like that." She turns off Charley's bedside light.

"Izzy's been saying it could have been her dad."

"What?"

"She said not to tell anyone but she remembered he'd got angry with Ash the night before. Then he left early the next day, which was the day Ash was found. He could've, you know, done something." She draws a noisy breath.

"Charley, who has Izzy been saying this to?"

"Me and Blake."

After she kisses Charley good night, she stands at the balcony staring out at the sunset. The sky is very clear. April already. Soon it will be another long, hot London summer. Martin wrote about swimming in the Kariba Dam as well, and elephants on safari. She didn't tell Charley that.

Melly said the police interrogated Paul about Ash's death six months ago now, and since. They were very sure it was an accident. She must ask Charley not to repeat Izzy's words in front of Poppy or Sorrel, or Eve; they could be intensely upsetting. She waits till the sun disappears and the lights begin to prick the twilight all over south London. There is no one in the parking lot below. The landlady was right, the gang has gone. Five thousand miles away, it will be dark in Zimbabwe; night descends suddenly, there is no lingering English dusk, which she has grown to love. She goes inside to write, shutting the balcony doors.

Melissa

Paul leans forward over the prison table, his voice is croaky.

"How's Sorrel?"

She stares at him in disbelief. His lawyer relayed that he had something urgent to communicate. The requests were repeated; eventually she agreed to go, one final time. Was it just another trick? A chance to ask questions about the little girl he left to die? She shakes her head in silence.

"Any memories yet?"

She doesn't reply.

"Okay. How's Izzy?"

She tightens her lips; he must be insane if he thinks she is going to give him a progress report on his daughter's recovery from the damage he inflicted. Perhaps he is; incarceration causes madness in some prisoners. A deep line encircles his neck like a jagged crimson thread, damage coming full circle.

"One of the blokes stole some wire from the workshop," he says, noticing her glance. "I thought I was going to die. So, about Izzy. I'm worried about her, really worried. Is she having therapy?"

Around them couples lean forward and touch. Two little boys dressed in matching outfits with gelled hair are fighting over a bag of chips while their parents hold hands and talk in whispers. Another couple is silent, the girl yawning, obviously bored; she is probably here for the last time, as she is herself. Paul's hair is whitening; she'd thought it was a cliché, stress making your hair go white. His hands are rough-skinned, the nails are short and torn. There are bruises on his arms, old ones and more recent ones; they merge, like the bruises he gave her.

"Listen to me, Paul." She meets his eyes in a way she'd never dared, not even at the beginning. "You have forfeited the right to ask about your daughter, now or ever. Please don't get your lawyer to contact us again."

He leans forward but she doesn't move back. If this is a game, she's not going to lose. His face tightens and his skin flushes a dark, blotchy red.

"You listen to me. Izzy was lying. I did nothing, none of it. I didn't touch her, I swear. I did none of the things she said. Of course I didn't." He looks more like the old Paul, though this Paul sounds desperate rather than angry, the words are pouring out. "She made it all up, everything she said was a lie. I had nothing to do with Sorrel's abduction either. Izzy's ill, she must be. It's the only explanation. You need to get her some sort of help." His voice rises. "You must promise me you'll find someone to help her. I'll be cleared of course when the police dig deeper, though to be honest, I'm far more worried about her than me."

"I can't listen to this, Paul."

"You have to, for Izzy's sake. What the hell's she up to? Why would she lie about me? And what the fuck was Sorrel doing in our freezer? It doesn't make any sense. I'm locked up while the real culprit is walking around somewhere; it could be dangerous. Dangerous for Izzy."

His fists on the table clench tight but she doesn't flinch. They stare at each other; he is breathing heavily, the veins in his neck stand out like tight cords. Then he leans back slowly, his eyes narrow. "Where do you plan to live?"

She stares at him calmly; there is nothing that will induce her to tell him. She returns to last week's unexpected phone call; she's turned it over in her mind since then, like a cache of secret treasure that you know will have the power to change your life.

We visited the house last week. I like what you've done very much." There had been a smile in Jean-Claude's accented voice. "You don't know us, yet it's perfect."

"You sent me photos of your place in France and I read between the lines; it wasn't hard," she'd replied, gazing at Eve's garden through the kitchen window, the phone to her ear. The house was quiet; the children were playing in the garden. "I'm so glad you like it."

"We love it. I am grateful."

"You're welcome." I love that house, the project saved me.

It had filled her mind for weeks: the careful refurbishment of the kitchen and the bathrooms, the antique beds, the paints she mixed herself. The exquisite curtains. It had all come together in the end like a work of art.

"I have bad news and good news," Jean-Claude had said, a little hesitantly.

He's run out of money. He'll sell the house; someone new will change the colors, knock things down or knock them through.

"We have decided to remain in France for two more years; my boy has to stay close to the hospital for treatment."

"I understand, I'm sorry to hear that." And she is, but she's right, he'll sell the house.

"Would you like to live there?"

"Sorry?" Had she heard properly? She gripped the phone tightly. "Could you repeat what you've just—"

"I'm greedy. I want to keep the house though it will be a long time before we live in it; meanwhile it needs to stay alive. It needs people. You need a house."

"How did you know?" She shouldn't have said that, she should have laughed it off as a joke, but her heart had begun to beat very fast.

"I read between the lines."

They had been on television, all over the internet for weeks. It's hardly surprising that he knows her situation. What's more surprising is that he wasn't put off. The families of criminals become contaminated with the crime, her therapist said; she could be labeled unlucky or dangerous to know. She's lost clients already.

"The thing is, it isn't just me. I have a daughter, and a young Syrian friend will be joining our family, she's having a baby soon."

"Any friends of yours are welcome. The more the merrier. I'd like the house filled up. Live there for us."

"I want to know where you'll be, you and Izzy. I know you're selling the house, I had to sign those papers too." Paul is watching her closely. "And I want my share of the money; I need a better lawyer."

"You have to repay the money to Izzy's trust fund first."

He shrugs.

"If you manage to get out, God knows how, stay away from us." She gets up, catching his look of astonishment. He was always the one who ended conversations, never her, and now she is ending everything for good. She makes herself walk out of the room despite wanting to run as fast as she can. She is going toward freedom, though she can feel his eyes boring into her back.

A week later she is standing next to Izzy in Eve's kitchen as they peel potatoes for supper. Izzy's red nails sparkle in the water, she cuts deep into the white flesh; her potatoes end up half the size but she's helping, she looks absorbed. This is a good moment to share plans.

"We've got somewhere to live, Izzy."

"Yeah, I know." Izzy's mouth curves in a little smile. "Poppy told me; Eve says we can stay as long as we like."

Through the window Melissa sees Eric walking slowly around the garden, Eve behind him holding Sorrel's hand as she skips along beside her. The little girl looks content, but her parents aren't talking or touching. "I mean I've found another house, for us."

"My counselor said no upheavals." Izzy's voice becomes hard, she's still scared. "She told you, no big changes."

"Think of them." She nods through the window. Eric has stopped to pin back a strand of wisteria that's blowing in the wind, Eve continues past him as though he were invisible. "They need to recover in peace if they're to survive everything that's happened."

"So do I." Izzy has stopped peeling potatoes; she stares at her mother, the old Izzy look.

"That's the best thing about it." Melissa speaks calmly. She is stronger now, she reminds herself, she needs to stand firm. "A client has offered us his house in Wiltshire while he's abroad. It's peaceful, and your father will never find us there."

"What do you mean?" Izzy steps back. "Is he getting out?"

Melissa puts her arm around her. "Of course not. The new case hasn't even come to trial yet and when it does, he'll be locked away for years. All the same, we need a new start somewhere else, we have to build new memories."

"What about school?"

"There are some great schools in Salisbury."

"I need to be with my friends." Izzy sounds frightened.

"We'll see them often, sweetie, they can come and stay during breaks whenever you like. And you'll make new ones."

Izzy doesn't reply. Melissa busies herself putting the pot of potatoes on the stove and clearing out the sink. "We're stronger now, we'll manage, you'll see. Lina's coming too." She turns to smile at her daughter but Izzy isn't there. The door to the garden is open. Through the window she sees her approach Eve and take Sorrel's other hand. Melissa's are full of wet peelings, soft and already disintegrating. It's natural Izzy would want to stay in familiar surroundings. She does too—she dreads leaving Eve and Grace—but Izzy's safety has to come first. If Paul gets out, Eve's house is the first place he would look. She puts the peelings in the trash bin and shuts the lid firmly.

Later Melly unscrews a bottle of wine. Eric is doing the bills. The girls have gone to bed. She pours out two glasses.

"I should say no." Eve picks up her wine. "But I find I can't."

"Just one glass, sweetie, surely it won't hurt."

"I meant your invitation, Izzy passed it on." Eve looks happier than she has in months. "Darling Melly, it would be perfect."

"My invitation?"

"It's come at just the right moment; I hadn't realized how much I needed to get away."

Eve is smiling as she continues but her eyes are full of tears. "When I'm in the kitchen, I see Ash running towards the door. Sometimes I hear him in the garden calling to Noah. I'll think if I'm quick I'll be in time to stop him. I find myself standing in front of the paddock gate to bar his way. What happened fills my mind, day and night. It's not fair on the girls." She stares out the window as if, even now, she can see her little son in the dark running across the grass toward the paddock with the dog. "In a different place, the good memories might have a chance to come back instead."

Izzy's been kind, more thoughtful than she was; she understood exactly what Eve needed, what they owe her. She puts her arm around Eve and hugs her. Eve gave them a home when they needed it, despite what Paul did to Sorrel; a less generous woman might have simply turned her back. It's time she repaid Eve's friendship, it's the least she can do.

She draws back and smiles warmly into Eve's eyes. "That's wonderful news. Eric's invited, of course, he'd love the garden. I'll ask Grace too; we should all go."

"Eric won't come; I know that without asking. He's got too much work and we need a break from each other." Her voice drops to a whisper. "I still don't know if he knows what happened between me and Martin, but if he does he's not saying. He doesn't say anything. It's lonely, like living with a stranger who doesn't seem to like you very much." Then she stops. "How tactless of me, Melly, you must be much lonelier."

"It's the opposite for me," Melissa replies. "I was lonely when I was with Paul. I'm not lonely now and neither is Izzy." She hands Eve her wine and they touch glasses. "To the future."

*B*lake thinks that if they have to be anywhere without Dad this is the best place. There are so many trees, it's mental. There's a tennis court; they got some rackets off Amazon, Melly is showing them how to play. He messaged Dad to tell him to come when it's the university holidays in Zimbabwe, but Mum said he probably won't because of having to be careful with money; she's writing a book, which is cool, but it's only Dad earning now. If Eric came, he'd go nuts for this garden.

Charley gets woken up by the birds' singing in the morning and just lies there, trying to believe her luck. There are ponies and sheep in the fields here; everyone is happier except maybe Izzy. Mum is, definitely; maybe because she's writing so she's kind of switched on all the time, you can tell. She's not saying what the story is about yet. Charley doesn't want to go back to London. They've actually talked about moving here and changing schools, though Mum thinks Dad might prefer to stay in London when he's back, but they'll cross that bridge when they come to it, apparently.

Poppy is kind of waiting to see what she feels; she likes it mostly because Sorrel looks more as she used to, though she hasn't grown that much; Mum says that's to be expected and she'll catch up eventually. She misses Dad and she's never not thinking about Ash, but she can't tell Mum. Grace was really helpful, she said it gets better; it's not that the sadness gets smaller exactly, but that you get stronger so it's easier to carry. She can just about imagine how that might work.

Izzy misses the noise and the lights. She's bored, to be honest, but they had to come, obviously. Sorrel's getting better, so everyone's happy about that, but her memory hasn't come back, maybe it won't. Mum's loads better; she talks about Dad sometimes, they're both just relieved he's in prison. Everyone loves tennis, but she misses the games they used to play. They could always start playing them again, you know, in a bit.

17. April

Eve

"Where's Ash's tractor?"

"Tractor?" Eve echoes Sorrel's question sleepily. Across the lawn, the old house glows pink or-ange in the spring sunshine, the windows are wide open. The interior will be silent and flooded with light. Grace is writing somewhere inside that quietness. Behind the house, sheep are dotted all over the Downs, smaller ones among the larger ones. April is hot this year, hotter than usual; it's as though summer has come early. The grass is thick. She hasn't worn shoes for a week. Sorrel is lying on her stomach next to her, drawing pictures on a pad of paper. Half awake, Eve feels, imagines she feels, another presence, a head near hers. A blond one, green eyes staring up into the branches of the cypress tree above them. A life unlived, alongside hers. For once the pain has receded enough so she can feel the edge of contentment—not happiness, not yet.

"You know, the red one."

"It's in a bag, sweetheart, in the loft, back at home." Then the question hits her; she sits up, the blond head disappears, she puts her hand on the grass where he would have been. Sorrel has a new memory. She must keep calm, mustn't exclaim, mustn't even hug her.

"What did he use to do with his tractor?"

"He ran it over my tummy. It tickled." Sorrel starts humming. She is coloring in: brown branches, green grass, a big yellow sun. "It was a nice tractor. I liked it."

"I liked it too, sweetheart. It was a lovely tractor."

Sorrel smiles, choosing a yellow crayon for the buttercups.

"He had some other toys too, but I can't remember them. What did we call his little teddy with the vest, for instance?"

"Sparkly Teddy. Honestly, Mummy."

Eve presses her palms to her eyes; she mustn't cry either. "I know. Silly me. How could I have forgotten that? It must be this place."

This place. The green branches stir like great flags above them; a group of ponies graze in the next field.

There are thrushes on the lawn. A place where Sorrel's memories can seep back safely. Across the grass Melly is playing tennis with Izzy, Poppy and Blake on the other side of the net. Charley is being ball boy. The children call out the score and make swooping runs to the ball, often missing. The white lines have disappeared into the grass, the net is full of holes.

"Anything else, darling?"

"Anything else what?" Sorrel's china-blue eyes study hers seriously. There was a time when she'd imagined them closed and covered over with earth.

"Anything else about Ash's toys?" She shouldn't ask but she can't help it.

Sorrel frowns and goes back to drawing; she's started a house now: a red block with a path, a brown door, symmetrical windows.

Eve texts Eric. *Sorrel remembered Ash's tractor and Sparkly Teddy. Out of the blue.*

Go carefully, he texts back.

Eve sighs. At least Melly will celebrate. "Let's go and see what the others are doing."

She takes Sorrel's hand and they walk across the lawn. Melly puts down her racket and walks toward them, she is barefoot too. Charley and Poppy collapse gracefully onto the grass, arms and legs spread wide. Izzy is leaning over the fence, feeding grass to a pony on the other side, her hand tightly cupping his muzzle. Blake begins to practice his serve and Izzy pulls up clumps of grass by the edge of the court where it grows dark green under the shelter of an overhanging apple tree. The smell of sun-warmed net mixes with the sharp ammonia smell of the ponies. Sorrel is lagging behind, staring at Izzy as if transfixed.

"Sorrel remembered Ash's tractor," Eve tells Melly, becoming conscious that Izzy's head is now inclined toward them, her body tensed; she seems to be listening. Eve stops talking; she doesn't want Izzy to start asking Sorrel lots of questions.

"That's wonderful." Melissa's eyes are shining.

"Let's play hide-and-seek," Izzy announces suddenly. "Sorrel, you can have a head start. There's lots of hiding places in the house." She covers her eyes and starts to count. "One, two, three . . ."

"I'm too sleepy," Charley murmurs from the lawn. "It's so hot."

"Me too." Poppy sighs. "I can't be bothered to move."

"Four, five, six," Izzy continues.

Sorrel's anguished scream catches them all off guard. She begins to run away across the lawn toward the house.

"Wait, Sorrel. It's only a game." Eve begins to hurry

after her, but Sorrel has a head start and is running fast. She is wearing sandals and her feet crunch rapidly over the gravel drive.

"Why's she so frightened?" Melissa has caught up with Eve and is jogging beside her.

"God knows. Ow, watch out, Melly."

They have reached the wide gravel sweep in front of the house. The sharp stones hurt their feet and slow them down. Izzy flashes past them with an easy burst of speed, her sneakers scattering the gravel.

"Thanks, Izzy," Melly calls. "Tell her we'll play rounders instead."

Izzy doesn't reply; she is running up the wide stone steps that lead into the house. Sorrel has disappeared already. Above them the house stands serene; the windows of every floor up to the attic are wide open to the sun.

Grace

The pencil makes soft scraping sounds that melt into the silence of the attic. Grace prefers writing with a pencil, the ideas seem to flow better. She brought a stool up from the kitchen and a camping table she found in the garage. She has placed them by the window for the breeze, though today there is almost none. She is nearly at the end of her story; this is the hard part. House or prison? Warm weather or cold?

Her own kitchen was bleak the day they left, the flat no longer felt like home. Martin had been gone for several weeks—was that why? Her concentration wavers, she glances outside. Blake is practicing his serves, Charley lying in the sun. The others have disappeared. Grace looks down at her writing, growing less certain. If the story begins in a home with the woman, should it end in prison with the man? Or is that too predictable? Begin in a kitchen overlooking a garden and end, with less certainty, in another garden.

The door to the attic opens. She hears the light patter of footsteps run up the wooden stairs. She puts the pencil down, listening to the harsh breath sounds. Boxes are moved in the next-door attic room, then silence descends again punctured by ragged breaths. Hide-and-seek, that delicious waiting fear. This is the perfect house for it; she starts writing again. A few minutes later there is the quiet click of the attic door shutting. Footsteps ascend, slower, stealthier ones. The seeker, playing the game. The steps reach the top of the stairs, pause, then enter the adjacent room. A bike or a carriage is wheeled out of the way, boxes are moved.

"Got you!"

Grace's smile lasts until she hears Sorrel's scream.

"I hate this game."

"Which one?" Izzy sounds amused.

Grace gets up quietly.

"Hide-and-seek." Sorrel is crying. "No one came to find me last time."

"But I've just found you," Izzy says; there is laughter in her voice now. "We can play something else if you like. How about the flying game?"

By the time Grace reaches the door, Izzy is by the large open window that comes almost to the floor, the kind that should have bars across it, because if you fell you would tumble at least forty feet to the ground. Izzy is lifting Sorrel, which looks easy because the child is still so small. She is swinging her around toward the window, which is very near where she is standing. Grace moves fast but Poppy moves faster. Poppy has climbed the stairs, Eve and Melly are right behind her.

Melissa

Melissa sits in the armchair in the corner of the kitchen she designed, with its ancient dresser and the saffron walls. The room is full of the people she loves but they won't stay much longer, they will leave soon and return to their own homes, their own lives. She's Izzy's mother, after all, Paul's wife. The kind of woman to be avoided from now on.

Izzy is in the ballroom at the front of the house being guarded by a policeman. Melissa has to restrain herself from getting up and going to find her; she wants to look into her daughter's blue eyes and ask her why. Izzy's angry, she might be in the mood for telling, although admittedly not to her mother. Izzy had stared at her with thwarted fury in the attic; she'd always gotten her own way, though no one, surely, could have guessed that would be murder.

Sorrel cuddles into her mother; she is holding a little blue woolen horse that Poppy bought her from the village shop last week. Poppy stands near her sister and Charley is on the floor by the stove, with Venus on her lap. Blake, looking dazed, sits next to Charley, his arm around Noah's neck. Grace leans against the wall by the door while the policewoman settles her broad frame onto a stool next to Sorrel and Eve.

Eve holds Sorrel tightly as though she will never let her go. "You're safe, my darling. You needn't be scared."

"I ran upstairs to hide, 'cause I was frightened."

"I know, poppet."

"Last time I hid no one came."

"Last time?" Eve puts her cheek on Sorrel's hair.

"Izzy made me go on a hide-and-seek adventure, just me and her; we walked along that railway line, well, we had to run." Her voice wobbles. "She put me in this thing and she said everyone would come and find me but they didn't and it was dark and I couldn't move properly and . . ." The tears overflow.

Eve holds her close, murmuring into her hair

Melissa's hands tighten on the arms of the chair. The car that was sliding over the road has hit the bank and overturned. Her life has smashed to pieces. It was Izzy, not Paul. Her daughter, not her husband. He'd tried to tell her. "Izzy's ill," he'd said. "You need to get her some sort of help." How was she to know, after all his lies, that he was finally telling the truth and that it was Izzy who'd been lying all along?

"So you ran upstairs today because you were scared." The policewoman's tone is soothing. Sorrel stares at her with unblinking eyes. "I'm wondering if you can tell us what scared you so much?"

The kitchen is silent, though there are lots of little background noises. The humming of the fridge, the cat purring, the children shifting positions on the floor, the dog sighing, the comforting sounds of everyday life.

"When she fed the pony she put her hand over his

nose; I thought he wouldn't be able to breathe. Then I remembered she did the same thing to Ash and he couldn't breathe." She pushes into her mother, twisting the blue horse in her hands; her voice lowers to a whisper. "He went all still after a bit."

The silence in the kitchen deepens, even the comforting noises seem to stop. Everyone is holding their breath. Sorrel looks up at Eve as if checking she is still there; Eve kisses her; her face is blank as though wiped clean by horror.

"I've already been told a little bit about what happened to your brother," the policewoman murmurs gently. "It would be so helpful if you could tell me more, just so I can get it straight in my mind. So you were there in your brother's room . . ."

"Yes, I was." Sorrel nods several times; her eyes are very wide. "I went to see him because he wouldn't stop crying, but Izzy was already there. She had her hand tight over his face then she took her hand off, then she put it back like she was playing a game."

Eve closes her eyes. Melissa wants to get up and run away, anywhere but here. She doesn't want to hear these words that will be in her mind forever; she will never be rid of the pictures that go with them.

"She picked him up." Sorrel is twisting the horse around and around in her hands. "His head was hanging in a funny way, a bit like a doll." She looks at Eve again; her voice gets higher. "She looked up and saw me." Eve's lips tighten but her hand strokes Sorrel's hair gently.

"And then?" the policewoman prompts quietly after a while. "What happened then, Sorrel?"

"She didn't say anything; she just took him away. I ran back to bed and pulled the cover up. When she came back, she pulled my cover down and said she would kill me if I told." Sorrel's voice drops to a whisper. "I wet the bed."

Eve lowers her face to Sorrel's. "You don't need to tell us anything else, my darling."

"I tried to tell you about him not being able to breathe, I really tried, but you didn't let me say."

"Oh, sweetheart." Eve sounds desperate and sorry at the same time. "I thought you meant when he was drowning. It was making you upset, so I stopped you. I'm sorry."

She tried to tell me too, Melissa remembers, but I'd thought the same as Eve; I hadn't allowed Sorrel to finish either.

It's agonizingly simple to work out what must have happened next from Izzy's point of view: when her first plan for Sorrel didn't work, the memory loss must have been a gift. No wonder she wanted to stay close to the family. She must have been watching Sorrel all this time; watching and listening for the first hint of her memory returning, as it did today. She would have framed the fall as a terrible accident and they would have all believed her. Melissa grips the arms of the chair tightly; her hands are sweating.

Grace pushes herself away from the wall. She touches Eve lightly on the shoulder, goes to the fridge, and, taking out a jug of lemonade, she collects three glasses and leaves the room.

Sorrel wriggles off Eve's lap, takes Poppy's hand, and walks out of the kitchen, pulling her sister after her. Poppy rolls her eyes at Charley but she doesn't let go of Sorrel's hand. The policewoman follows, Melissa thinks, to check that Sorrel's really all right. Charley and Blake hurry after them.

The room is quiet. If Eve shouted or screamed it would be fair; if she wanted to kill her, she would understand. After a few minutes Eve lifts her head; she looks bereft rather than angry, confused as though nothing makes much sense.

"I can't understand why Izzy had to kill Ash." Eve's face is white. "Even if I could, I don't think I'd be able to forgive her. I know she suffered at Paul's hands, but—" She is unable to continue.

"I don't know why either." Melissa stumbles over

her words. "I'm sorry. I'm so very, very sorry, though that sounds pitiful. Ridiculous. I had no idea, none. I don't think I know anything anymore—"

"Well, I suppose I know two things." Eve stands up. Melissa waits, head bowed.

"We let things happen which we shouldn't have done, all of us," Eve begins bravely. "And the other thing is . . ." Eve's voice begins to falter. ". . . something about us, about being friends, about how good that's felt this year. The trouble is . . ." She is speaking through tears. "I don't know what to do with that feeling now. Eric used to say I should do what my heart tells me to do, but . . ." She wipes her eyes with her sleeve and attempts a smile. ". . . how the hell does that work when my heart is broken?"

She leaves the room, and seconds later the front door bangs. She has gone to her children.

The wood in the range slips lower. Noah comes over and rests his head on Melissa's lap. She is glad of the warm weight, the gentle eyes. The low sun through the windows strikes the pans above the stove, the copper glows like flames.

18. April—Same Day

Grace

Grace gives the policeman a glass of lemonade and asks him if he wouldn't mind waiting outside. He has a tattoo around his wrist, nice eyes. Fit-looking. He parks himself, feet apart, just inside the door. "Sorry, love, I need to stay close. She'll forget all about me in a minute."

The police van and the social workers are due to arrive in half an hour. Grace and Izzy are alone in the yellow-painted room at the front of the house, the old ballroom. There are deep alcoves and an expanse of floor, constructed for dancing and perfect for secrets. You might think that your words would fly up into the dusty cornices and disappear among the cobwebs; you might imagine there would be no consequences. Grace pours lemonade into the two remaining glasses, pulls a couple of armchairs to the window and sits in one, sprawling a little, relaxed or pretending to be. Izzy is pacing in circles like an animal in a cage.

"Sit down, won't you? Try to relax, have a drink." Grace points to the glasses on the table between them.

Izzy sits in the armchair, her back to the door, and stares at Grace. She doesn't touch the lemonade.

"You're good, Izzy, very smart," Grace says, nodding. "We all thought it was Paul. The tiara in the car was clever. He didn't stand a chance."

"Don't forget the abuse." Izzy's mouth twists in a smile. "It mightn't have worked without that."

Grace pauses, the lemonade halfway to her lips; another piece of the puzzle slots in.

"Ah. Paul was already on trial; was that necessary?"

"I had to make absolutely sure. I had to think of something, and it fitted so well." Izzy laughs, she's warming up. The policeman was right; she's forgotten him completely. "You should have seen Dad's face."

"Your father loves you. Do you have any idea what you've done?"

"He's a monster." Izzy's voice sharpens. "He hurt my mother. He got what he deserved."

"You hurt her too," Grace points out, then stops;

Izzy's a child, after all. A damaged child. She may not have realized that her lies in court could make it harder for her mother to get justice for herself.

"Don't pretend you care about my mother," Izzy snaps back. "You must have seen how scared she was, but you didn't bother to think what that meant. You didn't have a clue about us kids either. None of you did." Her face has become pink with anger. "We could have been on a desert island for all you cared, as long as we kept out of the way."

The words hit Grace like little stones—the sharp-edged ones she saw under the bed in the attic. Had they all been that careless, that distracted?

"I gave you a chance," Izzy continues angrily. "I did things to wake you up."

"What kind of things?" Grace isn't sure if Izzy will answer, but Izzy is hitting her stride.

"I got Blake to steal your door keys for me, but you didn't notice, it made no difference to you at all."

"You're wrong there, it made all the difference," Grace replies. If those keys had been with my other ones on the night of my assault, she continues silently, I would have escaped back into my flat. I wouldn't have been attacked. I wouldn't have been terrified for weeks or pushed Martin away. I might have noticed what was happening to Melly or Sorrel.

"I didn't need keys to get into Eve's house, though," Izzy is continuing, contemptuously. "I walked right in and took her ring while they were having sex." She laughs. "Eve must've been so spooked when she saw it had gone." Then her face changes, a note of irritation creeps into her voice. "I let their dog into the garden by mistake, he messed up their shed. If Eve was brighter she might have suspected something." Then she frowns. "And you were supposed to discover the ring. I put it in your bed specially; Martin must have got there first, or you wouldn't've been so surprised by the photos."

Grace closes her eyes. It might have been better to have found Eve's ring in her bed; the images Izzy showed her on her phone are still vivid; they still hurt.

"I made Blake steal your money too." Izzy's eyes narrow as if watching for pain, but Grace feels an unexpected stirring of pity. All the coins in the world wouldn't have bought Izzy what she wanted. She'd needed precisely those things money can't buy: a stable home, parents who loved each other, who spent time with her. All kids do—including her own. Guilt twists inside her stomach.

"He did anything I wanted him to—anything." Izzy's voice is jubilant.

"Like stealing knives?"

Izzy shrugs, a careless little gesture. "I gave him those, we needed them for the games."

"What games?"

"Oh, you know." Then she shakes her head. "Actually, you wouldn't want to."

"Tell me."

Izzy unwinds gracefully from the chair to stand at the open window. Sorrel and the policewoman are on the lawn, throwing a ball for Noah. Poppy is sitting nearby leaning against Eve, whose head is lowered so she can't see her face. The police siren is so faint it could be imaginary.

"Tell me about the games," Grace says again; they might not have long.

Izzy turns and stares at her, triumph in her eyes. She's deciding not to talk about the bruises and the burns, the cuts, those bloodstained little stones under the bed. Why would she? Silence is power, the last she will have for a while.

The shadows are growing longer on the lawn and darker under the trees where they emptied the little bottle of earth from Ash's grave. The children troop back into the house; she can hear them in the hall.

"Why Ash?" Grace speaks softly. "Was he just another game to you?"

She didn't expect an answer, but neither was she prepared for the expression on Izzy's face, a flicker more than an expression, gone in a flash. A kind of impatience, but with herself, that look of regret people have if they feel they could have done better, given time. After all, she might have gotten away with it completely if Sorrel had died as she'd planned. They could have been playing upstairs right now: Izzy, Poppy, Charley, and Blake, somewhere out of sight. She and Melly would be cooking supper. Eve, twice bereaved, might not have come, but she would have let Poppy have a holiday with her best friend. The kids are fine, that's what she and Melly would have said to each other as they sipped wine in the kitchen, they're just playing games. Grace shivers. The house is unheated; spring evenings are chilly and it's starting to get dark. A police van pulls up; a policewoman gets out with another woman in plainclothes, probably the social worker they've been expecting.

Later she stands with the children at the front door as Izzy is led away; Melissa follows with bags she must have hastily packed. Izzy looks around for her mother at the last minute and they get in the van together.

Grace didn't get the answer to her last question—*why Ash?*—that final piece of the jigsaw puzzle is still missing. Children are born barbarians, Eric had said, and need to be tamed. Melly had been powerless to tame anyone, but as Izzy said, they were all at fault; they didn't notice anything; they didn't have a clue.

The children huddle together as if watching for a sign, a wave, one last look out the window as the police van pulls away.

"She didn't even say goodbye," Sorrel says, sounding disappointed.

19. May

Melissa

"Do you want to know whether it's a girl or a boy?" the ultrasound tech asks.

Melly holds her breath. Lina says that she knows it's a girl anyway and the technician smiles. Little girl or boy, it doesn't matter. A life that was conceived in fear is becoming itself, will be welcomed, cherished. Loved. The monitor glides over Lina's swollen abdomen. The technician is checking the position, the reason for this late scan. The baby is overdue but not breach; despite the obstetrician's concern, everything's fine.

Melissa's eyes fill. Her baby is in custody now, for at least fourteen years.

"Look," Lina whispers. "The hands."

She'd had to let go of Izzy's hands. The staff at the secure unit in Bristol had been kind but precise, very firm. The gates had shut behind her; the high fence barred her view.

"See the face, she's so beautiful." Lina's English is much better than it was. She can speak fluently; six months in the shelter has worked wonders. Lina retreats to her room to dress; Melissa waits in the corridor outside.

Izzy's face had been shuttered when it was time to part; she could have stared at those lovely features for hours and still not understood. In the end there wasn't much time to say goodbye. She'd put her arms around her daughter and Izzy had hugged her back. Melissa didn't cry until she was outside the unit and then she couldn't stop. Grace rescued her; she organized the overnight hotel in Bristol and met her there; they went back to the unit together the next day. Grace was with her in the youth court and later in the Crown court where Izzy was referred for sentencing. She came to the first meeting with the psychiatrist and counselors when Izzy's program was explained. She held Melissa's hand when the diagnosis of psychopathy was first discussed.

A couple walk down the corridor toward Melissa as

she waits for Lina. Their heads are bent over a photograph; she can't see their faces but the man has his arm around the woman and they are chatting softly, absorbed in the magic of the image. They don't notice her sitting there, watching them; they will be thinking of nothing else except the birth of their tiny baby. They won't be thinking of the child at three or thirteen; they have no idea at all of the complex life that will unfurl.

Visits to the unit are allowed weekly, more often once Izzy settles. Izzy's detention worker told Melissa that Paul had been informed and wanted to see her, but Izzy refused. Melissa watches the man's face as the couple walk past her, the love in his eyes. He looks kind, which is everything. The little baby will have a kind, loving father. Paul hadn't abused his daughter, as it turned out, but he'd possessed her all the same, while ruthlessly excluding his wife. He'd dominated them both and manipulated their lives. Izzy's rejection must have been hard for a man with his pathological need to control. For the first time ever, Melissa feels almost sorry for him. He's been released on bail with conditions, pending a retrial for marital rape; the case isn't due for several months. Melly needs the time to gather strength.

Lina reappears, dressed and still holding the photo; Melissa looks at her watch. "We've got lots of time before school's out. It's a sunny day, let's go into town and find a cup of tea. We could go round the cathedral."

Later they are walking around the ancient cloisters. It might have been something to do with the peace of the place, the way you can rely on time to make things right in the end. She is thinking about this and about Eve when Lina's gentle voice breaks across the bird-filled quietness.

"I wonder if she will look like her father." Lina's tone is interested. "I wish in a way I could send him a copy of this, despite everything."

Melissa glances at Lina, shocked. "It's your decision, of course, but I'd be careful, really careful. Paul has been released; if he hurt you once it could happen again."

"Paul?"

"He's out of prison, remember, at least for now. He's not allowed to come near me, but he might find his way to you."

Lina looks up, bewildered. "Paul never hurt me."

"He raped you," Melissa says softly. "If he finds out he is the father of your baby—"

"Paul didn't rape me. No one did. He is not the father of my baby." Lina shakes her head, her dark eyebrows are raised in surprise. She lifts her hands, clearly astonished. "It was my boyfriend."

It's Melissa's turn to feel stunned. "But I thought you finished with him, way back last autumn. The first time I found you in the kitchen, you said—"

"I had finished with him—at least that's what I thought. I'd just found out I was pregnant. Hassan wanted me to have an abortion. That's why I was upset; I told him it was over."

Melissa sits down on the stone ledge by the pillars that run around the cloisters; her legs are trembling. Lina sits with her.

"Hassan carried on pestering me," she continues. "He used to wait outside the door on my days off, he forced his way in to be with me sometimes. He began to hurt me; it was like he was punishing me for being pregnant. He said if I told anyone, he would let the authorities know I didn't have a work permit. That morning you found me in the kitchen, the second time—remember?" She pauses.

Melissa nods. She remembers everything about that morning: Lina asleep in the pantry, her bruised face, the swelling in her abdomen. It was the morning Melissa finally realized she had to leave her husband.

"Hassan had got into the house again. He hit me," Lina is continuing. "He would have carried on but there were noises from upstairs, so he left. I hid in the pantry in case he came back."

Melissa puts her arm around Lina. Reeling from Paul's vicious attack, she'd assumed he'd assaulted Lina as well; what Lina told her had seemed to fit, though she'd actually said so little. They could hardly communicate back then.

"Karen told me some men like to hurt their girlfriends when they're pregnant; she said it would have got worse. You rescued me." Lina touches Melissa's hand gently. "Hassan is in Syria now," she goes on softly. "He still texts me, he says he loves me."

"Do you believe him, Lina?"

She shakes her head. "He hurt me," she replies very simply. "That's not love."

Melissa nods, pushing herself upright, and then she helps Lina to stand. The photograph is still in Lina's hand; Melissa watches the tenderness in her face as she studies the grainy image. You are wiser than I was, she thinks, you've got to the truth much more quickly. What Hassan says isn't love, not even close. Love is what you are feeling for the baby you are carrying. It will survive everything. You will find this out for yourself, you are right at the beginning of love.

They link arms and walk through the wooden door of the cloisters into the bright sunshine of the Close.

20. December

Eve

Eve is outside in the herb garden gathering sage,
partly to escape. The house is noisy, Sundays are
always noisy. Jean-Claude's wish is coming true, according to Melly. He wanted the house filled up. There
are four women and five children; three when Grace
goes to London to meet her lawyer. It might be difficult to prove historical assault, but luckily she kept the
DNA, and once Grace has made up her mind, things
tend to get done.

Eve can hear Charley calling and Blake calling back;
Poppy shouting at them to shut up, she wants to do her
homework. Sorrel will be telling Noah not to worry,
that this kind of noise is normal in families. Charley

and Sorrel go to school in Broad Chalke; Poppy and Blake catch the bus into Salisbury. It's quieter on a weekday, Eve tells the sleeping baby in her arms.

The dark green sage has the scent of Greece. She holds a crushed leaf under the baby's small nose. "Your mother is sleeping," she says, "she's tired out. Well, you did keep her awake all night with your antics."

A car enters the gates and begins to drive slowly toward the house. Eve is surprised. They weren't expecting anyone. The car stops and two men get out and walk toward the house. They haven't noticed her. The taller man has the swinging gait of someone who spends much of his life outside, a wind-tanned face, a face she has known for most of her life. He looks around at the grounds, interested, as you'd expect him to be. The other is shorter, with gray hair straggling over his collar. His face is tanned. She knows him too, of course. She bends to pick another handful of sage. She'll have to make more stuffing now.

The baby sneezes.

She hears Grace calling the children down and then she goes inside.

Epilogue

Grace sits back, puts her pencil down, stretches and shakes out her hand. She walks to the window and opens it as wide as she can, which isn't that far. The new locks allow eighteen inches; Eve measured.

She looks at the photos on the floor, the old newspapers. It looks like a crime scene, and in a way it is.

She walks back and sits down again, then opens a new document. She calls it *Aftermath* for now. She starts to type, copying from her notebooks, slowly at first then faster, warming up.

It was surprising how quickly things took off in the end, like a bonfire, one of those big ones the children loved so much. Some nights I hear that sound of crackling again, like a bomb ticking down. I wait for the roar and see the flames; the scent of scorching fills the air. I can feel that searing heat.

The children danced around fires all summer, lit up and yelling like wild things.

The attic is quiet, apart from the tapping and the birdsong that comes through the window along with the noise of sheep. Some of them have tiny lambs already; she can hear them in the fields, calling for their mothers.

Acknowledgments

Warm thanks are due to the following.

Women's Aid staff: for information about admitting procedures and the running of shelters. This crucial charity provides vital support for countless victims of domestic abuse.

Sir John Royce, High Court judge and neighbor, for his reading of the text and invaluable advice. Any mistakes in the legal aspects of the book are mine alone.

Pat Jones, OBE, founder and principal of the Bristol Dyslexia Center, for much help and advice.

Simon Williams, deputy head of the Charter School North Dulwich, for meeting me at the school and for information about knife crime and school safety procedures.

Nick Shaw, police constable, for his invaluable advice about police procedures and investigations.

Erenie Mullens-Burgess, charity manager at Bell House, in Dulwich, for kindly showing me around the house, an educational center that provided inspiration for the setting of Eve's house.

Alan Grieg, whose bid to FundingNeuro's auction won the right for Karen McFetters's name to be included in this story. FundingNeuro is the charity that supports my husband Steve Gill's work with children's brain tumors, Parkinson's disease, and amyotrophic lateral sclerosis (ALS).

Julian Power, whose bid to the charity CLIC Sargent's "Get in Character" auction won the right for Marian Power's name to be included in my story.

I am very grateful to the following people and teams whose support throughout has been invaluable.

Eve White, my agent, and her assistant Ludo Cinelli, on whom I rely for help, wise advice, and friendship.

Jessica Leeke, Clare Bowron, Sarah Bance, Nick Lowndes, and the whole team at Michael Joseph, Penguin Random House, and Lisa Brewster, who designed the beautiful cover of *Little Friends*.

Rachel Kahan and all her hardworking team at William Morrow, especially Ashley Caswell, who designed the fabulous cover of *The Playground*.

My writing group for their reading of early drafts of this novel, including Tanya Attapatu, Victoria Finlay, Emma Geen, Susan Jordan, Sophie McGovern, Mimi Thebo, and, from farther away, Hadiza el Rufai.

Tricia Wastvedt, for her kind advice and wisdom, as always.

My husband, Steve, and our children, Martha, Mary, Henry, Tommy, and Johny, for everything.

About the Author

While working as a general practitioner, JANE SHEMILT completed a postgraduate diploma in creative writing at Bristol University and went on to earn a master's in creative writing at Bath Spa, gaining both with distinction. Her first novel, *The Daughter*, was selected for the Richard & Judy Book Club, was shortlisted for the Edgar Award and the Lucy Cavendish Fiction Prize, and went on to become the bestselling debut novel of 2014. Jane and her husband, a professor of neurosurgery, have five children and live in Bristol.